"The mystery has a touch of a gothic feel, with the killing happening on a dark and stormy night at a Victorian mansion tucked away in the mountains. The loyalty of the quilting friends makes me want to sit in with the Village Quilters guild even if I don't know how to quilt . . . and Craig's clever character development and sharp mystery kept me riveted to the story."

—MyShelf.com

Knot What It Seams

"Craig laces this puzzler with a plausible plot, a wealth of quirky characters, and rich local color as Beatrice and her friends try to restore peace for the piecers."

—*Richmond Times-Dispatch*

"There are plenty of descriptions of quilts, fabrics, and patterns, along with a solid mystery, to entice any quilt lover to put down their needle and sit a spell and read."

—The Mystery Reader

"Fans of cozy mysteries, quilting, and well-written fiction will enjoy this book and this series. I highly recommend it." —Sharon's Garden of Book Reviews

Quilt or Innocence

"A delightful new series as warm and cozy as a favorite quilt. Elizabeth Craig captures Southern life at its best, and her characters are as vibrant and colorful as the quilts they sew."

—*New York Times* bestselling author Krista Davis

"Sparkles with Craig's cleverness and plenty of Carolina charm."   —*Richmond Times-Dispatch*

"A warm and welcoming new series, *Quilt or Innocence* is full of eccentric and engaging characters. The women Beatrice meets are unique and quirky, but in a down-to-earth, believable way, not a silly, comic way that such characters are often portrayed."

—The Mystery Reader

"*Quilt or Innocence* is a delightful regional amateur sleuth due to the eccentric quilters. . . . Readers will enjoy touring Dappled Hills guided by colorful locals."

—Genre Go Round Reviews

Also by Elizabeth Craig

Quilt or Innocence
Knot What It Seams
Quilt Trip

SHEAR TROUBLE

A SOUTHERN QUILTING MYSTERY

Elizabeth Craig

AN OBSIDIAN MYSTERY

OBSIDIAN
Published by the Penguin Group
Penguin Group (USA) LLC, 375 Hudson Street,
New York, New York 10014

USA | Canada | UK | Ireland | Australia | New Zealand | India | South Africa | China
penguin. com
A Penguin Random House Company

First published by Obsidian, an imprint of New American Library,
a division of Penguin Group (USA) LLC

First Printing, August 2014

ISBN 978-0-451-46950-2

Printed in the United States of America
10 9 8 7 6 5 4 3 2 1

In memory of my grandmothers.

ACKNOWLEDGMENTS

Many thanks to my talented editor, Sandra Harding, my hardworking agent, Ellen Pepus, and to the team at Obsidian for putting this book together so beautifully. Thanks to my husband, Coleman, and my children, Riley and Elizabeth Ruth, for their enthusiastic support. And thanks, as always, to the writing community for their encouragement and selfless sharing of resources, which help all writers perfect their craft.

Chapter One

"The funny thing, Beatrice," said Meadow, beaming through her red-framed glasses, "is that all this time I never knew that Boris was a genius."

Beatrice looked doubtfully down at the aforementioned Boris. The massive animal of mixed bloodlines was grinning at her with his tongue lolling out. He actually looked rather slow. And this was the same dog who strong-armed his way into her kitchen on a regular basis and upset her canisters while searching for food. "How did you come to that conclusion, Meadow? I mean—I'm sure Boris is *smart*, but I wouldn't have said he was more clever than . . . well, Noo-noo." She looked with satisfaction at her own dog, a well-behaved, alert corgi.

"He's so incredibly intuitive and communicative. Lately, he's put his paw on my leg whenever he wants to tell me something. I've been amazed." Meadow looked wonderingly at the huge animal's tremendous paws. Boris yawned. "Yesterday morning, I had a real absentminded episode. I put eggs on the stove to boil and then something distracted me . . . I don't now remember what it was. Anyway, I walked outside to get the newspaper. While I was outside, I saw weeds were really making inroads into my flower bed. So I pulled weeds for a bit."

Beatrice took a bite of her shortcake cookie. She was used to Meadow's meandering stories and had confidence that she'd eventually come to her point.

"Out of the blue, Boris bolted out the door. I swear I don't even know how he opened it. Do you think he turned the handle?"

Beatrice didn't.

"Anyway, he galloped outside, giving me this incredibly intelligent pleading look. I get goose bumps whenever I remember it." Meadow thrust out her arm for Beatrice to view the indisputable truth. "He put his paw on my shoulder—that's because I was stooped over weeding—clearly telling me to come inside. He gave a few sharp barks and ran to the front door. I tell you, Beatrice, I started running. Sure enough, the pot was already blazing when I went in, so I sprayed my kitchen extinguisher on it and put it out. Boris saved the day!" Meadow choked up at this last bit and pulled a tissue out of her purse, blowing her nose loudly.

Noo-noo looked concerned and Beatrice reached over to rub the dog's head. "That's a very scary story, Meadow. Thank goodness that Boris paid such close attention. I'd hate for this gorgeous barn to burn down." Beatrice gazed around her. The old barn had been turned into a beautiful home. Skylights in the cathedral-like ceiling lit the large, open living area, illuminating vibrantly colored quilts hanging from the walls.

Meadow reached over to refill Beatrice's iced tea before she could protest. Meadow took her hostessing duties seriously, but Beatrice was wondering if she'd need to make a pit stop by the powder room before she and Noo-noo walked home.

Before she knew it, Meadow had put another couple of shortbread cookies on the china plate in front of her. "Meadow!" she groaned.

"Oh, please. Like you need to worry about calories. I've never seen a fitter sixty-something-year-old than you. Platinum blond hair, carelessly stylish button-down, and capri-length khakis." Meadow snorted. "How did I end up with the big bones and crazy hair? The least you can do is eat a few cookies with me in sympathy."

"I'm afraid my hair is white, not platinum. I'm not as fit as you're giving me credit for. And your hair isn't crazy at all. I've always thought your braid suited you." It was a long gray braid that did suit Meadow to a tee.

Meadow said, "Hey, how is your quilt coming

along?" Her eyes were wide and innocent, but Beatrice knew that this was a dead-serious follow-up.

"Oh, I figured I'd finish it the night before the quilt show. There's still plenty of time," said Beatrice in a studiously careless voice. Meadow gasped, choking a bit on cookie crumbs, and Beatrice chided, "Meadow. It's all finished, of course. You know how I am about meeting deadlines." She reached down and gave Boris a distracted pat as he laid his mighty genius head on her lap to look lovingly at her shortbread cookie.

Meadow flashed her a relieved look as she reached for her drink to wash down the cookie. She said, "Well, thank goodness. I only wish that everyone else in the guild had your work ethic. This show might be featuring a bunch of unfinished quilts from the Village Quilters." She frowned thoughtfully. "Do you think we can spin that somehow? Promote it as high art? 'The Process of Quilting,' or some such thing?"

"I don't think so, no." Somehow Beatrice didn't think a postmodern deconstructed-quilt exhibit was going to go over well in tiny Dappled Hills. "Are you sure that everyone is running so far behind? That doesn't sound like Savannah, for instance."

Meadow cleared her throat. "Well, Savannah has been busy doing other things lately."

"That sounds ominous," said Beatrice slowly. "Are you talking about her little borrowing problem?" Savannah, who looked like a prim and proper buttoned-up old maid, was a complete kleptomaniac.

"Let's say she's kept her sister busy lately," said Meadow with a sigh. "I happened to be in the quilt shop when Georgia came in to return a thimble that Savannah had swiped. Sometimes she goes through spells with it, you know. Just be sure to nail down your stuff when it's your turn to host a guild meeting."

"Okay. Well, I can understand the two of them being a little behind, then. But Miss Sissy? She's up all night with insomnia. You can't tell me that she hasn't finished her quilt. What else does she have to do?" Miss Sissy was the oldest member of the guild. She'd gotten a bit demented and was fairly arthritic, but she could still produce the best needlework of anyone in the state.

"Who knows?" said Meadow gloomily. "Whatever she's doing, it's not quilting. At least not on the quilt that's supposed to be in the show."

"And Piper?" asked Beatrice. "Surely my own daughter is enough like me to meet her deadline with lots of time to spare."

"I think Piper and my son have been spending a lot of time talking on the phone together lately," said Meadow. This, at least, put a smile back on her face. "Ah, they're really a lovely couple, aren't they? I can tell that Ash is just wild about Piper. Oh, and he's probably at the airport even as I speak, getting ready to fly here for a little visit."

It was a pity that Ash lived all the way over on the other side of the country. Beatrice was both happy for her daughter and sorry that she was in a relationship that might eventually result in a move. Piper had only recently returned from a long visit in California to see Ash.

"So Piper isn't done with her quilt, either?" This *was* looking bad for the quilt show. "I wonder how the Cut-Ups are doing with their quilts?" asked Beatrice. The Cut-Ups and the Village Quilters had a friendly rivalry with each other. Friendly *most* of the time, anyway.

Now Meadow's face looked even glummer. "I'm sure they're completely done, as usual."

"Well, why don't we set up some sort of bee?" asked Beatrice. "You know the Village Quilters love to socialize—maybe that would be the best way to keep everybody from procrastinating and finish their quilts."

Meadow brightened. "Great idea, Beatrice. Maybe Posy will let us use the Patchwork Cottage's conference room. We could set up a bunch of long tables, run some extension cords, and everyone would have plenty of space to spread out."

"A retreat," said Beatrice, nodding. "A quilting retreat. We could all bring some food—that'll lure them in if the quilting doesn't."

"Do you think Posy will go for it?" asked Meadow. "The shop has been so busy lately and it seems like she's always on the go."

Beatrice could tell when Meadow would keep stewing over this issue until it was addressed. "Tell you what. Why don't we head over to Posy's shop and find out right now? We can ask her about the retreat and I can pick up a few things for the new quilt I'm working on. Can Noo-noo visit with Boris while we run the errand?"

Meadow beamed at her. "Boris will *love* it!" she said as she snatched her keys off the kitchen counter.

Noo-noo apparently didn't share the sentiment and stared reproachfully at Beatrice as she and Meadow left.

Beatrice felt a smile pull at the corners of her mouth as soon as she entered Posy's shop. The Patchwork Cottage always made her feel a bit more relaxed, a little more mindful. Posy had soft music playing in the store, usually by local artists. The large room was a visual feast for the eyes with bolts of fabric and lovely finished quilts on display everywhere—even draped over antique sewing machines and old washstands. Gingham curtains hung in the windows. Posy had made the shop as welcoming and friendly as she was.

Beatrice and Meadow waited a moment while Posy was finishing up with a customer. Meadow elbowed Beatrice. "Looks like Miss Sissy has taken up residence in her usual spot."

Beatrice glanced over at the sitting section to see the cronelike old woman sleeping on the sofa. As if somehow feeling their gaze, she abruptly awakened, glaring around the store and muttering, "Poppycock! Poppycock!" She spotted Beatrice and Meadow looking at her and brandished an arthritic fist at them.

"Looks like she's in rare form today," murmured Beatrice.

Posy quickly walked over and greeted them and they filled her in on their idea for the quilting retreat. "Oh, I think that's a marvelous idea!" said Posy, twinkling at Meadow and Beatrice. She was a tiny bespectacled woman with a gentle smile. "Believe it or not, the store has been so busy that I haven't finished my own quilt yet."

Meadow said to Beatrice, "See? This is what I'm talking about. Even Posy can't get a quilt finished."

"Can we do it Friday night?" asked Posy. "You know the shop closes early on Fridays, and that would give us a little time to catch up before the quilt show. We can put long tables in the storeroom and extension cords for all the tables."

"May I come, too?" came a voice behind them, and they turned around to see an attractive woman who looked to be in her late fifties although she had a remarkably unlined face. "Sorry for listening in. But I'm way, wayyyy behind on my quilt for the show."

Posy quickly said, "Oh, Beatrice. This is Phyllis Stitt—she's a member of the Cut-Ups guild. I don't know if y'all have met."

Beatrice and Phyllis shook hands. Phyllis gave her a solid handshake.

"Do you mind, Posy?" asked Phyllis again. "It would really help me out."

Meadow looked a bit scandalized. "But it's a guild meeting for the Village Quilters!"

Miss Sissy wandered up from the sitting area and glared at Phyllis. "Village Quilters!" she repeated in a low growl.

"Pooh," said Phyllis, waving away Meadow's objections with a sweep of her hand and completely ignoring Miss Sissy. "We're not talking about industrial espionage or uncovering state secrets here. Quilting is quilting, right? I've gotten behind because things have been completely awful at the Cut-Ups lately. In fact, Meadow, I was planning on giving you a call and talking with you about it. I might be a refugee from the guild."

"Whatever do you mean?" came another voice behind them. This one was a good deal colder in tone. Beatrice turned to see Martha Helmsley standing nearby. Martha was also in the Cut-Ups and was their most elegant member with her loosely upswept red hair, pearls, and tasteful designer clothes in various neutral hues. She was usually fairly reserved when she spoke, but this time her tone was downright frosty.

Phyllis colored slightly at being overheard but raised her chin and said, "You heard me, Martha. The Cut-

Ups hasn't exactly been a fun group for me lately. I don't get the warm fuzzies when I go to the meetings anymore. Don't act like you don't know what I'm talking about, either. You're the one responsible for the rest of the group giving me the cold shoulder."

"That's ridiculous," snapped Martha. "You're imagining things. And I'm sorry to hear," she added in a censorious voice, "that you're behind on your quilt. You certainly shouldn't be." She stalked away to shop for fabrics.

"See what I mean?" asked Phyllis in a shaky voice. "So, what do you think, Posy? You'd really be helping me out."

"No room! No room!" snarled Miss Sissy. Beatrice decided she sounded very much like one of the demented guests from the mad tea party in *Alice in Wonderland*.

Posy, whose blue eyes had anxiously watched the standoff between Martha and Phyllis, said quickly, "Actually, I was just counting tables in my head. I'm sure we have room for you at the retreat."

"But for heaven's sake, don't tell anyone else!" said Meadow in her loud whisper that could likely be heard by passersby on the street outside.

"Thanks so much," said Phyllis, giving Posy and Meadow and even a startled Beatrice a hug. "I'll be here Friday evening."

"Let's make it five o'clock," said Posy.

"Remember to bring food," Meadow called out as

Phyllis started walking toward the door. "We have to have lots of sustenance for this kind of thing."

The door chimed as Phyllis left the shop. "That was interesting," murmured Beatrice.

"Those Cut-Ups with these silly melodramas," said Meadow with a sniff. "It's good to belong to a grown-up guild." She froze as Martha Helmsley gave her an unfriendly stare. "That is . . . well . . . oops. I have foot-in-mouth disease. Sorry about that, Martha."

Beatrice could barely see Martha's tense face over the huge pile she was holding. She held yards of several different patterns of fabrics—enough material for several quilts—and quilt batting, to boot. Posy quickly rang her up and Beatrice raised her eyebrows at the final total for the purchase.

"Thanks so much, Posy," said Martha smoothly. "You always have everything I need here."

"Thanks for being one of my best customers," said Posy brightly.

"Before I go," said Martha carelessly, "I wanted to see if I could join you ladies on Friday evening, too."

"Oh!" said Posy, startled. She looked helplessly over at Meadow and Beatrice for direction.

"No room! No room!" Miss Sissy repeated aggressively.

Meadow gave a ferocious frown, putting her hands on her wide hips. "I thought you told Phyllis that you were done with your quilt."

"No," said Martha, "I said that *Phyllis* should be done with her quilt. She procrastinates. I, on the other hand, have been incredibly busy. I have only a little ways to go, but this would give me a deadline for finishing my project." She looked expectantly at Posy over the bags of fabric still sitting on the checkout counter in front of her.

Posy nervously fingered the beagle pin on her fluffy blue cardigan. "I'm sure I can find a spot for you at the retreat, Martha. I'd love to have you come."

Martha rewarded her with a smile. "Thanks so much, Posy. See you ladies on Friday," she added coolly to Beatrice and Meadow.

"Now, why on earth would she want to come to your retreat when clearly she and Phyllis don't get along?" asked Beatrice.

"Isn't it obvious?" asked Meadow. "To get on her nerves, of course."

"Dangerrr," crooned Miss Sissy, right on cue.

Chapter Two

Beatrice had just finished doing some chores around the cottage the next morning when the phone trilled.

"Beatrice? It's Wyatt."

Beatrice felt a smile spread over her face at the sound of the minister's voice. Wyatt, a widower for many years, and she had seemed to have a connection between them since Beatrice had moved to Dappled Hills. "How are you?"

"Great! I was wondering—I know this is a little last-minute—if you would like to have lunch with me today." He hesitated, then hurried on, "I understand if you've already got plans, of course. I'm finishing up at the church office here and . . . well, I'd love to see you for lunch. Have you eaten yet?"

Was this . . . was Wyatt asking her out on a date? Beatrice's heart thumped in her chest and she said rather breathlessly, "I'd love to. No, I haven't had any lunch yet." At this point, even if she'd eaten enough for ten lunches, she'd still go out with Wyatt for a meal.

"Wonderful. I'll come over and pick you up in about—is thirty minutes all right?"

Beatrice touched her hair. It felt as if it must look like a squirrel's nest after she'd been working around the house all morning. "Perfect," she said weakly. And as soon as they hung up the phone, she hurried off to brush her hair and find something that looked nice—but didn't look as if she were trying too hard. She settled on her favorite pair of black slacks, a cotton blouse, and a red infinity-loop scarf that Meadow had told her set off her hair well. After carefully applying some makeup and brushing her hair, she looked at herself critically in the bathroom mirror. A definite improvement.

She found herself feeling a little nervous as she waited for him to pick her up. Silly. It was only Wyatt. But this was the first time he'd asked her on any kind of actual date, despite the fact that it was lunch. Lunch was low-key, wasn't it? Beatrice jumped as the doorbell rang, then fussed at herself some more. She paused for a couple of moments—it wouldn't do to swing the door immediately open as if she'd been waiting by the door. Although she *had* been waiting by the door.

When Beatrice opened the door, all her nervousness quickly vanished. Wyatt's eyes crinkled in a smile when he saw her. "Ready to go?" he asked. "You look

wonderful, as always. Thanks for coming with me."
Beatrice flushed with pleasure.

Wyatt drove them to the Dappled Hills Eatery downtown. It was a popular meat-and-three-vegetable restaurant with Southern-inspired dishes that would melt in
your mouth. Beatrice and Wyatt had a nice view of the
park from their table by the window, and the little restaurant was filled with delicious aromas. "I thought a warm
lunch would be a nice change," said Wyatt, pulling off
his jacket and hanging it neatly on the back of his chair.
"If you're like me, then you usually eat sandwiches for
lunch."

She did. And frequently, lunch would even pass her
by completely and she'd realize she'd forgotten to eat
it when her stomach would start rumbling in the middle of the afternoon.

After perusing the menu, Beatrice settled on chicken
and dumplings with side orders of fried okra and black-
eyed peas and Wyatt got the meat loaf with butter beans
and fried green tomatoes. She'd ordered and Wyatt was
still giving his order to their server when Beatrice glanced
up and saw several tables of diners staring goggle-eyed
at them. Most of them she recognized as members of Wyatt's congregation. When one table of older ladies saw
that she was staring back in their direction, they waved
delightedly at her, grinning. Beatrice gave a small smile
back, and then determinedly gazed down at the check-
ered tablecloth. Small towns.

Wyatt, on the other hand, seemed completely unfazed. He noticed the diners staring at them, too, but he immediately waved and smiled at them, even inquiring after one of the diner's health. He was a bigger person than she was, reflected Beatrice. This might be expected, however, considering that he pursued the ministry.

"You've got the kind of job where you're always on the clock," said Beatrice ruefully. "Does it bother you sometimes?"

Wyatt considered this for a couple of moments. "Hardly ever. Maybe after a very long day or if I'm especially tired. But overall, I really enjoy being around people—you really have to, to be a good minister. What about you, though, Beatrice? I'd imagine you spent a good deal of time with people in your role as art museum curator."

"Sometimes I did. We'd host special showings and events there—evenings with museum patrons and members. The difference was that there was a definite end to it—there'd be an event from eight o'clock to ten o'clock and then I could sort of decompress at ten. But there were plenty of times when I'd be by myself at the museum, too—setting up exhibits or planning events," said Beatrice.

Their meals arrived, steaming hot to warm them up on the cool morning. There was something about comfort food that was just so . . . comforting.

Wyatt said interestedly, "Tell me more about the

kinds of things you'd do as curator and the sorts of exhibits you'd put together."

Beatrice talked a little about planning, preparing, and promoting exhibits, organizing community outreach activities, and developing relationships with museum patrons and collectors as Wyatt listened intently and asked questions at various intervals.

Wyatt said, "So although you worked a lot with artwork, and you're remembering a lot of the time spent alone, it was also a job where you needed to foster relationships."

Beatrice smiled at him. "Maybe our jobs were more alike than I'd thought. Although I have a feeling your relationships with your congregation might be a lot closer and more rewarding than the ones I developed. What does your usual day look like?"

She found herself listening with genuine interest as Wyatt talked about being a pastor in a very small town—the different generations he'd known and ministered to. The kinds of situations, both humorous and heartbreaking, that came up every day. And she found, as she listened to him and enjoyed her lunch, that the rest of the world faded away. They talked about books they always found themselves returning to, places they'd like to see, and music they enjoyed. And through it all, Beatrice realized that what she really missed was this type of companionship—this type of intellectual and spiritual connection.

Fortunately, they were both finished with their meals when Wyatt's phone made a soft chime. "I'm sorry," he said as he picked it up to look at it. "I'm afraid I'm going to have to go. Constance Bradley, one of my oldest church members, has been doing poorly for a while and has taken a turn for the worse. Her daughter says she'd like me to visit." He quickly signaled for the check and gave Beatrice a rueful look. "I'm very sorry about this," he repeated. "I guess this is one of those occupational hazards we were talking about. But I did enjoy our lunch and time together. Can we repeat it again soon?"

Beatrice smiled at him. "I'd like that, thanks." She tamped down the twinge of disappointment that she felt. This was just the nature of Wyatt's profession, after all.

Wyatt walked over to the cash register to stand in line to pay their bill. As Beatrice was waiting for him, she heard voices from the table behind her. A woman was saying, "I don't know how you keep your temper around her, Jason. Every time I turn around, it's like Phyllis is there, smiling in your direction. Doesn't she realize that you're not interested? That you're with me now?"

Beatrice turned surreptitiously to see a woman near her age with red, upswept hair and a determined expression sitting with an older man with silver hair and very white teeth set in a tanned face.

The man's voice was deep and soothing. "Martha,

you can't think that Phyllis wants to get back together with me. She can see how delighted you and I are in each other's company—it's plain to everybody. Besides"— and now his voice had an embarrassed edge to it— "you do know how Phyllis's and my relationship went the last time. It didn't exactly end on a good note."

"She's the kind of delusional person who just might believe she can get you back," came the woman's voice. She sounded put out.

"You've got nothing to worry about, Martha. I'd simply ignore her behavior. After all, won't you have to learn to deal with her? She's in your quilt guild, isn't she?" asked the man.

"Not for long. Not if I have my way," said the woman darkly.

That night, Noo-noo growled at the door and Beatrice, laying down her book, looked down at her in surprise. "What's wrong, Noo-noo? What is it?" She listened for a moment, but didn't hear anything, so she picked her book up again.

Then there was another growl from the dog, this time more persistent. Beatrice listened, harder, and this time she heard something. "Is that an animal out there?" she muttered. Noo-noo gave a small woof of agreement.

Beatrice flipped on the porch lights and peered out the window next to her front door, looking first to make sure there were no people out there lurking on her porch, then gazing down at the floor of the porch. But she didn't see anyone, or anything, out there. "Noo-noo, I'm not sure what you're hearing, sweetie. . . ." And then she stopped short, hearing the noise herself. She squinted, peering intently out the window at the corner of the porch. But she still couldn't see anything.

Beatrice cautiously opened the door just a crack and a little gray fuzzy paw immediately came through. She opened the door farther and a gray kitten bounced through the door, rubbing against her legs and purring. She was a beautiful bluish gray with blue eyes. "Where did you come from?" asked Beatrice as Noo-noo growled at the cute intruder. The growling didn't faze the kitten whatsoever and she ran over to lovingly rub against the growling Noo-noo. The corgi gave Beatrice a helpless look.

"Well, Noo-noo, it's a chilly night, and our visitor did single us out to visit. She doesn't seem to have a collar or belong to anyone. I guess she's our guest until we figure out a long-term plan for her." Somehow the little dog seemed to understand . . . and looked rather dejected.

Clearly, something would have to be done about a makeshift litter box. Beatrice thought this through for a moment and then found a small cardboard box that she lined with a trash bag. She tore up some newspaper into strips for the inside and then put the kitten inside. Apparently, she didn't have to go, though. And Beatrice was ready to turn in.

Both animals followed her into her bedroom—Noo-noo probably to keep an eye on the little intruder. She lay down on the floor close to Beatrice, and the kitten somehow managed to jump and scramble and claw her way to the top of the bed, where she lay curled up against Beatrice's leg.

Chapter Three

The next morning was the perfect day for a fall quilt retreat. The skies were sunny and wispy clouds blew quickly through. There was a brisk breeze in the air, although it wasn't quite cold—only a little crisp. Beatrice's unexpected furry guest had behaved herself remarkably well and even figured out the temporary litter box. That afternoon, she went to the store and picked up cat food, toys, and a real litter box. Noo-noo had settled into wary acceptance of the kitten.

With the animals set, it seemed that the best course of action, as the sun started to sink, was to enjoy some tasty food and the company of quilters in the cozy quilt shop.

Meadow beamed when she saw her and immediately relieved Beatrice of half of the things she was carrying and led her to the store's large back room, where long tables were set up next to one another. "Good. You came early. Figured you would, since you're one of those strictly punctual types. Here, take this table." She laid down Beatrice's things with a flourish. "See, you're here in between me and Miss Sissy." Meadow gestured behind Beatrice.

Beatrice turned, repressing a sigh. How was Miss Sissy today, on the lucidity scale?

Miss Sissy glared fiercely at Beatrice, her black button eyes narrowed. "Wickedness!" she growled.

Apparently, Miss Sissy was not having one of her good days. Fortunately, Beatrice now knew how to make her a bit more even-tempered. "Could you help me out with my quilt today, Miss Sissy? I'm finished with my quilt for the show, because it was an easy pattern, but I wanted to try something harder for myself."

Miss Sissy's harsh gaze relaxed and she trotted spryly around her table until she was on Beatrice's side. She gently helped spread out the quilt and ran a hand over it. "Double wedding ring," she grunted, smiling down at the colorful arcs that Beatrice had started. Instability aside, Miss Sissy was a fantastic quilter. And Beatrice would take all the help she could get. Particularly if, in the process, it meant keeping the peace.

"Hoo-boy!" said Meadow, looking over Beatrice's shoulder at her project. "That's not a pattern for the faint of heart, is it? You're a very brave quilter."

Beatrice said, "Well, I figured the fastest way to learn

was to do something really tough—and probably to fail at it. Besides, if I try a pattern this difficult, I know I'll have experts volunteering to help me out." She smiled over at Miss Sissy, who rewarded her with a small smile in return.

Meadow grabbed her arm and gave it a squeeze. "Ash is here. Isn't that exciting? I know he and Piper have already gone out a few times. Hope Piper can tear herself away from Ash to finish that quilt of hers. We need to get cracking to get ready for this quilt show." She looked toward the door. "Hi, Georgia!"

Georgia Potter, one of the younger quilters, in her early thirties, gave Meadow a quick wave and then wrinkled her brow as she looked around the shop's back room.

"Something wrong?" asked Beatrice.

"Have y'all seen Savannah?" she asked them.

Meadow gestured toward the store. "I saw her— looked like she was shopping for quilting supplies."

Georgia sighed. "I was afraid of that."

Meadow said, "Don't worry about it." She lowered her voice. "If she nicks something, you know Posy will just tell you about it later on. It's not a big deal. Posy doesn't even care."

Georgia gave her a grateful smile and then said, "I know. And it's sweet of y'all to cover for Savannah and work around her . . . problem. I'll admit—lately, she's worn down my patience a little." Georgia's eyes were tired.

Beatrice and Meadow exchanged glances. That was a huge admission for Georgia to make. She always seemed to have endless patience for Savannah. "Has Savannah been especially . . . challenging . . . lately?" asked Beatrice.

Georgia nodded. "When Savannah gets stressed out about anything, these incidents seem to happen more. With the quilt show coming up, she's really been tense—she's fallen behind on her quilt and wants it to be perfect . . . but she also wants it finished on time. She and I even had a little spat a couple of days ago, and that made her even worse." She noticed that Beatrice and Meadow were giving her a surprised look and she explained, "We can't agree on getting a pet. I want one and Savannah thinks they're really untidy. I guess they are. And I know Savannah is already making a lot of concessions for me—it was her house, originally, before she let me stay with her after my divorce." She shrugged.

"But Savannah has always been delighted to have you stay with her," said Meadow stoutly. "You can tell how much she loves having you there. You're her sister!"

"I know. I feel the same way. But I'm very different from Savannah and she's had to make a lot of adjustments to the way she wants to live. She likes everything perfectly straight and organized. And I'm more . . . loosey-goosey." Georgia gazed ruefully at the pile of quilting materials she'd brought in. Loosey-goosey was an understatement.

Beatrice said, "It's probably only natural that y'all would have disagreements like that. After all, you spend so much time together. Maybe you need a little bit of a break from each other."

Beatrice expected that Georgia, always so loyal to her sister, would immediately pooh-pooh that suggestion. To her surprise, she seemed to be seriously considering it. "Maybe. Maybe I should, just for a little while. It might be really good for Savannah, too. Actually, it's funny but I have a good friend who asked me to pet-sit while she's visiting her mother in Alabama. I was planning on checking in over there a few times a day . . . but she'd love it if I house-sat and stayed there." She smiled and said, "She has the cutest little pets in the world—Snuffy and Mr. Shadow. I especially love Mr. Shadow—he's this fluffy gray butterball of a cat."

Meadow said, "See? It's perfect . . . something like that has got to be fate. A break will do you good— maybe it will do Savannah good, too." She cleared her throat. "And maybe it will give you both the opportunity to finish those quilts of yours in time for the show."

Beatrice murmured, "Savannah is on her way over."

They stopped talking and Meadow said breezily, "Hi there, Savannah!"

Savannah gave them a gruff greeting. She was wearing her customary long floral dress and had her hair pulled into a tight bun. But Beatrice noticed she seemed less put-together than she usually did. Savannah spotted Georgia's pile of fabric and notions on a table and carefully took her place at a table across the room from it. Georgia sighed and gave Meadow and Beatrice a meaningful look.

A small woman with a round face and a constantly startled expression peered through the door to the back room. Meadow clapped her hands when she saw her. "June Bug! And you've brought cakes for us to eat. Perfect!"

Posy hurried over to relieve June Bug of the desserts. "Since we all know that June Bug makes the best cakes in town, I thought I should ask her to make some for our retreat. But I do wish you'd stay for the quilting, June Bug," she said to the little woman.

June Bug flushed at the praise but shook her head swiftly. "I'm not in the quilt show." She gave a hurried glance at her large watch. "I'd better run," she said. And she was gone just as quickly as she'd arrived.

"That June Bug!" said Meadow. "I can't believe I can't convince her to enter one of her gorgeous quilts into the show."

Beatrice said, "*I* can't believe you managed to persuade her to join the Village Quilters." June Bug was extremely doubtful about the quality of her quilts or her craftsmanship. And, from what Beatrice had heard, she had no idea that she was as gifted as she was.

Meadow said gloomily, "Not that she ever goes to any of the guild meetings."

Posy said, "Slow and steady wins the race, remember? We just have to build up her confidence, that's all." Then a frown suddenly creased Posy's gentle features. She anxiously fingered the beagle broach she'd pinned on her fluffy pink cardigan. "Oh dear. It looks as if Martha Helmsley and Phyllis Stitt might have tables next to each other. I hope that's going to be all right."

Meadow gave a dismissive wave of her hand and said in a low voice, "Phyllis is looking for a little creative growth, that's all. They'll be fine. Remember, Phyllis is a professional in the community. She knows how to play nicely with others."

"What does she do?" asked Beatrice.

"Phyllis is a wedding coordinator," said Meadow.

Beatrice said in a low voice, "Is there some animosity between them because of a man? I overheard something recently and was trying to figure it out."

"That's right. Phyllis used to date Jason. Maybe Martha is worried Jason still has feelings for Phyllis. But that's ancient history. I'm sure they'll get along fine."

Meadow stopped talking as Phyllis approached Posy. She looked a little nervous and said quietly, "Do you have another seat available? I'd rather not sit next to . . . well, you know."

Posy gave Meadow and Beatrice a helpless look and

quickly said, "I think there's one over here that's still free, Phyllis. Let's take a look."

Phyllis abruptly vacated the table as Martha watched with a derisive smile on her face. Phyllis called over to Beatrice, "You've got quite a project on your hands there." She nodded at the table to indicate Beatrice's double wedding ring quilt.

Beatrice said, "That's exactly why I decided to bring it today. This retreat is the perfect place for advice." She looked over at Phyllis's quilt—a very complex tumbling blocks pattern. "You haven't really got an easy quilt yourself."

Phyllis laughed. "I sure don't, sweetie. But I've got some great tools to help me with it." She held up a pair of eight-inch stainless steel quilting shears. "This is my new favorite notion. It'll clip threads like nobody's business. Posy pointed them out to me a couple of weeks ago. She sure does stock this store well."

Beatrice looked around her and sighed. "Well, I brought my quilting things in, but I apparently left my pocketbook in the car. I'm starting to think I'd lose my head if it weren't attached. I'd better go grab it."

Everyone was either getting their notions and fabrics set up or talking to one another. Meadow and Posy were keeping a watchful eye on the Phyllis and Martha situation. Martha was still throwing icy glares in Phyllis's direction, and Phyllis appeared blithely unconcerned or else completely ignorant of the malice directed at her. Beatrice found her keys—fortunately, she hadn't left *those* in the car along with her purse—and walked out to the parking lot.

When she'd retrieved her bag and was heading back toward the shop, she saw the much-talked-about Jason Gore walking in. He was speaking with Posy and his white teeth flashed as he threw back his head and laughed at something she said. This made her flush with pleasure. Beatrice looked Jason over with a discerning eye. He certainly was tanned. What on earth did he do for a living? Or perhaps he spent a lot of time on the golf course. Jason had silver hair and something of a corporate world appearance. He wasn't classically handsome, though, and had rather a large nose, although it did seem to fit his face well. A man from the shop next door walked out and Jason hesitated briefly while talking to Posy, as if he'd forgotten what he was going to say. The younger man, very lean and fit in jeans and a white T-shirt, gave Jason a look of complete contempt. Jason averted his gaze and quickly resumed his conversation again, stuttering a bit as he talked. He glanced back over a few seconds later and saw the man still standing there, arms crossed, as if determined to make Jason nervous.

Beatrice watched as Jason deftly put an arm around Posy and lightly motioned her into the shop and away from the brooding man on the sidewalk. Interesting. She'd have to ask Meadow who the young man was. Or maybe Piper knew. Beatrice entered the shop behind them.

Jason's appearance inside the Patchwork Cottage created a multitude of different reactions. Several ladies were primping with surreptitious lipstick applications. Posy and Meadow looked a bit anxious. And Phyllis seemed—well, Beatrice couldn't decide exactly what the expression on Phyllis's remarkably unlined face meant. Perhaps it was longing? Perhaps it was exasperation? Frustration? Beatrice really didn't know her well enough to be able to read her. Her usually mischievous eyes were solemn and she impatiently brushed an errant strand of her artfully careless hair from her eyes. She hurried from the back room into the shop.

But Martha seemed delighted to see Jason. "You're here. I didn't know you were coming." She leaned against him and beamed as she looked up into his face.

"Just trying to be supportive," he said with a grin.

Martha gave a giggle that didn't fit either her age or her sophisticated style. Then she abruptly glanced across the room. "Oh, splendid, my son is here. I asked Frank to bring by some fat quarters that I'd accidentally left at the house."

Martha's son, Frank, was wearing his customary black. Beatrice always thought he'd carefully constructed his appearance to make it scream "artist." He had a scraggly Van Dyke beard and occasionally sported a beret in case someone didn't get the point. He smelled like cigarettes. He also seemed invariably moody. Although he was probably nearly thirty, there was an air of immaturity about him.

Frank was moody today, in fact. As he handed his mother a plastic grocery bag full of fabric roll, he shot Jason an icy glare and said, "I don't suppose you could have asked your Special Friend to get your forgotten items."

"Don't be silly," said Martha sharply. "Jason doesn't have a key to my house."

Frank rolled his eyes at this. Apparently, there was some disagreement on this point. "Whatever. You're certainly adults. But don't pretend I don't know what's really going on. Remember, Mother, we're family. He's . . . not."

"Not right now he's not. That's open to change," said Martha stiffly.

"Not if I have a vote," muttered Frank between gritted teeth. "He's always trying to tell you what to do. Whispering lies in your ear. I know all about this guy. He's nothing like the man you think he is, Mother. He's putting on a front."

"Now, look here," said Jason, his genial expression hardened, "you can't talk to her like that."

"I can talk to her any way I please," said Frank. "She's my mother."

Frank spun on his heel and stalked out the door into the store. Jason stared after him, and then followed him out. "I'll be back soon, love," he called over his shoulder to Martha.

In an attempt to divert everyone's attention back to quilting, Posy greeted the ladies, made sure everyone had entered their name for the door prize, and they all started working. There were quiet moments, but in general, the room was filled with laughter and conversation and, almost, a sense of family.

There was also a lot of coming and going. Sometimes the quilters found that they could use a bit of different fabric to add to their quilt. There were also women visiting the table of food and drinks that Posy had provided in the store—she'd put out a tray of mini quiches, some prosciutto-wrapped cheeses, vegetables and fruits, and punch. And, of course, there were June Bug's delicious cakes—a German chocolate five-layer, a peanut butter swirl cheesecake, and a carrot cake with cream cheese frosting.

Beatrice, as she'd expected, had run into some trouble with her pattern fairly early on. Cutting the pieces for the quilt was a lot trickier than she'd guessed. But Miss Sissy glanced over, saw she was having problems, and skillfully put her on the right path. Surprisingly, Miss Sissy advocated a shortcut—an acrylic template that Posy sold in the store. Miss Sissy helped Beatrice tape the fabric to the back of the templates and use a tool to cut the center blocks for the quilt.

In general, the retreat seemed like a very smooth

and organized event. Posy was relaxed and happy and also seemed to be making a fair number of sales, including the templates and tool to help Beatrice with her quilt. The only person who appeared to be having any trouble was Phyllis.

"Where did my new shears go?" she asked plaintively. It was her nearly constant refrain for the next twenty minutes. She'd looked under bunches of fabric and peered under her table.

Posy helped her search. "Could you have set them down on someone else's table while you were chatting, maybe?" she asked.

Phyllis pursed her lips thoughtfully, and then shook her head until her frosted blond hair tumbled around her face. "I don't think so." Then her eyes narrowed and she said in a hard voice, "But they're expensive shears. Maybe someone took them."

There was a small gasp from the assembled quilters, and the feeling of family quickly dissipated. Beatrice raised her eyebrows. Was Phyllis seriously leveling an accusation of theft at these quilters? These were all neighbors, all friends of hers. Over shears? Now she *was* seriously wondering if Phyllis was a good candidate for the Village Quilters.

"In fact," she said, "if I had to guess, I'd say that Martha might have taken them." Phyllis turned to stare at Martha Helmsley.

Martha gave a startled laugh. "Me? Why on earth would I take your shears? Even if they *were* nice. I have the means to go into the store and purchase my own, you know."

"I bought the last pair," spat Phyllis.

"But I can always order more!" said Posy, hurriedly, anxiously fingering her beagle pin.

"I wouldn't want yours," said Martha. She had a slightly disgusted expression on her face as if she suspected that Phyllis's shears might have some terrible, transferable germs on them.

"Something wrong, Mom?" came a grim voice. Beatrice turned to see Martha's son, Frank.

"What are you still doing here?" she asked sharply. "I thought you had things to do today."

"I wanted to check and see if there was anything else you needed," he said in an innocent tone. Beatrice noticed that he was holding a paper plate loaded down with food. Apparently, hunger had kept him at the store. Or, perhaps, the realization he should smooth things over with his mother a bit, considering that she was his sole provider.

"Everything okay?" Frank repeated, this time somewhat impatiently.

"Yes," said Martha in a chilly voice. "Everything is fine. Phyllis and I were simply having a misunderstanding."

Phyllis was opening her mouth again, as if to dispute that fact, when Beatrice quickly broke in. "Phyllis, I can help you find your shears. I'm sure they'll turn up."

Phyllis continued looking under various quilts and fabrics and notions on different tables, searching for the scissors.

Hadn't the storeroom been searched enough? Beatrice had the feeling that the missing shears were likely in the main area of the store. Maybe Phyllis had absently laid them down as she was entering the retreat. "I'll check the store," she offered. It was a relief to get away from the bickering in the back room, anyway.

Beatrice first checked out the most likely areas of the store where Phyllis might have absentmindedly put down her scissors: the buffet table and the ladies' room. No shears. She also looked at the checkout counter to see if she'd laid them down while fumbling with whatever she was carrying. Nothing.

Beatrice walked into the sitting area with the sofa and chairs and peered at the coffee table and the seat cushions—she saw nothing. Then she headed to the far end of the store near the windows.

And saw Jason Gore, unmoving, behind a display case. Phyllis's missing shears were stuck into his chest.

Chapter Four

Beatrice sharply drew in her breath, drawing back from Jason's body, her heart pounding. She pulled her phone out of her pocket and dialed police chief Ramsay Downey, Meadow's husband. She punched the numbers with trembling fingers. "Ramsay," she said hoarsely as he answered, "there's been a murder at the Patchwork Cottage. Jason Gore is dead."

"What?" said Ramsay in a voice that was a mixture of surprise and exasperation. "All right, I'm on my way. Keep everyone far away from the body. Actually, have everyone step out of the shop entirely. I'll be right over."

As Beatrice was hanging up the phone, she heard a startled cry. She turned to see Phyllis right behind her, weaving unsteadily on her feet, a hand to her throat. "Jason," she said in a soft voice.

"Did you find the silly shears?" Martha impatiently asked behind them. She stopped short, gazing at Jason with a horrified expression. "Jason!" she shrieked.

Beatrice said in a gentle but firm voice, "I've called Ramsay. We're to keep away from this area and wait outside for him to arrive."

Her words went unheard, though, as Martha turned on Phyllis. "You. This is your fault—your doing!" she spat out.

"Of course not," said Phyllis with a gasp, blinking in a dazed manner. "I'd never . . . I couldn't . . ."

"They're *your shears*," bellowed Martha. "And you're the one who wanted revenge on Jason. He left you at the altar, didn't he?"

Now Phyllis's voice had an edge to it. "No, actually, he didn't. It was weeks before the wedding when he left. And, by the way, you can't have it both ways, Martha. Did I want Jason back, or did I want him dead? You've told everyone in town it was the first. Now you're claiming it's the second."

"Because they're *your shears*!" Martha's pretty face was mottled with a blotchy red as her voice rose. "And now he's dead!" Now there were other quilters peeking out behind her with their own gasps.

"I told you, they went missing!" Phyllis, trembling, appeared to be ready to launch herself at Martha.

A deep voice behind them murmured, "What's this?

My, what a shame." Beatrice turned around to see Martha's son, Frank, gazing at Jason's body with more than a hint of satisfaction on his face.

Miss Sissy's grizzled face peered out around Frank to stare at the body on the floor. "Evilllll," she hissed.

"All right," barked Beatrice in as commanding a voice as she could muster. "Everyone outside the shop. Out!" She pointed to the shop door. "Let's head out all the way to the parking lot."

Martha and Phyllis reluctantly left, still looking as if they were both furious and shocked at the same time. Meadow muttered to Beatrice, "At least Phyllis's shears were found and we don't have to hear about them anymore." Beatrice quickly stuck her head in the storeroom, explained there'd been an accident, and that Ramsay had asked everyone to please congregate in the parking lot. The quilters quietly followed.

The young man who'd acted so aggressively when Jason was entering the shop gazed at the women curiously as they gathered in the parking lot. He walked over to their group. "I don't think we've met," he said quietly. "I'm Tony Brock—I work at the hardware store there. What's going on?" he asked Beatrice.

She hesitated and then said, "Jason Gore has been found dead in the shop. He was apparently . . . murdered."

Beatrice watched as an indefinable emotion crossed

his features. It was quickly suppressed and he said, "That must have been awful for all of you. Who found him?"

Beatrice swallowed. It had, actually, been awful. But everything had happened so fast that she didn't think it had had time to sink in yet. It was starting to, though, and she thought she might be plagued with some bad dreams in the nights to come. "I did," she said quietly.

Tony asked, "Did you call Ramsay? Did he ask you all to stay out here?"

Beatrice nodded.

She watched as another man, tall and spindly with glasses and gray hair, hurried toward the group of quilters standing in the parking lot. He rushed right up to Martha and said, "Someone in the hardware store said there'd been a murder at Posy's shop! I was worried sick about you."

Martha, who'd been staring blankly into space, gave him an irritated look. "I'm okay, John. But it's Jason. He's gone." He reached out as if to give Martha a hug, but she pulled away from him, wrapping her arms around herself and delving back into her thoughts.

The sound of a car made Beatrice turn and they saw Ramsay's police cruiser approaching the group. He parked and got out to walk over to speak with Posy, who'd been anxiously standing away from the others, feeling a strong responsibility as store owner. Ramsay was a short, balding man with a stomach that had seen its share of Southern cooking. But Beatrice had found him kind and fair, although he certainly seemed to have a dislike of police work. He'd much rather be at home, rereading his beloved *Walden* . . . or maybe watching *Wheel of Fortune* on television.

Posy handed Ramsay the shop keys and he secured the scene. Ten minutes later, he left the shop and motioned Beatrice over.

"You okay?" he asked, squinting in concern. "You're looking a little pale, there."

She'd been feeling a little ill, as a matter of fact. Beatrice, unfortunately, had had occasion to discover other murder victims. But they'd always appeared as if they were sleeping somehow. This was a much more violent, furious crime. She nodded at Ramsay, though, in reassurance.

"So . . . what happened, Beatrice? It sounds like you happened on Jason Gore's body?" he asked. "You didn't see or hear anything? No clues as to who might have done this?" Ramsay watched her intently.

"I didn't see or hear a thing. I was looking for Phyllis Stitt's lost shears," said Beatrice. She sighed. "And I found them."

Ramsay raised his eyebrows. "Lost shears? Like the ones that were used . . . ?"

"I'm afraid so. The very ones," said Beatrice. "For what it's worth, she'd claimed all along that they were missing. That's why I set out to look for them. She was blaming Martha for swiping them up until the shears were discovered."

"And now they'll be taken away in an evidence bag," said Ramsay grimly. "I suppose I should speak to Phyllis first."

"You might want to tread softly," warned Beatrice. "She's apparently ultrasensitive right now about being blamed for anything. She is trying to get into the Village Quilters guild because she thinks everyone in the Cut-Ups believes she was trying to steal Jason away from Martha."

"Was she?" asked Ramsay.

"I guess that remains to be seen," said Beatrice with a small shrug. "But she really didn't seem love-struck to me. *Or* bent on revenge for him running out on her." She lowered her voice. "Although it sounded as if Martha thought so. Martha is apparently the main reason why Phyllis wants to get out of the Cut-Ups guild."

Ramsay gazed over at the assembled group of quilters and sighed. "Here goes nothing. Hopefully the state police can get over here soon and give me a hand. Let's hope somebody saw something helpful."

"You've got to solve the mystery, Beatrice. I'm counting on you."

It was way too early in the day, decided Beatrice, for a visit from Meadow. Apparently, discovering bodies took a real toll on Beatrice. She'd slept in for the first time in ages, although that probably had a lot to do with the fact that she'd had such a hard time falling asleep last night. Now she was sitting in her nightgown and robe, drinking a very dark cup of coffee with great determination.

Meadow, on the other hand, looked fresh as a daisy. She was dressed in a very colorful tunic and flowing pants in a different bright color. Her eyes gazed earnestly at Beatrice through her red-framed glasses. Boris, the Genius Dog, was with her. Beatrice watched them both with tired eyes. The kitten watched Boris with wary ones. She'd chosen to sit up on the top of the cabinets. How she'd gotten up there, Beatrice couldn't say.

"Why are you counting on *me* to solve the case, Meadow? You have a police chief husband. I'm pretty sure that Ramsay's investigating techniques are a lot better than mine are. Besides, I can't imagine that Ramsay would be very happy with me getting in the middle of his murder investigation."

"That's where you're wrong," said Meadow. "I'm sure he'd be eternally grateful if you'd help. After all, Ramsay despises police work. He's always just praying that somehow it'll all go away so that he can write poetry again or read some big, boring book. You have a real talent, Beatrice—you're a Gifted Amateur. I'm convinced you can use your skill to find the real killer—because Ramsay is very shortsightedly focused on poor

Phyllis right now. Can you imagine how stressful that is for her?"

"That's only natural," said Beatrice mildly. "After all, those *were* Phyllis's shears that were used as the murder weapon. And she did have a history with the victim."

"Oh, anyone could have gotten hold of those silly shears," said Meadow. She waved her hand impatiently. "And Phyllis wasn't the only one who had a problem with Jason. Honestly, Phyllis could possibly be an asset for the Village Quilters. Although I don't think we really need another member in the guild right now— after all, we recently took on June Bug, even if she doesn't come to meetings very often. But even if the guild votes *not* to induct Phyllis, I know we have to get to the bottom of this mess. It's not good for our community."

"I'll ask some questions and see what I can find out." Meadow's face lit up. "And I'll start with you. I need all the dirt on Jason Gore."

"Didn't I already do that? Tell you what I knew?"

Beatrice shook her head.

Meadow heaved a great sigh and absently patted Boris for a moment. "I'm not too sure I know a lot. You heard about the Phyllis/Martha/Jason relationship thing."

"The love triangle you mentioned at the retreat. Yes. But what's going on with Tony Brock?"

Meadow frowned. "Tony Brock?"

"Yes. You know—the young guy who works at the hardware store next to the Patchwork Cottage. He was glowering at Jason when he was walking into the quilting retreat," said Beatrice. She took another sip of her coffee, although she was starting to feel more awake now. "And he seemed interested in finding out what happened when he saw us all standing out in the parking lot."

"Oh. That's right," said Meadow. She let go of Boris and leaned back in her chair. Boris immediately shuffled off into Beatrice's kitchen, although Beatrice was now paying little attention to the dogs as she focused on Meadow. "You see, Jason Gore might have been a bit of a con man."

"A con man. In Dappled Hills?"

"Where better?" asked Meadow, spreading out her hands. "After all, when you're in a small town, people trust you. Everyone knows everyone here. And the people in the town might not be particularly sophisticated or have much experience with crime. It's the perfect place to find a mark."

"Maybe that's what Frank meant at the retreat when he told his mother that Jason wasn't the man she thought he was. When did Jason move here? Or was he a part of the town for a long time before he decided to run a scam?" asked Beatrice.

Meadow gave a hooting laugh. "*Run a scam?* You

sound like a gangster yourself. I guess that's what living in Atlanta teaches you, right? Okay. Well, he was here for a couple of years, I think. He moved in, saying that he was some sort of a financial consultant and wanted to take some time off from city life. He'd come from New York, he said. He did seem to have very expensive clothes," she said musingly.

"Did he buy a house?" asked Beatrice. "Was he acting as if he was going to settle down here?"

Meadow nodded. "He *said* he wanted to settle down. In fact, his mother and brother followed him down later on. They didn't seem to have much income, and we all understood that he'd persuaded them to join him in Dappled Hills because he wanted to help look after them. Although they didn't seem to corroborate his story that they were all from New York. A little confusing, that. Anyway, he wanted to rent first, so that he had plenty of time to make a decision before buying a house. He was also considering building a house, he'd said. So the fact that he was renting a house made sense. And he was so charming, Beatrice," added Meadow with a sigh. "Half the town must have fallen in love with him."

"I guess, if he was a con man, he must have gotten himself put in positions of trust right away," said Beatrice.

"That's apparently how it works," said Meadow.

"He volunteered over at the church all the time. He was even a greeter on Sunday mornings. The best greeter ever. Oh, he'd ask you how your quilt was coming along or if your arthritis was doing any better. He'd even give me dog treats in a sandwich bag to give to Boris after church. I think he got along very well with Wyatt, and for a minister, Wyatt is a pretty discerning judge of character, I think. And he seemed as if he had plenty of money. He always tipped nicely and bought sweet gifts for Phyllis or flowers or took her out to restaurants. He advised people on their retirement savings when they asked him about it. And they usually *did* ask him about it because Jason explained that he'd made a comfortable living by day trading." She startled a bit as something occurred to her. "I guess he wasn't even certified for that."

"When did everybody find out that he was trouble?" asked Beatrice.

"When he left town. He left at night, just like a thief. Apparently, he didn't even tell his mother and brother that he was taking off. Poor Phyllis was a disaster. She'd really loved him. She felt totally humiliated. I've always wondered—did Jason even care for Phyllis or was it always a scam? Phyllis is really well off, you know," explained Meadow. She frowned. "Or—at least— she *was* well off. I wonder how much she spent on Jason. It seems as though she's living a very simple life these days. Not buying a lot of new clothes, driving the same car year after year. I think she's definitely cut back on her spending."

"You'd think, if he was only dating Phyllis for her money, that he would have gone through with the wedding," said Beatrice.

"You'd think. Although Phyllis did dote on Jason. She was always giving him things. But remember, we all thought he was really well off. Who knows—maybe he was taking her gifts and selling them," said Meadow. "I'd never thought that Phyllis was all that well off until she started giving Jason all those presents." She gave a small gasp as a thought occurred to her. "Do you think that maybe Jason bankrupted her? Or ran through most of her money? Maybe that's why he didn't go through with the wedding—because he knew she didn't have any money anymore."

"It's possible," said Beatrice. "But what about Tony? Where does he figure into all of this?"

"The way that I understand it," said Meadow in a hushed voice as if someone were listening in right there in Beatrice's living room, "Jason got to be friends with Tony's grandfather. Tony's grandfather trusted Jason and decided to invest in some kind of scheme that he was promoting. But the only savings he really had was the account he'd set up for Tony's college education." Meadow shook her head sadly. "Tony was always a very bright kid. Everybody said he had a lot of promise. When Jason skipped town seven years ago, he took that money with him, and that was the end of all of Tony's dreams. His grandfather died soon after Jason left. Such a pity."

"Why didn't Tony's grandfather press charges?" asked Beatrice. "He didn't pass away *that* soon, did he?"

"He was just too embarrassed, I think. I only heard about it through the grapevine and then only in whispers," said Meadow, shaking her head. "But the Phyllis thing—that was a lot more open and gossiped over. Jason's family never recovered from the shock of having him skip town like that. His mother died very soon afterward and then his brother . . . I never even saw him around town after Jason left. It's almost as if he didn't want to show his face around Dappled Hills."

Beatrice asked, "Do you think that Phyllis could have killed Jason, Meadow?"

Meadow vehemently shook her head, making her long gray braid sway. "I certainly do not! After all, Phyllis *loved* Jason. Why on earth would she want to kill him?"

Why indeed? But love could be very close to hate sometimes . . . and how might Phyllis have taken it when Jason started dating Martha? Her fellow quilter in the Cut-Ups? Wouldn't it have felt like a double betrayal?

"I wonder why he came back to Dappled Hills after being gone for seven years," said Beatrice. "Doesn't that seem a little strange to you? After all, he'd basically gotten away with a crime. Why would he want to come back to town and possibly face charges? It seems really risky to me."

"Maybe he wanted to try to make up to the town for what he'd done," said Meadow with a shrug. "I haven't heard of any bad behavior from him since he returned a few months ago. He could have wanted to make amends. And he certainly seems to be head over heels over Martha."

Beatrice wasn't convinced about Jason's ability to change. It seemed likely to her that he might have needed more money and thought that Dappled Hills had made an easy mark in the past. And she wasn't at all surprised that he'd focused in on Martha Helmsley. After all, she did seem to be very financially secure—plus, she was a lovely woman. Even if she did seem like a jealous one.

"Speaking of love," said Meadow, batting her eyes. "How are things going between you and Wyatt? I saw the two of you at the grocery store the other day—looking like you were sharing an intimate moment."

"An intimate moment? At Bub's Grocery?"

"Well, when you're in love, everywhere is romantic."

Beatrice said, "No, there was no romantic moment at the grocery store."

"But maybe there was . . . at the Dappled Hills Eatery?" Meadow looked as innocent as she possibly could."

"For goodness' sake. Were you in there, too? It seemed like half the town was in that restaurant and staring at Wyatt and me," said Beatrice, exasperated.

"So it *is* true! No, I wasn't there. But Emily Sue was there and she said that she saw the two of you having a nice lunch." Meadow clapped her hands. "Oh, Beatrice! I couldn't be more thrilled!"

Beatrice gave a weak smile in return. Was the whole town talking about their date?

"Have you cooked Wyatt a meal yet? That's one of the most romantic dates you can have, you know," said Meadow earnestly.

"Ah . . . no. No, I haven't gotten around to that yet. Besides, I think Wyatt and I have a more—well, cerebral relationship."

Meadow stared blankly at her. "Cerebral? See, that's why this relationship has been so slow to get off the ground. The way to a man's heart is through his stomach, remember?" Meadow suddenly jumped up and started opening Beatrice's cabinets and rooting around. The kitten hunched down on the top of the cabinet, staring down at Meadow as if she were thinking about jumping down on top of her head. "Where's your food processor? And your cake tin? Where are all the tools you need to create your culinary masterpiece?"

"Meadow, as a reminder, I've been cooking for one

for about the last ten years. Plus, I downsized to this cottage. I don't have the space for kitchen tools," said Beatrice, trying to sound firm. Really, she'd gotten very used to cooking herself very simple meals. Or picking up a sandwich at the deli. "But, since you're asking, here they are." She walked across the kitchen to open a small cabinet. There lay a glass casserole dish, a cookie sheet, a frying pan, a mixing bowl, a measuring cup, and a covered pot.

Meadow stared at the equipment in amazement. "I don't think I've ever seen such few things to cook with." She opened her mouth and then shut it back again. "Beatrice, this is serious. If Wyatt sees this, he'll realize that you really don't cook."

"Meadow, as I was saying . . ."

Meadow was shaking her head and continuing on as if she hadn't heard Beatrice interrupt. "I know. I've got a few duplicates in my kitchen. Especially the food processor. How can you cook your masterpiece with no food processor? I'll bring them over later."

Beatrice was about to talk this point over with Meadow when there was a tap on her door. Noo-noo quickly started barking and the forgotten Boris came galloping out of Beatrice's kitchen. His mouth was covered in peanut butter.

"How did Boris get into the peanut butter?" asked Beatrice. She clenched her teeth as she walked to the front door.

"Pure genius," said Meadow in satisfaction, reaching out to grasp Boris's collar. She watched as Beatrice turned the door handle. "Hey, check the window first, Beatrice. Since we have a murderer running around and all."

Chapter Five

Beatrice cautiously peered out the side window. "It's Wyatt," she said with a small smile.

Meadow gave her a hug. "Okay," she said in a conspiratorial manner, "we're going to work on your cooking stuff. All right? I'll come back another time with the kitchen equipment."

"Beatrice," he said, giving her a warm smile and reaching down to pet Noo-noo. "Are you all right? I heard about what happened yesterday evening. . . ." At that point, though, Boris couldn't be restrained any longer and pulled away from Meadow and galloped to Wyatt, sticking his massive head in the way so that Wyatt had to pet him instead of Noo-noo. Beatrice sighed.

Wyatt scratched Boris behind the ears. "Oh, you've got company," he said.

"It's only me," said Meadow, "it's not company." She

was already glancing futilely about her for Boris's leash. "And I should be going," she added hastily, giving Beatrice a broad wink.

"Don't leave on my behalf," said Wyatt. "I'm about to head to the church office to do some work, so I won't be but a minute."

Meadow settled back into the sofa with a sigh. "In that case, I'll hang out." Her gaze settled on Beatrice. "Beatrice was just going to change, weren't you?"

Beatrice looked down and realized she was still in her robe and slippers. Perfectly respectable garments, but . . .

"Sorry," said Wyatt, "I'm here pretty early."

"Not as early as Meadow was," said Beatrice wryly. "I had a slow start today."

Meadow apparently thought she needed to improve her appearance a bit. "Boris, Noo-noo, and I will entertain Wyatt while you get ready," she said in a rather bossy voice.

Beatrice hurried to her bedroom to change into khaki pants and a pale blue button-down shirt. When she returned, Meadow had already poured Wyatt a cup of coffee and he was protesting that he didn't need any more muffins. Meadow was always determined to feed people—even if she wasn't in her own house.

Meadow said, "So, I'm sure you've heard by now what happened at poor Posy's quilting retreat, right?"

Wyatt nodded and gazed sympathetically at Beatrice.

"And, Beatrice, you were the one who found Jason? I'm sorry—that must have been so awful for you."

Beatrice said, "It was, actually. I didn't sleep so well last night, which is why I hadn't gotten out of my robe and slippers yet this morning. But, of course, it was a lot more upsetting for Martha and Phyllis."

Meadow sighed. "Believe it or not, those two used to be good friends in the Cut-Ups. That's another reason why I want you to get to the bottom of this, Beatrice. Right away, they started blaming each other for Jason's murder. Jason created discord between them in life and he's going to do it in death, too."

Wyatt cleared his throat a little. "I'm actually officiating at Jason's funeral service."

Meadow's eyes opened wide. "What? You want to do that for him? After all he'd done?"

Beatrice said, "Meadow was explaining before you arrived, that Jason had used the church to help build up his position of trust in the town."

"Before he ran away with some money!" added Meadow. "He acted like he really cared about people at church, but he used that trust to lure them in and steal from them—like he did with Tony's grandfather."

Wyatt nodded, but his eyes were tired. "Jason has been working hard to repair ties with the church since he returned a few months ago."

"I should hope so," grumbled Meadow. "He had plenty of ties to repair."

"It wouldn't have been right for me to hold his past against him," said Wyatt gently. "Besides, Martha has been active in the church for years and she personally asked me to perform the service. It's an honor, as it always is."

Wyatt did seem a bit uncomfortable, though, despite what he was saying. Beatrice said, slowly, "It seems as though Jason must have been very optimistic about his return to town. After all, he started settling right back into life here. He started dating someone, he returned to the church. And it was only seven years ago that he left. He seemed determined to return, get on good terms with everyone, and perhaps repair some of the damage he'd done. Do you think that people can change? I'd really like to believe they can, but I'm not sure."

Meadow gave a hooting laugh. "Well, don't ask Ramsay that question. He'll start muttering about tigers never changing their stripes. But he's looking at it from a law enforcement perspective and not a faith-based one."

Meadow and Beatrice waited expectantly for Wyatt to answer.

Wyatt said, "Yes, I do believe people can change. I'm in the wrong business, if I don't. I've seen change throughout my years as a minister. Although . . ." He paused. "I do feel as though it's very *difficult* for someone to change." And his face was troubled.

*   *   *

After Wyatt, Meadow, and Boris left, Beatrice figured out a plan for casually interviewing suspects in Jason's murder. She decided that she might as well start with Phyllis. Phyllis had, after all, made herself central to the case. She drew attention to the love triangle by trying to leave the Cut-Ups. She'd once been engaged to Jason. And the murder weapon was her very own pair of shears.

Of course, she didn't have an excellent reason to just drop by Phyllis's today. It wasn't as if she and Phyllis were good friends—she barely knew the woman. Beatrice hoped that if she just went over and rang the doorbell, Phyllis would invite her in.

And, surprisingly, that's nearly what happened. Beatrice had parked in the driveway in front of Phyllis's small brick house with black shutters. The little yard had obviously been cared for and had meticulously trimmed bushes and fall-blooming flowers. Phyllis even had a small pumpkin on her porch for an autumn decoration.

Phyllis, in a wide-brimmed hat, was deadheading late-blooming roses. Beatrice saw that her eyes were exhausted, though, and figured that Phyllis had slept as little as she had.

Phyllis gave her an immediate hug. "I'm tickled pink you came by, Beatrice! How incredibly kind of you. I could tell right off the bat that you're a really sensitive person. You obviously picked up on how isolated I'm feeling right now and knew to come by and be a friend. You don't know how much I appreciate it."

Beatrice felt a twinge of guilt, although she was also relieved that Phyllis was so eager to invite her in that she wasn't asking a lot of questions.

Phyllis took her inside, sat her down in a room that was small and rather sparsely furnished with some threadbare antiques, and scurried off for lemonade for both of them. While she was gone, Beatrice glanced around her modest living room. Then she swiftly got up to take a closer look at a picture that was on her tidy desk. It was a photo of Phyllis with Jason Gore. In the background was a luxurious Cadillac. They were both giving wide grins in the photo and she noticed that Phyllis looked very happy.

Beatrice knew that Phyllis no longer drove a luxurious Cadillac. As she recalled, she drove a small, older-model sedan with a few dents in it. Maybe Meadow was right. Maybe Phyllis had spent most of her money on Jason.

Beatrice heard footsteps coming back toward the living room and hurried to sit back down. Phyllis handed a glass of lemonade to Beatrice, exclaiming as she did, "Oh my. Beatrice, you must have slept as badly as I did. I'm so sorry. It would have been traumatic finding poor Jason that way."

Phyllis gulped hard as she said Jason's name as if it

were difficult to get the words out. Beatrice, fearing tears, quickly said, "It was a terrible day for all of us, wasn't it? What a shock for everyone."

Phyllis nodded, taking a sip of her own drink. "Maybe I should have poured some alcohol in these lemonades," she said with a strangled laugh.

She stared blankly out the window at her tiny backyard for a moment. An angry flush colored her cheeks. "I think the shock is quickly turning to total fury," she said quietly. "Somebody set me up."

"I think you're right," said Beatrice. "Someone wanted to make it look as if you'd killed Jason. What's more, whoever is behind this murder has a lot of gumption. After all, they committed a terrible crime only yards away from a roomful of quilters. It was a very brazen murder."

Phyllis eagerly added, "And they swiped my shears from right under my nose, apparently."

Beatrice actually doubted this. There was brazen, and then there was crazy. Who would lean over and take Phyllis's scissors from right in front of her? To use in a murder? Why take that risk, even if you were setting someone up? "I'm not so sure about that, Phyllis. After all, we were all in that room together, talking. Couldn't you, a bit absently, have laid them down when you walked into the shop? You'd have had your arms full and probably set them down for a moment to adjust your load."

"Maybe," said Phyllis, excitement rising in her voice. "Then anyone could have gotten them. Someone could have seen the shears lying there as they came through the door, and then gone back into the store later and taken advantage of the fact that they were there." She took a thoughtful sip from her drink. "I can't understand why I'm getting blamed for this. I really can't. After all, my relationship with Jason was over. I wished him well. Why would I want him back after what he did to me? He humiliated me in front of the entire town of Dappled Hills. He wasn't the kind of beau I needed."

"Perhaps," said Beatrice delicately, "people aren't thinking that you wanted to continue your relationship with Jason. Perhaps they think you wanted revenge."

A flush spread across Phyllis's face and she turned again to better look out the window. "That's silly," she muttered. "What's done is done." She stared broodingly out at the goldfinches on the nearby bird feeders. "I moved on. It's important to move on."

Beatrice cleared her throat. "I've had a bit of success in the past in poking around in these cases. I guess it gives my brain something to do," she said with a slight shrug. "I thought I'd try to ask some questions and see what I can find out about Jason's death. See if I can clear y..."

A... ble expression passed across Phyllis's f... vanished and she smiled at her. "Would you? Oh, Beatrice, that would be wonderful! It's fantastic living in a small town—until it isn't fantastic."

"What I need to know from you, then, is what you were doing while the retreat was going on. That will really help to clear your name, naturally. Of course, I was in there with you for some of the time, but I wasn't exactly tracking your movements or anything." Beatrice smiled at Phyllis. "I was trying to get a handle on that double wedding ring quilt that I've been working on."

"I was mainly in the back room with all of you. But I left the room briefly a couple of times. For food and something to drink," said Phyllis.

"And you didn't see or hear anything while you were in the store?"

"I sure didn't," said Phyllis regretfully, after thinking for a moment or two. "Of course, it was pretty noisy in the back room, wasn't it? We were all chatting and the sewing machines were running. It wasn't the quietest place in the world."

"I meant, though, while you were in the *store*, not the back room," said Beatrice.

"I didn't. But I was so focused on those cakes that I don't think I'd have noticed if a pink elephant stampeded through the shop," said Phyllis made a rueful face and patted her stomach as if chubbier than it was.

"Have you got any ideas who mig Jason's death?" Beatrice took a last sip of her lemonade and set it gently down on a rather rickety antique coffee table.

"A few ideas," said Phyllis. "Well, one idea in particular. I thought it very convenient that Martha's son, Frank, showed up. Why on earth would he be hanging out at a quilting retreat?"

"I believe he had a legitimate excuse for being there," said Beatrice with a frown. "As I recall, he was bringing some sort of forgotten item to Martha. Fabric or something."

"True. But he could have delivered it to her and been gone in a few minutes. He was still there, though, when you made that awful discovery. Frank could have had a genuine reason to show up, and then could easily have taken advantage of the setup. Jason was in the shop, perhaps even had his back to Frank. My shears may have been lying on top of a nearby display. It would have been easy for him."

"Why would Frank have wanted to kill Jason?" asked Beatrice curiously.

"Because he hated him, of course!" said Phyllis in surprise. "Didn't you know? You see, he depends on his mother for absolutely everything. Martha supports him completely. That's fairly scandalous right there—a grown man who sponges off his mother to survive. Ridiculous!" she snorted.

"He's an artist, isn't he?" asked Beatrice, remembering the Van Dyke beard and the dramatic black clothing. And the moodiness.

"That's what they say. He certainly tries to look the part, although I think he looks silly. You know, I've never seen any of his art for sale or seen anything that he's done. I think he's probably loafing around all day instead of painting, or whatever it is that he's supposed to be doing. I kept hearing from other quilters that Frank and Martha were arguing with each other all the time—he told her not to have anything to do with Jason. I'm sure he was terrified that they'd end up getting married and that Jason would persuade her to cut him off—Jason did seem to have remarkable influence over Martha." Phyllis shrugged and took a sip of lemonade.

"So you think that Frank is the most likely suspect," said Beatrice.

"Or maybe Martha herself," said Phyllis.

"Martha? But you were saying that Martha was so taken with Jason that she would even consider siding with him against her own son."

"Well, yes. But Martha has also been troubled lately by Jason's behavior. You see, Jason was a tremendous flirt. I wasn't irritated myself by it when he and I were engaged . . . because that's just how Jason was. You could tell that it bothered Martha, though. He'd be flirting with some woman and she'd be stewing nearby."

"Maybe," said Beatrice doubtfully. Murdering someone like that, though—she couldn't really picture Martha doing it.

"Or maybe," said Phyllis in a pointed tone, "Martha killed Jason in order to set me up and make it look as if I were responsible. She might very well have. After all, she absolutely loathes me. It might be exactly the kind of mean thing she'd have done—implicate me in murder."

Phyllis paused and asked brightly, "Would you like some more lemonade, Beatrice?"

On the way back home from Phyllis's house, Beatrice ran by the store and bought more cat food, and another cat toy for the kitten. When Beatrice arrived back at her cottage, she saw a grinning Boris the Dog sitting at her front door. An indignant Noo-noo looked out the front picture window.

"If he's such a genius," muttered Beatrice, "why does he keep forgetting where he lives?"

Boris bounded around her as she fumbled with her keys, trying to open the door while fishing her cell phone out of her pocketbook and holding on to the bags from the store. "Meadow," she said, when she'd finally found the phone and punched her number in, "Boris is over here paying a visit."

"What an intuitive, brilliant boy he is!" Meadow said effusively. "He senses you've had a rough time and wants to bring you comfort."

The comforting Boris galloped past her into the cottage, making a beeline for the kitchen with Noo-noo scampering behind him as fast as her legs would allow her. "I'm not sure that's why Boris is here, Meadow. I believe he may have ulterior motives." She followed the dogs into her small kitchen and noticed that both sets of dog eyes were focused on the canister of treats she kept on her counter. The kitten was nowhere to be seen. She was probably up on as high a surface as she could find.

"Let me give Ramsay a quick call," said Meadow. "He just left in the cruiser a minute ago—he can swing by and pick Boris up."

Beatrice was still trying to decide whether to reward Boris's bad behavior with a treat when Ramsay opened her front door, poking his head through cautiously. "Beatrice?" he called.

"Come on in," she called back. Boris, hearing his master's voice, joyfully bounded out of the kitchen, ending her dilemma.

Ramsay quickly snapped a leash onto the dog's collar and then squatted down to give him a hug and accept Boris's wild kisses.

"Can we trade dogs?" he asked Beatrice. "Owning Boris is like having a toddler in the house again. Noo-noo is always well-behaved."

Noo-noo grinned at Ramsay as if she understood every word.

"She's got a different temperament, that's all," said Beatrice. "She doesn't get as . . . well . . . excited as Boris does. I hear Boris has other talents, though." Ramsay gave Beatrice a curious look. "I understand he's gifted," explained Beatrice, hiding a smile.

Ramsay made a *pish* sound and waved his hand dismissively. "Meadow's madness. Boris . . . gifted—ha!"

Ramsay slowly stood back up as if his back hurt a bit. He had smudges of circles under his eyes from lack of sleep, and his uniform didn't look as pressed and neat as it ordinarily did. "I've got some coffee," she offered. "You look as though you've had a long day."

Ramsay brightened. "That would be great, actually. I didn't even have a chance to get a full cup this morning." He kept a tight hold on Boris's leash as Beatrice walked off to get them some coffee.

Beatrice poured him a cup and they both sat down in the living room. "Are *you* doing all right?" asked Ramsay, scrutinizing her face. "Yesterday's . . . event . . . must have come as a huge shock to you."

Beatrice nodded. "It was, of course. But now I've moved on and would simply like to know what happened. It always seems incredible that there would be murders in Dappled Hills. I feel as if we live in the safest place in the world."

"We do, we do," Ramsay hastened to say. As police chief, perhaps, he felt a strong sense of responsibility to defend that point. "But people are people, no matter where you go. I'll get to the bottom of this, don't worry." He clumsily patted Beatrice's hand, and then knitted his brow as a thought occurred to him. "Meadow's not trying to rope you into investigating this murder, is she?"

Beatrice hesitated. She didn't want to throw Meadow under a bus, but she didn't feel right lying to Ramsay, either. "Let's just say that I'm keeping my ears open, that's all. If I hear something, I'll be sure to let you know."

This answer seemed to satisfy Ramsay and they sipped their coffee in comfortable silence for a few moments. Then Ramsay said, "You haven't heard anything so far, have you? Any hints are welcome. As usual, I want to wrap up this case as fast as I can so that I can get back to what *really* matters." Which, to Ramsay, would have little to do with police work.

"No, I haven't really gotten anywhere yet. Except that Jason seemed to be disliked by several people."

Ramsay nodded, absently reaching down to scratch Noo-noo behind the ears until Boris bumped his hand to grab his attention. "Oh yes. I guess you've been hearing about Eric, then. Small towns do gossip, don't they? I bet when you lived in Atlanta, you likely didn't come across it, did you?"

Eric? Who on earth was Eric? Beatrice decided she might get more information if she played along. "Oh, I'd say there was plenty of gossip in Atlanta, too. But, yes . . . Eric. I suppose he couldn't help being upset with Jason, though." Beatrice waited, hoping that Ramsay would ruminate on that point a while.

Apparently, Ramsay was happy to oblige. "I suppose so. After all, he moved to Dappled Hills to be near his half brother. He likes it here, liked the people. Then Jason got half the town riled up with him for one thing or another and ran off like a thief in the night. Poor Eric was left behind to face the music. Reckon I wouldn't be too happy myself."

"No, I guess not." Beatrice paused. "I don't want to ask you anything you shouldn't talk about, but I was wondering about Jason's death."

Ramsay took a long sip of his coffee and then nodded at Beatrice to continue.

Beatrice spread out her hands in a supplicant manner and said, "Maybe you can help me to understand it. Here we are, in a roomful of women. About a dozen of us. We're not staying in the room, either—we're leaving regularly to find the refreshments or to visit the ladies' room or even to buy a different fabric or a needed notion from Posy from the shop. And a man—a grown man and a healthy one—is murdered with a pair of scissors and we don't hear a thing." She shrugged. "I can't wrap my mind around it."

Ramsay sighed. "It does beat all, doesn't it? At first, I thought I was going to have more information than I could handle, considering all the potential witnesses.

But then I realized y'all had been wrapped up in your quilting too much to really focus on much else. And I guess it was pretty noisy in there, too—what with the sewing machines running and everyone talking at once."

"And there was a bit of drama between Martha and Phyllis," said Beatrice.

"I did hear a little about that from Meadow," said Ramsay.

"What I'm thinking," said Beatrice carefully, "is that there was probably another reason that this murder was so quiet. Perhaps he was unconscious when he was stabbed."

Ramsay raised his eyebrows. "Have you got an informant in the state police?"

Beatrice smiled at him. "Sounds like I guessed right."

"Some sort of blunt-force trauma knocked him out first. Then he was murdered with the shears."

"I've always heard that stabbing is a very personal type of crime," said Beatrice.

Ramsay gave a short laugh. "I think most victims would say that *any* type of murder is personal. But yes—I think stabbing implies a certain level of dissatisfaction with a victim. It shows anger." He reached up with his free hand and rubbed his eyes.

"I'd better go," he said with a sigh. "Especially since I need to drop Boris by the house before I head to work again." He stood up and Boris followed his lead. Ramsay's gaze dropped to Beatrice's coffee table and he squinted at the title of the book there. *"Golden Summer,"* he read. "Hmm."

"I can't recommend it," said Beatrice. "Although everyone tells me it's a terrific book if I stick with it."

"Looks a little lightweight to me," said Ramsay doubtfully. "I've got some books that I'd love to let you borrow, Beatrice. I'll bring one to you the next time I see you. I can tell you're a person who gives back books."

She was. And she had the feeling that she'd be only too eager to hand Ramsay's literary tomes right back to him.

Chapter Six

One thing that Beatrice had learned since moving to Dappled Hills was that Posy's Patchwork Cottage was a major town hub. It was one of the best spots to see people, gossip, and gather information. Beatrice found her pocketbook and peered into her wallet. It was also, clearly, a good place to spend money. She'd have to stop by the bank along the way.

As she'd hoped, the Patchwork Cottage was bustling with activity. Posy gave her a quick wave as she continued checking out a quilter. Miss Sissy was, as usual, snoring away in the sitting area. She'd apparently tried to work on the jigsaw puzzle that Posy had put on the table in the sitting room, since there were several puzzle pieces in her lap. Beatrice was glad to see that Martha Helmsley was there. And, actually, surprised to see her there, considering the large amount of fabric she'd recently purchased and the scary scene from yesterday.

Martha spotted her and walked over, holding a bunch of fabric. "Beatrice, it's good to see you here. I wanted to let you know that I was so impressed with you yesterday—the way you kept your head and did all the right things. I felt—well, I felt as though my world were coming to an end. Your attitude really helped me to keep calm. Although I know I didn't handle everything as well as I could have." She put the pile of fabric on a table and sat down in a chair next to Miss Sissy.

Beatrice sat down next to her and spoke in a low voice. "I don't think you should be too hard on yourself. You were facing a crisis and you reacted to it. That's only natural. And look at you now—you're picking up with your life again and trying to move forward."

Martha's eyes grew misty and she blinked a few times to chase the tears away. She cleared her throat and said, "That's the best way of handling a tragedy— don't you think? Although I nearly broke down before coming over here." She gestured to the fabric with a well-manicured hand. "Jason had gotten me these fabrics as a surprise. Bless him. As soon as I saw them, I knew there was no way I could use them in any projects, but I didn't want to hurt his feelings. Now . . ." She shrugged, fishing for a tissue from her purse. "I figured I could return them. But it makes me so sad."

Beatrice waited a moment while Martha dabbled at her eyes and Miss Sissy snored loudly beside them. "I was talking with Ramsay earlier," she said finally, "and he was saying that it was tough investigating since none of the quilters had really seen or heard anything while we were in the retreat. I knew that I hadn't witnessed anything that seemed important. Did you?"

Martha's eyes hardened. "I certainly did. I saw that Phyllis lost her shears. And then I saw that she'd found them again. That's what I witnessed. I don't understand why Ramsay is trying to talk to people when it's clear who is responsible for Jason's death. Phyllis."

"Phyllis says that her shears were taken from her and that anyone could have murdered Jason with them," said Beatrice. "She thinks that maybe someone was trying to set her up by taking her shears and using them for the crime."

"Well, of course she says that. Wouldn't you?" Martha gave a short laugh. "The facts are that Phyllis's shears were responsible for killing my Jason." Her eyes filled again with tears. "I suppose she thinks that *I'm* somehow behind Jason's death. Since she thinks someone is setting her up, it's pretty definite that she'd blame me."

"Which is ridiculous, of course," murmured Beatrice.

"Naturally! Does she think that I went out in the store, stabbed Jason, and returned to quilting without even a wrinkle or a spot on my white outfit? She's insane. Or desperately trying to switch blame from herself over to me."

Beatrice said, "So you didn't leave the conference room or notice anyone else who did?"

"I was very, very busy with my grandmother's flower garden pattern, actually. It's a tough pattern—have you attempted one, Beatrice?"

Beatrice shook her head. "Those hexagons—they seemed as if they might be tricky."

"If you had, you'd know what I mean. You really have to focus on it," said Martha smoothly. "And it's all hand-stitched. The hexagon pieces are paper pieced."

"You didn't get up even once from it?" asked Beatrice. "Not even with all the snacks to tempt you?"

"Perhaps I got up once," said Martha slowly. "One quilter came back in the back room with some really yummy-looking cake that I understand June Bug made. And June Bug is such a fabulous cook, as well as a housekeeper—you know she helps me out a couple of times a week. I do believe I got a slice of cake at one point, but then I got right back to work on my quilt."

Beatrice knew that Martha had left the room more than once. She knew this because she'd been keeping an eye on both Phyllis and Martha. The two women had certainly seemed to be gearing up for some kind of fight, and Beatrice was going to try to defuse the situation before it happened—mostly for poor Posy's sake.

"I could have sworn that you left the room more than once, Martha," said Beatrice.

Martha's eyes narrowed. "Are you trying to investigate Jason's death?" she asked coldly. "Really, Beatrice. I think that's something better left to the police. Don't you?" Her hands tightened on the fabric she was holding in her lap. She glanced around the store for a moment as if trying to collect herself. "I might have gone back into the store for a napkin. It was a very moist cake, you see."

"I know you think that Phyllis is behind this, but is there anyone else that you can think of who might have wanted to do Jason harm?" asked Beatrice.

"Jason was a *lovely* person," said Martha in a censorious tone.

"I'm sure that he was."

"It's very difficult for me to imagine that *anyone* would want to do him harm." She gave Beatrice a stern look.

"Of course it is," said Beatrice, nodding and waiting.

"Although I sometimes wonder about John," said Martha. She sighed. "I guess each of us has our trials in life. I do believe that John might be mine."

"John. Let's see. John is a friend of yours, right? I believe that I saw him right after we left the retreat—didn't he come over to make sure you were all right?" Beatrice remembered that John Simmons had been trying to win Martha's affections for years—but that apparently she was unswayed by his efforts.

Martha looked away. "That's right. He's—I suppose he's always hoped that we might end up married."

"You've known him a long time?"

Martha sighed again. "All my life. I think he's been pining after me since nursery school."

She clearly didn't want to talk about it. But Beatrice was sure that Meadow would be able to provide her with some more insights later on.

"I should get going," said Martha, slowly standing up and looking tired. "By the way, Beatrice, I wanted to let you know that I'm going to be planning Jason's service and holding a small reception afterward. You're most welcome to come. I don't know exactly when it will be, but I'm thinking in the next couple of days. The police have to . . . well, you know."

Beatrice realized that Jason's body must not have been released from the police yet. "I'd be happy to come, Martha, of course."

Martha took her fabrics to the counter to return them. Beatrice glanced over at Miss Sissy, who had one eye open, watching her. "How much of that conversation did you hear, Miss Sissy?"

Miss Sissy opened the other eye and sat up. She looked more disheveled than usual, with iron gray hair falling loose out of her bun. "Wickedness," she muttered.

But there was a gleam in those old eyes that made Beatrice suspect that Miss Sissy was actually having one of her good days. "Which part was wicked?" she asked.

"Everything!" spat the old woman. "And lies. Lots of lies."

Beatrice had realized that Miss Sissy knew a lot more about things going on in Dappled Hills than she really let on. "What do you know about this John that Martha was talking about? Have you seen him around?"

Miss Sissy nodded and more hair fell out from her bun. "Stalks her."

"John stalks Martha?" asked Beatrice, startled. "Martha doesn't seem like the kind of person who might put up with that for years."

"Stalks her!" said Miss Sissy sharply. "All foolishness." She gave Beatrice a canny look. "June Bug knows. Ask the June Bug."

"I will, I will," said Beatrice in a soothing voice. She studied the old woman for a moment and then asked, "Did you see anything during the retreat? You left the room a few times, didn't you?"

"A body has to eat," muttered Miss Sissy. Miss Sissy was never one to let snack time pass her by. "June Bug brought cakes!" she said, rather defensively.

"Well, that's what the food was there for. But did you see or hear anything suspicious?"

Miss Sissy paused. "Men's voices. In the quilt shop."

This was hardly a revelation and Beatrice tried not

to show her disappointment. "Wouldn't there have been men's voices, though? After all, Jason was there. And Martha's son, Frank, came through to bring her something she'd forgotten."

Miss Sissy glared at her and slapped her hand on the table next to her, making her glass of lemonade shake precariously. "Not Frank. Another man. Talking to Jason—the dead boy."

If Beatrice needed another reason to discount Miss Sissy, she'd just gotten one. Jason was no boy. Could she possibly be talking about Tony Brock? The young man at the hardware store that Meadow said had been cheated out of his college education? Or was Miss Sissy simply delusional again?

She must have looked skeptical, because Miss Sissy shook her fist at her. "I heard them talking!"

The old woman seemed to be returning to a familiar chorus now. Beatrice stood up. Time to go, for sure. "Well, it was nice speaking with you, Miss Sissy."

Miss Sissy, with her usual surprising spryness, jumped to her feet with an agility that Beatrice admired. "Remember," she said, urgently staring into Beatrice's eyes, "it's always the money. The love of money is the root of all evil."

The two women stared solemnly at each other for a few moments. Beatrice felt again that Miss Sissy still had some shrewd ideas bouncing around in that head of hers. She could also be incredibly intuitive.

This train of thought was derailed, however, as Miss Sissy spotted a bowl that Posy had set out for customers on a nearby table. "Peppermints!" she hissed. And she was gone.

Later, back at home, Beatrice found her mind drifting to thoughts of Wyatt. She'd really like to see him—to spend some time with him and even bounce a few ideas off him regarding the investigation. She knew he was busy now, though, especially as he planned for the upcoming funeral. Well. This was the twenty-first century, after all. Shouldn't she also reciprocate an invitation? What did other widows do in these cases? She found it hard to believe that they sat around in their ivory towers and waited for the handsome prince to show up.

Meadow had mentioned a dinner. Maybe that would be a good idea. Something simple. Then, if she pulled it off, she could keep the food warm and invite Wyatt over for an off-the-cuff meal. That would still keep things low-key, but intimate.

But where were her cookbooks? She didn't dare look up recipes online because she'd end up spending hours looking through them and then get distracted by her e-mails. No, better to go with something out of one of her cookbooks. Beatrice walked into her kitchen and stared at the cabinets. She couldn't remember having seen the cookbooks lately. Maybe they were in one of the high cabinets, out of the way.

She pushed a chair into the kitchen and carefully stood on it to look in the highest cabinet. Sure enough, there was her old cookbook, complete with frayed edges and old food stains. She reached for it, straining. She could barely feel the book with her fingertips. She stretched some more, grabbed the book enough to knock it off of the shelf, and then to her horror, realized the chair was sliding backward on the floor. Beatrice fell to the floor, hitting it right after the book fell and narrowly missing hitting her chin on the counter on her way down.

Beatrice lay for a few moments still on the floor, heart pounding. Then she carefully tested her arms and legs. Everything seemed in working order, although she felt a little sore. She glared at the cabinet. How on earth did she get the book up there to begin with? She carefully returned to her feet, wincing. Next time she'd get out the step stool. It had rubber feet.

Later, she decided that the fall had been an ominous start to her cooking project. Because what she then launched was definitely not the culinary masterpiece that Meadow had charged her with cooking. First of all, she decided, for the meal to truly appear casual, she needed to make it from ingredients she already had in the house. After peering around her pantry and kitchen, she felt a little like Old Mother Hubbard. She had some frozen vegetables, some shredded cheese, some eggs, and a bit of ham. Maybe a quiche?

Beatrice flipped through the old cookbook, shoving old newspaper and magazine clippings back into it as she went. No to the Beef Bourguignonne. There was no way she could make that look like a last-minute thing. Where were the quiche recipes?

She found the quiche section of the cookbook and then frowned. Did she have a pie shell? She pulled open her freezer and saw one. She should be in good shape, then. They could have quiche and a bit of fruit and maybe some ice cream for dessert. And wine . . . she had wine in the fridge.

It all should have gone well. She even felt a sort of creative surge when she was cooking . . . enough to confidently throw in some mushrooms that she'd forgotten she had. But then she apparently put in too much broccoli and ham and mushrooms in the pie shell, because the egg mixture wouldn't all fit in. And surely . . . shouldn't she be pouring in all the mixture? Wasn't there something important in the mixture that would help gel this quiche together? She forced as much into the pie shell as she could and slid it into the oven—as the filling sloshed over the bottom of the hot oven.

Beatrice fussed at herself, and used a metal spatula to try to scrape out what was quickly becoming fried egg. There was an unfortunate burned smell, too. And fifty minutes later, when the quiche should have been done, she peeked into the oven. The outside of the quiche was pretty brown, she thought as she studied it critically. She pulled it out and cut into it . . . and found the inside was all mushy and uncooked.

"*That* didn't go well," muttered Beatrice. It was a good thing that she hadn't invited Wyatt over. Although she disagreed with Meadow that men were simple enough creatures that a good meal would win them over, she certainly didn't need to push Wyatt *away* with an awful one.

She tossed the quiche into the trash and decided to clean up all the dishes and drippings a little later. For a simple meal, she'd sure made a huge mess. It was enough to make her wonder—was she able to take on a serious relationship at this point in her life? She was so set in her ways . . . ways that included food from the grocery store deli . . . that she wondered if she could adjust to life with a man again.

The police apparently released Jason's body sooner than Beatrice had thought might be the case. The following morning, there was a funeral announcement in the Dappled Hills newspaper. And the day after that was the graveside service itself.

Wyatt officiated at the service and kept it fairly brief, which was in line with Martha's wishes. Beatrice saw that the attendees were somber, but no one looked teary. Phyllis looked a bit pensive. Beatrice, standing near the back of the gathering, thought again that Phyllis seemed an unlikely suspect, despite the evidence against her. She was the only one, besides a stoic Martha, who seemed genuinely saddened by Jason's death.

Martha's son, Frank, arrived late to the service and stood near Beatrice at the back. Beatrice noticed that Martha turned and that her eyes hardened when she spotted her son walking in, finally fitting in with his trademark black since everyone appeared to be wearing darker colors. Beatrice also saw that Frank appeared a bit unsteady on his feet. She glanced at her watch. It was eleven o'clock in the morning. Rather early to have been hitting the bottle.

Frank was entertaining to watch during the service. He sneered throughout it, weaving more and more as he tried to stand still. At one point when Martha rose to speak a few words about Jason, Frank couldn't seem to keep himself from rolling his eyes. That was the point when he finally noticed that Beatrice was looking at him. Thinking that he'd found someone who agreed with his opinion of Jason, he staggered over to Beatrice. She could tell he wanted to talk, so she gestured for him to follow her a little farther out so they wouldn't disturb anyone.

"Can you believe this drivel? So bourgeois," he snorted. "I should never have come. But I couldn't win, could I? Either Mother would have been furious that I skipped the funeral, or else she'd be mad that I came. Couldn't win," he repeated, with a self-pitying sadness in his eyes.

"You didn't like Jason very much, did you?" asked Beatrice in a soft voice.

Frank gave a hoarse laugh. "Of course not. Why would I? The guy was determined to get rid of me. He got his kicks by telling Mother what a waste I was— that she shouldn't support me. Then he'd act all concerned about me and say, 'Frank, the best thing that could happen to you is if you were forced to earn a living.' Really? And that would help my art *how*? Jason Gore didn't *get* art, that's what the problem was. Fascist."

Beatrice winced as Frank's voice got louder as he became more agitated. A few people turned around to look in their direction and Beatrice took Frank by the arm and led him farther away. "Your art is the most important thing to you, isn't it?"

His gaze finally softened a little at the mention of art. But his voice still had that hint of superiority in it as he said, "Of course. Naturally, a philistine like Jason Gore isn't going to understand that. Money is the only thing that drove him. And he saw money flying out the door to me. I've always gotten along with Mother and she always supported my art. Until Jason came along." Frank stared, broodingly, in the direction of the casket.

"He wasn't even good to her," he muttered unevenly as he took a stumbling step to keep his balance. "Somebody told me he cheated on her. Wasn't even faithful. Couldn't even manage *that*." He finished his rant with a sneer.

"It sounds," said Beatrice carefully, "as if you had many reasons to be glad that Jason is dead."

Frank's attention snapped back to her again as he suddenly realized what he'd been saying. "Look," he said in a gruff voice, "I had nothing to do with that. Nothing."

Beatrice nodded at him but allowed herself to appear doubtful.

"I didn't," he repeated, his voice rising. "I know his death worked out well for me, but I couldn't kill somebody. No way."

Beatrice led him even farther from the assembled mourners since several toward the back were turning around to stare at them again.

"All right. So you had nothing to do with his death. But somebody did, Frank. And you were on the scene that afternoon," she pointed out.

Frank nodded. "Just bringing Mother some stuff she forgot. Very inconvenient," he added in a slightly whiny tone.

"But you stuck around for a while, didn't you? You were still there when the retreat ended so abruptly," probed Beatrice.

Frank's face flushed with color. "There was food there," he muttered. "June Bug had made cakes. She cooks for Mother sometimes and I thought I'd hang out and maybe get a bit of a meal out of it."

Frank Helmsley really was a sponger. "At one point, it looked as though Jason was following you into the store to talk with you. What did he have to say?" asked Beatrice.

"Same old song and dance. I should be very grateful for Mother's kindness to me. And I should treat her better. I should stand on my own two feet. Blah, blah, blah." Frank narrowed his eyes at the memory.

"While you were in the shop, did you see anything or hear anything?" Beatrice remembered Miss Sissy's adamant statements and added, "Men's voices, for instance?"

A cagey look crossed Frank's face. "Maybe I heard something. Maybe I saw something. Maybe I know who did it."

A certainty rose in Beatrice as she looked into Frank's bleary eyes. He did know who did it. "Frank," she said urgently, "you need to let me know who's behind this. Whoever it is, he's obviously dangerous."

Frank said nothing and Beatrice continued. "If you don't want to tell me, you should at least tell Ramsay. He's right over there." She gestured to Ramsay, who was standing opposite them at the other side of the group. Ramsay, in fact, was leveling his gaze right in their direction with a questioning look. Beatrice had a feeling that she'd be hearing from him later about the tête-à-tête she and Frank were having.

"I'm not telling Ramsay anything," said Frank, in a suddenly childish tone. "That's for me to know and him to find out. Let him do his job for once. Besides, that kind of information can be useful."

His eyes had a greedy gleam that made Beatrice wonder.

Chapter Seven

After Frank had staggered off, the service wrapped up quickly. Beatrice was surprised to see Tony Brock there. Wasn't he supposed to have a huge grudge against Jason? She was so focused on staring at him that she didn't notice Miss Sissy walking up to her until she growled, "Tony is a nice boy."

Beatrice jumped. The old woman was standing right at her elbow, watching Tony with her. "That's right. You're friends with Tony, aren't you?" Miss Sissy, fortunately, seemed to be having a good day.

Miss Sissy nodded fiercely. "Tony visits me a lot. Helps me around the house. Brings me groceries."

Nice of him. Particularly since Miss Sissy could be a handful. And Beatrice knew from personal experience that Miss Sissy sometimes didn't pay you back for things. Debts were conveniently forgotten by her on a regular basis.

Beatrice said, "I'm surprised to see Tony here today. I don't think he and Jason were friends at all, from what I've heard."

Miss Sissy gave her a sharp look. "Weren't friends. Wickedness."

Beatrice moved ahead quickly before Miss Sissy could harp on her favorite topic. Things always went downhill quickly from that point. "Jason cheated him. Is that right?"

Another nod from Miss Sissy as hair flew out of her loose bun. "Tony is a clever boy. Should have gone to school. Stole his money. Evil!"

Looking for clarification from Miss Sissy could be tricky. "It was his grandfather's money, right? But it was earmarked for Tony's education?"

Miss Sissy gave her a scornful look. "Tony's money. For school."

Beatrice glanced over in Tony's direction and saw that he was only a couple of yards away and seemed to be coming to talk with them. "We'd better hush," she muttered to the old woman. "Tony is walking over."

"Tony is good," said Miss Sissy fiercely.

"But you heard men's voices. In the shop before Jason was killed."

"Not Tony!" spat out Miss Sissy.

Beatrice shushed her as Tony finally joined up with

them. She could tell that Miss Sissy was completely besotted with the young man and would refuse to think badly of him, no matter what. He smiled warmly at her and said, "Ready to head over to the reception? And then Posy said she'd take you home afterward since I'm not going to stay."

Ah. So he'd driven the old woman to the funeral. That would explain his presence there. Naturally, Miss Sissy would have wanted to attend—her curiosity alone would have propelled her there.

"Tony, do you mind if I talk to you for a couple of minutes?" Beatrice asked quickly.

Tony raised a quizzical eyebrow. "Of course not. Mrs. . . . Coleman, isn't it?"

"Beatrice," she said, nodding.

"Miss Sissy, do you think you could wait out in the car for us?" asked Tony. He handed over his keys.

Her gaze fell greedily on the keys. She grabbed them and sprinted off.

"I hope you know what you're doing," said Beatrice. "You're pretty brave to give Miss Sissy your car keys— you've got to know she's a holy terror on the roads and she might even hijack your car. How did you get her to accept a ride from you in the first place? She always seems to want to drive herself just to scare the populace of Dappled Hills out of their wits."

Tony grinned at her and she realized that, when he smiled, he really was an attractive young man. He was lean and fit and today wasn't wearing his customary T-shirt and blue jeans, instead sporting khakis and a dark button-down shirt. "You have to know how to work Miss Sissy, that's all."

"Clearly, that's a skill I haven't yet acquired. How did you manage it?" asked Beatrice.

"Easy. I work on cars a lot—I'm not certified or anything, but I know a lot about them. All I had to do was to disable Miss Sissy's spark plugs. She realized her car wouldn't turn on and called me. I used my buddy's tow truck to tow it away. Now Miss Sissy thinks that her car has some sort of really odd and serious problem," said Tony. "She's not asking many questions, either, since she likes me and I've been giving her lifts. Figure it's my good deed for Dappled Hills."

"I'll say," said Beatrice fervently. It would be a relief not to suddenly have to dodge when Miss Sissy's aging Lincoln started veering onto the sidewalks.

Tony gave her a bow. "My pleasure."

"That was very smart of you. In fact, I've been hearing from various Dappled Hills residents how bright you are," said Beatrice.

Tony looked questioningly at her.

"I'm still new to town, and folks have been trying to get me caught up. I understand that Jason Gore actually left town with the money that had been set aside for your education. Is that correct?"

Tony's eyes darkened. "Let's just say that if people

liked him, it's because they didn't really know him. Jason wasn't the friendly, helpful, great guy that everyone seems to think he was. I know better. He changed my life—and not in a good way."

Beatrice said, "I know you were working right next door to the Patchwork Cottage on the day of the murder. . . ."

"Hey, I didn't have anything to do with that, Beatrice." Tony looked searchingly at her as if wondering who this sixty-something-year-old actually was.

"Of course not," said Beatrice in a soothing tone. "I was only going to ask if you'd seen or heard anything that might help track down who did this."

"You seem awfully interested in who killed Jason," said Tony, squinting doubtfully at her.

"I'm a fan of puzzles and of figuring things out," said Beatrice. "And the murder is having an unfortunate effect on my quilting guild."

"Okay. Well, I wish I could help you out, but I was up to my eyeballs in work. I didn't see anything, didn't hear anything."

Tony's eyes were shuttered and Beatrice couldn't help getting the feeling that he knew more than he was letting on.

"There's no one you can think of who might want Jason out of the way?" pushed Beatrice gently.

Tony gave a harsh laugh. "Besides me, you mean? I'm sure I could think of a few. Martha's son, Frank, for one. Maybe he was giving you a nice story when he was talking to you a little while ago, but I promise you that he was always thinking about money and the fact that his mother was lavishing it on Jason."

"He doesn't work, I believe."

Tony shook his head. "No. It sort of burns me up, to be honest. Here I am, working my tail off every day, and Frank is dabbling in a little paint or squishing some clay into shapes. Living off his mother. It's not right." He gave a quick shrug. "If you ask me, he wanted to protect his cushy lifestyle. He's the one the police should be talking to."

A loud, repetitive honking rent the air. Tony and Beatrice swung around to see Miss Sissy in the driver's seat, staring at them as she honked.

"I'd better run," he said quickly. "She might decide to drive through the cemetery to pick me up."

Beatrice stared at his back as he dashed away. Tony Brock must have the patience of a saint. But had he had that much patience with Jason Gore?

Meadow had driven Beatrice to the funeral, although she'd stood with Posy through the service. She caught up with Beatrice and they walked to Meadow's van together. "How was the sleuthing?" she asked in her pseudowhisper.

Beatrice glanced around them and was glad to see that no one was within earshot. "Not too bad. I wasn't sure when I'd have a chance to talk with Frank Helmsley, so I was glad I was able to ask him a few questions."

Meadow snorted as she unlocked the doors for them. "It looked like he was three sheets to the wind to me. He could barely stand up straight, could he?"

"It did seem to be a challenge." Beatrice opened the passenger-side door and stared at what looked to be a five-thousand-page book on the seat of the car. "Um . . ."

Meadow snorted. "From Ramsay, of course. Did you encourage him, Beatrice? I warned you about encouraging him when it came to books. Now you've got to read . . ." She squinted at the title. ". . . *The Brothers Karamazov* by Fyodor Dostoyevsky. And if you encouraged Ramsay in his big-boring-book obsession, then you deserve it. Oh, and I have a food processor and some other stuff in a bag in the backseat. I'll try to remind you about it when I drop you back off."

Beatrice hefted the tome and placed it in the backseat of the van. "He just happened to notice I was reading something lightweight. *Literally* lightweight. This thing must weigh a ton."

"Russian literature. You know. Good luck with that." Meadow gave a short laugh.

"It's supposed to be a masterpiece," said Beatrice with a sigh as she climbed into the front seat.

"Well, whatever you do, don't tell him you like it, or else you'll be saddled with more."

Beatrice carefully fastened her seat belt as Meadow started the engine. Meadow's driving wasn't nearly in Miss Sissy's league, but it could be fairly hair-raising as she sped around the mountain bends. "At least Frank didn't embarrass his mother too badly, although he was clearly drunk. He sure wasn't much of a fan of Jason Gore."

"Martha was keeping an eye on him, though. She probably half expected him to mess things up." Meadow pressed on the accelerator as if getting to the funeral reception was of the utmost importance.

Beatrice clung to the passenger door and felt a bit queasy as they started rounding the mountain curves on the way to Martha's house. "Slow down a little, Meadow. We're in no rush to get there, are we?"

Meadow glanced her way in surprise. "I didn't realize you liked a poky pace, Beatrice." But she obediently hit the brakes. "So, do you think Frank is responsible for getting rid of Jason? What was his motive? Greed?"

"That *would* be his motive. He admitted that he lived off his mother's generosity while he made his art. Frank called Jason a philistine and said that he was trying to persuade Martha to cut him off. But he swears he had nothing to do with Jason's death," said Beatrice.

"Well, naturally, that's what he'd say, right? He was hardly going to admit his guilt to you right at his poor victim's funeral, was he? Can you imagine? Ramsay would have had to make a huge scene by interrupting the service and arresting Frank on the spot." Meadow shuddered.

Beatrice hesitated. "I know. Of course he'd try to convince me that he was innocent. He was drunk, though. And he was telling me that he *knew* who was responsible for the murder. He really convinced me that he knew the killer."

Meadow took her eyes off the road to stare at Beatrice until the van swung into the shoulder and she swerved to get back on track. "For heaven's sake! If he knows who the killer is, then why doesn't he get with Ramsay and fill him in?"

"I got the feeling that he might be wanting to do something with that information," said Beatrice slowly. "He did say that it was Ramsay's job to find it out and that he wasn't going to tell him."

"How is Ramsay supposed to solve cases if people won't tell him what they know?" demanded Meadow, giving the steering wheel a whack with her palm.

"I was wondering if he might be planning on using his information to extort money out of someone," said Beatrice. "He said something about knowing information that could be useful somehow. He's obviously not swimming in cash right now. Maybe he's thinking he'd like another revenue stream besides his mother. It's got to be a little scary to be solely dependent on one source of income."

"So he's wanting to diversify?" Meadow clucked. "I

never did think that Frank Helmsley was the sharpest knife in the drawer." She pulled into Martha's long driveway and drove toward a very large home with white bricks and black shutters. "Wow, there're a lot of cars here. I wouldn't even have said there were this many people at the funeral."

"You know how folks are about free food around here," murmured Beatrice. "Although I'm pretty sure Frank won't make it. And Tony mentioned that he wouldn't be here."

"It's not like Miss Sissy to miss free food," said Meadow, shaking her head.

"Tony was planning on dropping her off."

Meadow said in a mulling voice, "You know, I half fancy Martha for this murder."

"What? But she was so crazy over Jason. She seemed devastated at his death."

"Now, hear me out. Yes, Martha was crazy over Jason. But she did have access to those shears. Maybe she *did* swipe Phyllis's scissors when she wasn't looking. And I keep hearing these rumors that Jason was flirting with other ladies. I could see Martha wanting to shut that down. Can't you?" asked Meadow. "And using Phyllis's shears would have been the perfect way to get revenge on her if she was trying to steal Jason back."

"Cutting off her nose to spite her face? Because she

wouldn't have had Jason, either—not if she killed him with Phyllis's shears. It just doesn't make any sense at all, Meadow. Besides, I don't think Martha would have seen any woman as a serious threat. After all, her financial situation was part of her appeal to Jason—and no one in town could match it," said Beatrice. "You said yourself that it looked as if Phyllis was living on a budget."

"Well, you could be right. I'm still keeping Martha in the suspect pile, though. Oh, I know what I was going to ask you about. You spoke awhile with Tony, too," said Meadow as she parked and turned off the car. She turned in her seat to look at Beatrice. "Did you find out anything from him?"

Beatrice shrugged. "He was pretty cagey. He hinted at past trouble between him and Jason but didn't really spell it out. He did basically tell me that he wasn't Frank Helmsley's biggest fan."

Meadow laughed. "No, I guess he wouldn't be. Tony works like crazy and I can't see him holding much stock in somebody who has never held down a real job. Not to put down Frank's art, but as far as I know, he's never sold anything. It would be different if he were making an income off his art and just needed his income supplemented. It's sure never been on sale here in Dappled Hills—no art shows, nothing. Tony, on the other hand, works in the hardware store, makes deliveries for folks who don't drive anymore, does odd jobs, puts up with Miss Sissy, works on cars . . . whatever he can do to make a few extra dollars."

Beatrice watched as a bald man in a well-worn suit glanced in a nervous way around him, straightened his suit jacket, squared his shoulders, and walked into Martha's house. "Who's he?" she asked, gesturing.

Meadow said, "That's Jason's half brother, Eric. I guess you wouldn't have met him . . . there would be no reason for your paths to cross. He doesn't even work in Dappled Hills—he drives to Lenoir to work. He's a movie usher there or takes tickets in the booth or something."

"Ramsay was telling me a little about Eric," said Beatrice. They got out of Meadow's van and started walking to Martha's house, which was a columned historic home with a meticulously upkept yard. Beatrice smoothed down her cream-colored blouse, which had gotten a bit wrinkled in Meadow's van. She removed what appeared to be a few stray bits of dog fur from her black slacks. "I was a bit surprised when he was filling me in, because somehow I'd gotten the impression that Jason didn't have any remaining family."

"He didn't. Except for Eric. In fact, Eric is supposedly his last living relative," said Meadow in one of her stage whispers.

"He's a half brother. Is that right?"

"Yes, and it's all a very tragic story, Beatrice," said Meadow, seemingly just getting geared up to tell the story as they walked through the doors.

"Tell me another time," hissed Beatrice as Martha came up to greet them.

"Thanks so much for being here," said Martha solemnly. Her eyes were red from crying, but she was poised and elegant as usual in a black dress with pearls. "It means so much to me that you're both here."

"Of course. Happy to come. We were so sorry about Jason," murmured Beatrice, and Meadow reached out to give Martha an impulsive hug.

Her large home seemed full of people, and the conversation after a bit rose to a chatty volume. Meadow quickly homed in on the food and there was quite a bit of it and it was fairly heavy in nature—ham biscuits and pimento cheese sandwiches, potato salad, egg salad, ham salad, pasta salad. And cakes. "I feel like I'm on a picnic!" said Meadow, trying unsuccessfully to hide her delight. She took a big bite of an angel food cake. "These are June Bug's. I can tell. That June Bug does beat all. That little woman can flat cook! *And* she's a fantastic quilter. And modest as all get-out. If I'd that much talent, I'd be yelling out my accomplishments from the rooftops."

Beatrice was sipping from a glass of iced tea when she noticed someone else coming through the door into the crowded living room. "Isn't that John?" she asked, leaning forward so that Meadow could hear her over the din. "The man who wants to date Martha?"

"You mean the man who wants to *marry* Martha," corrected Meadow stoutly. She squinted across the room. "Yes, that's he. I'm sure that Martha won't be any too pleased to see him here. She was certainly interested in shooing him away at any opportunity."

She and Beatrice gaped as Martha spotted John, burst into tears, and threw herself into his arms. "Well, that's certainly a change," muttered Meadow, blinking.

Beatrice witnessed a very satisfied expression cross John's lean face. A sort of fierce, protective pride. Yes, he'd been waiting for that particular change for a very long time. What did it feel like to wait and wait and wait for someone who couldn't care less? Who dated others? Who was dismissive? And then what was it like when she finally came around and ran into your arms? Could a person possibly kill for that feeling? Had John gotten rid of Jason Gore to finally win Martha?

Meadow nudged her. "There's Eric." She bobbed her head in the direction of the food. Eric Gore stood near the table, holding a glass plate with only a little bit of fruit on it. He glanced awkwardly around the room as if not sure who to talk to.

"He's acting as if he doesn't know anyone here," murmured Beatrice. "But it's his brother's funeral."

"He hasn't exactly spent a lot of time hanging out in Dappled Hills," said Meadow. "He's sort of got issues. He probably *doesn't* know anyone here. Maybe he knows Martha. But Martha is a bit busy right now."

Beatrice looked back over at Martha, who was still crying heartily in John's arms. "Maybe I'll go over and chat with Eric for a while." It might be a way to get some information. Besides, it always made her uncomfortable to see *others* uncomfortable.

"Good idea. I'm going to see if there's enough food for me to have seconds." Meadow sidled over to the table of food. "Oh no—here comes Miss Sissy. Better eat before she gets over there. She's sure to wipe out everything on the table."

"Hi, I'm Beatrice Coleman," said Beatrice, extending her hand to Eric. He switched his plate of fruit to his other hand to shake, giving Beatrice a grateful smile in the process. "I hear you're Jason's brother."

"His half brother, yes," said Eric automatically. Beatrice felt almost as though he were trying to add some distance between himself and Jason. He set down his plate of fruit, putting his napkin carefully on top of it as if he'd suddenly lost his appetite. "And his last living relative."

"I'm very sorry for your loss," said Beatrice. "It must have been a tremendous shock, losing him so suddenly."

Eric nodded absently. He said, "Beatrice. Weren't

you . . . didn't I hear that you were the one who discovered Jason? At the shop?"

"That's right," she said quietly. She cleared her throat and glanced around the room. No one was looking in their direction or seemed even vaguely interested in giving their condolences to Jason's one remaining family member. It just seemed very odd. It was almost as if no one really knew who Eric was.

"Were you very close?" she asked. "I mean—I'm sure you must have been. It must have been nice for you when he moved back to Dappled Hills after such an absence."

An unreadable expression passed across Eric's face. He stared down at the floor. "Well, you know how it is with adult siblings. Sometimes you grow apart through the years."

Actually, that hadn't been what Beatrice had observed at all. It usually seemed that siblings who might have had childhood rivalries grew closer as adults. She peered at him. So Eric was not only alienated from the entire town; he'd been alienated from his one relative, too. "And losing your last living relative must have been especially difficult."

Eric gave a harsh laugh. "Difficult? I wouldn't say that. Difficult was when I lost my mother. That was difficult."

"I'm sorry," said Beatrice softly. "Was that recent? That's a lot of loss to go through at one time."

"Not recent, no. It coincided with Jason's escape from Dappled Hills seven years back."

Escape? What an odd word to use. Beatrice frowned.

Eric ran a finger around the inside of his shirt collar, pulling it as if he weren't used to wearing dressy clothes. His face was flushed as if he were aware that he'd said something he shouldn't have said. "It was good to meet you, Beatrice. I should probably go now. I'll need to thank Martha."

Beatrice glanced back in Martha's direction, wondering if she was still in John's arms. Instead she saw Martha back at her iciest—and then saw why. Phyllis Stitt had arrived and was busily talking with a group of women as if she had every right to be there. Judging from Martha's expression, however, she strongly disagreed.

Meadow's gaze met hers from across the room and she raised her eyebrows at the development. Would there be drama at the funeral reception?

Eric wandered up to thank Martha, however, so she was momentarily diverted from what Beatrice guessed would be Martha's expulsion of Phyllis from the reception. She saw Martha's gaze soften as she spoke with Eric, giving him a quick hug before he left. Beatrice wondered if they'd actually really known each other, though. It certainly hadn't sounded as if Eric and Jason had been very close. And Eric apparently didn't spend all that much time in Dappled Hills.

After talking with Eric, Martha removed herself with difficulty from Phyllis's proximity. Martha walked up to Beatrice and said, "I certainly think it's in very poor taste of Phyllis to come here. Really. I've half a mind to toss her out on her ear."

Chapter Eight

"I suppose she's trying to show that she had no hard feelings for Jason," murmured Beatrice.

Martha rolled her eyes. "But there were hard feelings. Many of them. It's all an act for the police."

Phyllis glanced their way, her gaze falling for a moment on Martha before she quickly looked away. She noticed Eric was walking out the door and she gave him a friendly nod and a sympathetic smile before he left. He looked searchingly into her eyes, causing Phyllis to pause. Eric, seeming unable to help himself, reached out an arm toward Phyllis. She hesitated and then gave Eric a quick hug before hurriedly leaving. Phyllis was probably the only person there who'd reached out to Eric besides Beatrice and Martha.

John joined Beatrice and Martha. His face was appropriately solemn for the occasion, but his eyes were glowing. He greeted Beatrice and handed Martha a plate of food he'd put together for her. Beatrice noticed many curious glances from around the room.

Beatrice walked across the room for another glass of tea and Miss Sissy intercepted her on the way over. "They go out, you know."

Beatrice frowned. "Who goes out?"

Miss Sissy scowled at her. "*They* do."

Meadow joined them and Miss Sissy repeated her statement. Meadow said, "Who goes out with each other? We don't understand."

Miss Sissy looked at both of them as if she were surrounded by imbeciles. "Phyllis and that guy."

Meadow finished swallowing down a bit of mixed fruit, rolled her eyes at Beatrice, and said, "No, no, no, Miss Sissy. You've got it all wrong. Phyllis went out with *Jason*. The man who died. Whose funeral we're attending—you know."

"Vile!" fumed Miss Sissy.

Meadow shrugged and picked up a pimento cheese sandwich square with no crusts, which made Miss Sissy glare hungrily at her until she scampered off for another plate of food.

Wyatt had been busy speaking with Martha and others since Beatrice arrived, but now he came over and gave her a smile. "It's good of you to come and support Martha," he said. "The quilting community is really amazing."

Beatrice felt a small tinge of guilt. Well, she supposed she *had* wanted also to support Martha—it wasn't only that she was keeping her ears and eyes open for any potential clues to the murderer in this case.

Meadow winked at her and quickly said, "That's exactly the kind of person Beatrice is. Always looking for ways to support her fellow quilters. Isn't she wonderful?"

Beatrice flushed and shot Meadow a look as Wyatt murmured in agreement.

Meadow was gazing out into Martha's living room when her eyes opened wide, and then she shut them again briefly as if she were trying to erase an image. "I saw Savannah swipe something. Just now."

Beatrice glanced across the room to where Savannah was surreptitiously sticking something in her pocketbook. She squinted and saw that it appeared to be a clip intended to keep potato chip bags closed. "I have a feeling Martha really won't mind," said Beatrice. "It's not as if she'll probably even miss it. And clearly, her budget would cover replacement of it, even if she did notice."

Unfortunately, it was at that moment that Georgia joined them. She followed their gaze to Savannah, who was drawing her hand away from her pocketbook. "Oh no," said Georgia. "Is she at it again?"

"I'm afraid so," said Beatrice. "But it was only a chip clip."

"It's always something very insignificant," said Georgia with a sigh. "But it doesn't matter—what's wrong is wrong." She gave Wyatt a pained look. "I'm so embarrassed about Savannah's actions. You know she's not really like that."

Wyatt said gently, "I know that it's her stress that makes her act this way. If there's anything that I can do at all for her or for you, I hope you'll let me know. I'm always happy to talk to her."

"Thanks," said Georgia sadly. "I know that you are. But when we bring up this . . . problem . . . she really acts as if she doesn't know what we're talking about. She doesn't like discussing it. I'll have to try to get the chip clip back to Martha at some point later. After I'm done staying at my friend's house."

"How are things going with the house-sitting?" asked Meadow.

Georgia gave her a warm smile. "Oh, it's really nice. She has such a great house—lots of sunshine coming in the windows. The animals have sunny spots on the floors to sleep in. And she has the sweetest pets. I love her dog, Snuffy. And her cat, Mr. Shadow, is a real charmer." But Beatrice noticed the smile didn't go all the way up to her eyes and wondered if she might miss her sister's company. Maybe she wasn't quite as happy as she seemed with the house-sitting.

Later that afternoon, as Meadow drove Beatrice at the same breakneck pace back to her cottage, Meadow said, "I simply can't get how Martha was so happy to

be with John today. She's rebuffed him again and again
through the years. Then today, she acted like she loved
him or something." She snorted.

"Maybe she simply gave in," said Beatrice. "It's got
to be exhausting to keep turning down a devoted ad-
mirer, year after year. Besides, after losing Jason, she
must feel as if she needs some support. John seems
nothing if not supportive."

"Just the same," Meadow said darkly as the car sped
around the mountain curves, "I'm thinking that John is
behind this whole thing."

"I thought you were sold on Martha as the murderer.
Now you think that John is the killer?" asked Beatrice,
clinging to the passenger door and bracing herself with
her feet on the floorboard.

"Why not?" Meadow shrugged. "Martha is all that
old John has ever wanted. Most people want riches or
fame or something, but John has only ever wanted Martha. If getting your heart's desire was that easy and it
only meant getting rid of someone who's caused plenty
of pain and suffering in his time, then why not go for
it?" She turned to look at Beatrice and then had to
quickly swerve to stay on the road.

"Maybe," said Beatrice thoughtfully. "Love makes
people act in odd ways."

"Speaking of love," said Meadow, glancing sideways at Beatrice, "I think our precious lovebirds are
going out tonight for a special dinner."

Meadow was a devoted matchmaker. It really fell into hobby territory with her. She spurred on the relationship between her Ash and Beatrice's Piper at any opportunity. In some ways, it was probably good that they enjoyed a primarily long-distance relationship.

"I'd imagine every dinner is a special dinner when you're with someone you care about," said Beatrice. "It's not as if they get to see each other as often as they like."

Meadow was now wriggling in her seat with barely contained excitement and appeared in danger of not paying attention to the road at all. "That's what's so special about this dinner! Oh, I can't wait to tell you. I know I promised Ash, but you're not going to tell anyone." She shot Beatrice a worried look. "You *won't* tell Piper, will you?"

Beatrice gritted her teeth. "Tell Piper *what*, Meadow?"

"That Ash has been looking for a job in North Carolina since he met Piper. Nearby. He didn't want to let her know he was looking, because he didn't want to disappoint her if it fell through. But he found one. He's going to let Piper know tonight that their relationship will no longer have to be a long-distance one. I was about to be disappointed that Piper couldn't make the retreat, but then when I found out they were having a special evening, it was all worthwhile."

Beatrice's heart made a leap. She'd had such a mixture of feelings about Piper dating Ash. For one thing, she'd been glad that her daughter was so happy. For another, she was delighted that Ash was such a good match and a nice guy. But then—she had to admit there was a side of her that had been really upset. She hadn't wanted to lose Piper by having her move all the way to the other side of the country. If this worked out . . .

A thought occurred to her. "Meadow. I thought Ash was a marine biologist. How could he find a job in the mountains of North Carolina?"

Meadow beamed at her as she pulled into Beatrice's driveway. "That's the best part. It's a teaching position at Harrington College. So it's taking what he knows and using it in a totally different way. He doesn't have a PhD or anything, so he's an adjunct professor. But they're delighted to have him on board there and it means that *he gets to live here*!" Her eyes shone. "I can hear the wedding bells already." She gasped. "Or the pitter-patter of precious grandchild feet!"

"Remember, Meadow, it's only dinner," said Beatrice, trying to put the brakes on before Meadow was picking colleges for their unborn grandchildren. Meadow came to a jouncing stop and Beatrice opened the door to climb out of the van.

"Get the stuff from the backseat," Meadow reminded her.

"Oh, right," said Beatrice. She picked up the big book, and then gaped at the huge bag that was wedged between the two backseats. "You don't mean *this* bag, do you? This huge bag? Meadow, I thought you were just giving me a couple of your kitchen castoffs."

"I went through my cabinets and couldn't believe the amount of kitchen utensils I had!" said Meadow breezily. "There were gobs of duplicates, too. I put the food processor in there and some other things."

Beatrice peered into the bag. "I see a colander, a cutting board, a whisk, a grater, a hand mixer . . . Meadow, I can't take all this. For one thing, you might need them. For another, I'm simply not sure if I've got the room. And then . . . well, I tried cooking the other day. It was completely disastrous."

"Oh, please!" said Meadow, waving her hand dismissively. "That cabinet of yours was just as empty as it could be. All that stuff could easily fit in there. And I already told you that I don't need any of it. As far as disastrous cooking goes . . . you simply need to *practice*, Beatrice. I told you that you *couldn't* really cook—not with the equipment you had on hand. I'm surprised that you even tried."

Beatrice opened her mouth again to argue the point, but Meadow waved her hand at her again. "No, no— no, thanks! You can thank me by preparing your culinary masterpiece for Wyatt. Be sure and take pictures!"

And in the blink of an eye, she was gone.

The next afternoon, Beatrice was again taking a stab at Ramsay's *The Brothers Karamazov*—which wasn't growing on her—when there was a light tap at her front door. Noo-noo ran to the door in front of her and she peeked out and saw Piper standing there, wearing a tunic top and leggings that complemented her cute figure and her pixie haircut. Noo-noo ran off to find a toy as soon as she saw Beatrice's daughter at the door. Piper's gray eyes looked tired, but she grinned and gave her mother a fleeting kiss before she sat down on the floor to cuddle Noo-noo when she came back with a toy. "It's always flattering to come over here and get this kind of reception," she said.

"I'll get us some tea," said Beatrice, and she was back soon with two tall glasses. Piper moved to Beatrice's overstuffed sofa and took a big sip from her glass. Then she squinted, looking over near the door leading out to the backyard. "Is that a *kitten* you've got over there?"

Beatrice sighed. "I'm afraid so. I'm actually dropping her off at the vet tomorrow morning to get all her shots and then I'm going to try to find a home for her."

"Where did she come from?" asked Piper with a smile. The kitten was all curled up in a fuzzy ball, sleeping soundly.

"She found me," said Beatrice with a shrug. "Out of the blue the other night, she started mewing and pawing outside the front door. Noo-noo was most alarmed about it. But she's settled in just fine, actually. Except for the fact that Noo-noo doesn't care for her."

"I bet she doesn't. I'll try to listen out at school to see if anyone is looking for a pet. She should be easy to place with someone if she's so well-behaved and has her shots," said Piper.

Piper lived right down the street, but with her busy schedule, Beatrice didn't see as much of her as she liked. Piper was a teacher, and her move to Dappled Hills was the reason Beatrice was here. She'd always been sad at the thought that she'd see much less of her if she moved to California to marry Meadow's son. Beatrice was dying to ask her how her date with Ash had gone last night, but, after all, she wasn't supposed to know about it.

Instead she asked, "How is your quilt coming along for the show tonight? Is it all done? You know Meadow was fussing about all the quilts that were yet to be finished."

Piper nodded, reaching down to scratch behind Noo-noo's ears. "I managed to finish it up late last night."

"Oh, it was a late night for you, then? That's probably why you look a little tired," said Beatrice. Maybe it had nothing to do with Ash, after all.

To her surprise, Piper's eyes filled with tears. "It's more like I couldn't sleep." She put her face in her hands and her voice was muffled as she said, "I've messed everything up."

Beatrice reached over to hug her. "What's wrong, sweetheart?"

"Ash was so excited, Mama. You know he flew in for a visit yesterday. So we went out for supper last night. I just thought it was a time for us to catch up with each other, share a nice dinner, and relax. But he meant it to be so much more than that. I was caught off guard." Piper choked up. The snoozing kitten woke up, looked sleepily in their direction, and padded over to curl up in Piper's lap . . . as if she knew she needed the comfort.

Piper gave a half sob, half laugh and buried her face in the kitten's fur. If there was one thing Beatrice knew that she and Piper shared, it was a dislike for surprises . . . even for surprises that were supposed to be fun. Being prepared felt so much better. "Did he propose?" she asked.

"Not exactly," said Piper. "Only because I must have looked so stricken. You see, he found a job nearby, knowing that was the one thing that really stood in the way of us being together. But I had no idea he was doing that—preparing to move to the other side of the country and doing something completely different from what he's doing now. It was such a surprise that I didn't know how to react. I was just trying to take it all in, digest the news, and I guess I didn't exactly look thrilled." She stopped. "I *know* I didn't look thrilled."

She raised her head from her hands and said tearfully, "It's not that I don't care for Ash—I do. I think I even love him. It's simply such a tremendous move and means such a huge change in our relationship. I was caught off guard. With a move like this—well, it means that there are plenty of expectations as far as the direction of our relationship goes. I simply wasn't prepared for it. I guess I should have been."

"What happened after he made his announcement and you looked so taken aback by it?" asked Beatrice quietly.

"Ash was very hurt," said Piper sadly. "I guess we haven't spent enough real time together for him to see me when I'm trying to figure things out. We both lost our appetite and picked quietly at our meal, and Ash took me home." She shrugged, choking up again.

"I'm sure you and Ash can work it out," Beatrice said quickly. "It's just a misunderstanding." She paused. "You do want to work it out, I suppose?"

Piper nodded silently.

"Then I'm sure you will. Maybe you can give him a call later and talk with him about it over coffee or something."

Piper nodded and fished in her pocketbook for a tissue. She cleared her throat and said with a smile, "I hear that you and Wyatt finally went out on a real date."

Beatrice sighed. Small towns and gossip. "Since half

the town was in the restaurant, I guess it was only natural that you'd hear about it. From Meadow, I'm guessing?"

"Several different sources," said Piper with a grin. "All delighted, though, that you two were out with each other. Believe me, it was wonderful news to me—at least one of us has a love life that's going well."

Beatrice held up her hand in a slowing-down gesture. "We're moving very slowly, Piper. After all, we've both been widowed for a long time. It's a big change to spend time with someone after all these years. It was only lunch."

Piper could apparently tell that Beatrice didn't want to talk too much about Wyatt yet. "Is your quilt ready for the show?" she asked.

Beatrice relaxed now that they were clearly moving on to other subjects. "I've been finished for a while. Although there's another quilt I'm working on that's a bit trickier. It's a double wedding ring pattern."

Piper whistled. "That's a tough one, all right. The cutting alone is tricky."

"That's what I found out. But I was in the right place because Miss Sissy, believe it or not, recommended some templates and a cutting tool that was specifically made for double wedding ring patterns. I thought she was relentlessly old-fashioned about her quilting, but it seems like she'll use some modern tools, if they're available."

Piper gave a small laugh. "Well, she does spend a lot

of time in the Patchwork Cottage with Posy. I guess she might be an expert on what's available."

"It did help out. Although I was hoping to get some more guidance than that from the guild at Posy's retreat." She shrugged. "Of course, things didn't work out that way."

Piper shuddered. "They sure didn't. I was having nightmares that night, too, and I didn't even discover Jason, like you did. What an awful thing to happen."

Beatrice said, "It sure was. And poor Posy, having it happen right in her shop." She paused. "Who do you think might be responsible for it?"

"I was kind of hoping that some stranger passing through town came in and murdered Jason," said Piper with a sigh. "A random act of violence." She looked at her mother with a hopeful expression. "I guess that's impossible, isn't it?"

"I'm afraid so. This was a very personal crime. Someone really disliked Jason Gore."

Piper examined Beatrice closely. "You're not trying to look into this crime and do any of your investigating, are you?" Beatrice tried not to look guilty. "Because whoever is behind this is very dangerous, Mama. They clearly mean business. I just hate the thought of you putting yourself in any danger."

"Of course I won't do anything dangerous," said Beatrice. "You know how careful I am. I'm certainly not an investigator of any kind. I'm simply a fairly observant person who's interested in restoring order and peace to a very quiet town. I'm giving Ramsay a couple of extra eyes, that's all." She tried to deflect the conversation back to the case. "So, besides the random stranger, who do you think disliked Jason enough to do something like this?"

Piper shook her head. "That's what I don't know. I'm hearing whispers that Phyllis is behind this, but I can't see it. Can you? It's such a violent crime. I feel like a man has got to be behind it—after all, Jason was a pretty big guy."

"But after the killer knocked him out, anyone could have done it," said Beatrice.

"Is that what happened, then?" asked Piper. She thought a moment. "I still don't see Phyllis doing that. She really cared for Jason at one point, you know? Maybe Frank—he always acts like he's furious at the world. I don't think he was real happy about his mother going out with Jason. I overheard Jason telling Martha one day that she should cut Frank off and let him see if he could make a living from his art—that surely he had enough to sell by now to get him started."

"What did Martha say to that?"

"I could tell that she wasn't wild about the idea—but that she was thinking about it," said Piper.

After Piper left, Beatrice's thoughts kept returning to Wyatt. She decided that, since the dinner she'd attempted hadn't worked out, she'd at least offer to help Wyatt set up for that evening's quilt show. It was going to be in the church's basement recreation area and she knew that chairs and tables would need to be moved and refreshments set up on one side of the room. She picked up the phone and called over to the church.

"That would be wonderful, Beatrice. I could sure use the extra help. Tell you what . . . why don't we grab a quick supper before we start setting up? Is it all right if I pick you up in about fifteen minutes?"

Beatrice's heart gave a happy leap and she told Wyatt that would work well. But five minutes later, there was a phone call from Wyatt. "Beatrice, I'm so sorry. I've had a call that a member of the congregation is requesting a visit from me. Can we take a rain check on our supper? And then I'll meet you at the church for the setup, if that still works for you."

"Of course," said Beatrice. "I'll see you over there." She'd no idea that the ministry was such a demanding job. Wyatt must live the kind of life where his work intruded constantly on his personal time. At the same time, though, she couldn't help feeling a quick disappointment that she wouldn't be spending one-on-one time with Wyatt at supper. It seemed as though this was something she was going to have to learn to deal with if she wanted to be part of Wyatt's life in any way.

The next phone call was from Meadow, calling to see if Beatrice wanted to ride with her to the quilt show.

Beatrice explained that she was going early to help Wyatt set up. Meadow said, "That's so sweet of you to help Wyatt out! I declare, y'all are the cutest couple ever."

Beatrice closed her eyes.

"If I help you two, that won't mess up any romance before the show, will it?" asked Meadow. "Because I'd love to help with the setup."

"There was no romance planned—just work," said Beatrice, feeling a little tired. But at least Meadow wasn't asking about Piper and Ash. If she had to choose between the two, she'd rather have Meadow diverted by her relationship with Wyatt.

At about an hour and a half before the start of the show, there was a tap at Beatrice's door. She looked out the window and saw Meadow there in a pair of cranberry red slacks that matched her glasses and a tunic of bright reds and yellows. Meadow gave her a quick wave and she let her in.

"I know the church is close, but I thought we'd better drive over—don't you think? Carrying the quilt and everything? I can drive us," said Meadow. She gave her a critical look and then a thumbs-up. "You look gorgeous, as always, Beatrice. I love that creamy top with the black slacks."

They got in the car, Beatrice being careful to lift her quilt so that it didn't drag on the ground.

Meadow gave Beatrice a sideways glance as they set

off. "Did you notice anything funny about Piper today? If you saw her, I mean."

"What do you mean?" asked Beatrice, deliberately avoiding Meadow's gaze by looking forward through the windshield.

"Oh, I don't know. When Ash came in from their date last night, he hardly said a word. Kind of barked at me when I asked how the evening went. He was really grumpy. I was wondering if something went wrong." She sighed. "I hope nothing went wrong. Ash was so happy when he first flew in."

Beatrice knew one thing—she sure wasn't going to share what she knew with Meadow. Meadow tended to try to bulldoze people into doing what she wanted them to do. With the best intentions, of course. "He was probably just tired, Meadow. And maybe a little jet-lagged." She quickly changed the subject. "Piper did say that she'd finished her quilt."

Meadow heaved a sigh of relief. "Well, thank goodness for that. I was thinking that we weren't going to have much of a quilt show if half our guild hadn't finished their quilts. I'm sure the Cut-Ups were able to get theirs done. In record time, probably." Her face was glum as she pulled into the church parking lot. Then she brightened. "Let me tell you about the next quilt I'm doing. It's going to be a collage of Boris. I figured he was such a bright dog that he deserved to be immortalized in cloth."

"I'm sure it will be very cute." Beatrice tried to think up a different topic to forestall talk of Boris the Genius Dog before Meadow got going on his latest brilliant exploit. "Um, Meadow—you don't know anyone who is in need of a kitten, do you?"

"You're not trying to unload that little bundle of fur, are you? What a sweetie she is!" said Meadow.

Beatrice said quickly, "She *is* sweet. And she's house-trained—a very smart kitten. It's just that I hadn't planned on having a cat. And Noo-noo is less than thrilled."

"I'll keep my ears open," said Meadow. Then she squinted over at the church as they pulled in. "We *are* early, aren't we? I don't even see any lights on. I wonder if Wyatt is even here."

"Wyatt had a member of the congregation to visit before the show," said Beatrice with a shrug. "It's a good thing we're here to get everything set up."

A car came up behind them. "Oh, here he is," said Meadow.

Wyatt hurried out of the car. "Running later than I wanted to," he said breathlessly. "And it was a sort of odd visit, too," he said a bit absently. His eyes crinkled as he smiled at Meadow and Beatrice. "Thanks so much for helping." He fumbled for the key in his pants pocket and Beatrice watched him surreptitiously: The dark brown button-down shirt nicely offset his silver-streaked hair.

Another car roared up behind them and Wyatt pulled Beatrice into his arms and out of its path as Meadow nimbly jumped out of the way.

"For heaven's sake," fussed Meadow. "It's Miss Sissy. I thought Tony was going to drive her tonight. She's here so early, too. She'll eat all the food before anyone even arrives." Meadow looked at Wyatt with pleading eyes. "Can you do something about her? You know how she gets. And she *likes* you—she'll do whatever you say."

"Maybe I can assign her some sort of job," said Wyatt a bit dubiously. "I'll see what I can do." He handed the keys to Beatrice with a smile. "Could you open up the basement rec room for me?" He looked toward the stairs. "Sorry there aren't any lights on." He paused. "You know what, maybe that's something I should do. I don't want you tripping on those stairs in the dark."

"No, it's all right—I'll be careful," said Beatrice, taking the keys.

"I'll get all the quilts," said Meadow.

Beatrice walked down the pine-tree-lined walkway toward the old stone church. There was a narrow set of rather steep stairs on the side that led down to a roomy recreation area in the basement that was used for all sorts of activities—from senior bingo nights to quilt shows to youth group gatherings. She smiled as she heard Wyatt's voice behind her speaking soothingly to Miss Sissy, "It's a good thing you're here early, Miss

Sissy. I've got an important job I'd love for you to help me out with." His voice suddenly changed and he said, "What on earth . . . Boris?"

There was a deep-throated, urgent barking and Meadow said, "*My* Boris? Boris, you bad boy, have you run away from home again? Missed your mama? Wyatt, have I told you that Boris is a very bright dog? A genius, really. . . ." She broke off. "Boris. Come back here. What's wrong with you?"

Some genius. Beatrice shook her head and focused on her footing as she descended the stairs. The evening was cloudy, which wasn't helping with the visibility. And now Boris was barking persistently behind her as if he wanted her to drop everything and play fetch with him or give him a treat.

Beatrice gripped the metal railing and carefully walked down the stairs, feeling with her foot to find each step since the stone staircase was very old and the steps weren't exactly evenly spaced.

As she reached her foot down to the bottom of the stairs, her foot came in contact with something that definitely wasn't the stone floor leading into the basement. Beatrice gasped and pulled her foot back.

"Something wrong, Beatrice?" called Meadow from the top of the stairs. Then she said sharply, "Boris, come!" to the frantically barking dog.

Beatrice suddenly felt cold and clammy. She drew back a couple of steps and fumbled in her pocketbook for her cell phone, which had a flashlight on it. "Meadow, you might want to wait just a second. Can you grab Boris?" When her trembling fingers were finally able to switch on the light, she shone it down in front of her. And saw the open-eyed, glassy stare of Frank Helmsley.

Chapter Nine

Beatrice drew in a sharp breath. Although she felt sure that Frank was past the point of being helped, she put a shaking hand to his neck to feel for a nonexistent pulse.

"What's going on down there, Beatrice?" asked Meadow.

"Frank Helmsley," said Beatrice. "He's dead, Meadow."

"Dead? Nonsense. *Nonsense!* We're having a quilt show!"

"Can you call Ramsay? And keep everyone away from the area." How awful it would be if the quilters stumbled across the crime scene—and Martha, especially.

"Are you *sure*? You're sure." Meadow's voice was wavering. "Okay, let me put Boris in the van. He's absolutely going berserk!" The barking was even more urgent now and Boris pulled at his leash. "All *right*, Boris, all right. Let's get in the car."

The barking, no less frantic, at least diminished as they headed to the van. Beatrice took a deep breath (and a step back, not wanting to contaminate the crime scene any more than she already had done) and trained her phone's flashlight on Frank's lifeless form in front of her.

Beatrice couldn't see any injuries, besides the fact that his head was bent in a very unnatural angle and the blood was pooling behind his head, possibly from injuries sustained from falling down the steep stone steps. There were no gunshot wounds, no cuts, and no blunt objects lying nearby. And judging from the fact that he was lying partly on his back, it almost looked as though he'd fallen backward down the stairs. Which made her wonder—was he pushed?

"Wickedness!" hissed a voice above her, and Beatrice quickly turned around. She could see the vague outline of the cadaverous old woman.

"Miss Sissy, can you find Wyatt for me? There's a problem." An understatement, for sure, but Miss Sissy was the excitable type.

"Isn't here. Busy."

A light came on at the corner wall of the church, shining a comforting glow over the area. Wyatt must have gone to turn some of the exterior church lights on.

"Miss Sissy, I'm sorry, but I'm afraid the quilt show is going to be canceled tonight. Could you drive yourself back home? Or do you want me to call Posy or Tony and see if they can give you a lift?"

"Evil!"

"I know." She supposed that Miss Sissy was talking about the body that she must see at the bottom of the stairs. Unless she was talking about the cancelation of the quilt show. "I'm sure Ramsay will be here in a few minutes and that he'll want us out of the way. So if—"

"I'm greeting," said Miss Sissy in an aggressive tone. "Greeting the quilters."

"That's perfect," said Beatrice quickly. "But let's change your greeting, since we can't have a quilt show tonight. Let's have you greet them right as they come out of the parking lot—on the walkway. And, instead of just greeting them, let's have you tell them that the show is canceled and they need to stay at their cars."

"Depravity!"

"Thanks, Miss Sissy," said Beatrice.

The old woman scampered off, the barking was now only a faint sound, and there was light. Beatrice gave a sigh of relief and then studied the scene again. She couldn't really *see* anything in addition to what she was already seeing. But she could *smell* something—alcohol. It seemed that Frank might have been drinking this evening. Could his fatal fall possibly have been an accident? Or did someone take advantage of his unsteadiness and push him down the stairs? And—what was he doing out here to begin with?

A few moments later, she heard footsteps running on the concrete sidewalk above her and Wyatt's voice, low and concerned, calling her name.

"It's okay, Wyatt—I'm fine. You should probably stop where you are. I think this area is going to have to be taped off by the police when they look for evidence." Beatrice felt very tired suddenly. She seemed to have become quite the expert on crime scenes.

"You're sure you're all right? I should have been the one to unlock the door," said Wyatt, sounding frustrated.

Beatrice didn't have a chance to answer, because they both heard Meadow's voice giving a high-volume explanation of what was going on. Ramsay must have arrived. Moments later, she saw his tired face peering down at her from the top of the stairs. "Sweet Mary," he muttered. "What's all this?"

"I suppose it could be an accident," said Beatrice. "But somehow I doubt it." She climbed the stairs toward him. "Here, I'll get out of your way. I wish I had more information to add, but basically I was descending the stairs to open up the basement recreation room and turn lights on, and my foot brushed against Frank's body."

Ramsay gave Beatrice a sympathetic look. "You've had a hard week. And an unfortunate predilection for discovering murder victims. Thanks for keeping the crime scene—if it is a crime scene—protected. I saw that you'd stationed Miss Sissy up front. She nearly didn't let me pass. She's a heck of a sentinel."

"I'll help her now that you're here. I have a feeling that the quilters aren't going to be immediately leaving, either—they're going to want to talk about what's going on and the fact that our quilting events all seem to be coming to tragic ends," said Beatrice.

"You're not telling me anything I don't already know," said Ramsay sadly, as he looked down the stairs. "Meadow now has a huge bee in her bonnet over the fact that there is an evil conspiracy to shut down quilting in Dappled Hills. She's sure of it."

Beatrice shivered and Ramsay said kindly, "Go into the church and have a seat. I bet Wyatt can rustle up some water or a hot chocolate for you. I've got to call the SBI in again." The state police were always called whenever there was a serious crime in the town.

Wyatt was standing with Meadow when Beatrice walked up to the top of the stairs. He wordlessly gave her a hug and Meadow did the same. "It's awful. So awful," said Meadow.

Wyatt said, "Beatrice, why don't you come sit down? I can rustle up something for you to eat or drink, too." Beatrice wearily followed him toward the sanctuary doors, but paused as she saw the quilters huddled together in the parking lot. "Thanks, Wyatt. I'll head over there in a minute. I'll fill in the other quilters first." She walked over to them and was surrounded at once.

"What did Ramsay say?" asked Georgia anxiously. "Was it just an accident?"

"I've said all along," said Savannah in her firm, bossy voice, "that someone was going to take a tumble on those stairs one day. They were an accident waiting to happen."

"Was that it, Beatrice?" asked Posy, her brow knitted. "Was it only an awful accident?"

The women all waited for Beatrice's reply, eyes wide. Beatrice sighed. "I wish I had more information for you, but I don't. I think that the forensics people might be able to tell if it was an accident . . . or not. All I can say was that I didn't see any obvious signs of foul play."

Miss Sissy growled from behind them, "Murder! Murder!" Beatrice turned and saw the old woman brandishing an arthritic fist at them. That should keep quilters away from the church, for sure.

Beatrice said, "We don't know that it's murder. But we do know that we can't have access to the basement tonight—not with the state police on the way to investigate. Meadow, we'll need to cancel the quilt show. Or go ahead and come up with an alternative date and tell everyone who comes."

"I could put up a sign," said Posy, brightening. "I could ask Wyatt to unlock one of the Sunday school classrooms and get some poster board and markers."

"Good idea," said Meadow glumly. "I hate to be

such a poor sport, and I feel sorry about Frank. It's just that we were all looking forward to this for so long. And getting ready for it."

"Why don't you go ahead now and see if you can quickly figure out an alternative date with Wyatt, so that Posy can put it on her sign?" Beatrice looked at her watch. "We're still a few minutes before the time that the show was to start."

Meadow headed off to the church to find Wyatt.

Savannah said in a gruff voice, "Georgia, I thought you might need this." She reached in her tote bag and pulled out a five-pack of replacement blades for Georgia's rotary cutter. "I know you've done a lot of cutting lately, so some new blades might come in handy." She flushed a little and looked shyly at her sister.

Georgia took the pack of blades and gave Savannah a quick hug. "That's very thoughtful of you, Savannah. Thank you."

Savannah cleared her throat. "Well, I should be getting along, seeing as how there won't be any quilt show tonight. See you soon." And she walked briskly away.

Posy said gently to Georgia, "That was very sweet of Savannah, wasn't it?"

Georgia sighed. "It was. And I do miss her. Oh, part of me loves being in my own place and playing with Snuffy and Mr. Shadow and taking care of them. But I'd gotten so used to being roommates with my sister that it somehow feels as if something is missing."

Beatrice said, "Maybe it's the adjustment from spending *all* your time with Savannah to spending no time at all. It might have gone easier if y'all had still seen each other for lunch or gone shopping together or something."

Georgia made a face at the word *shopping*. "I'm a little worried about going shopping with Savannah in her current state." She hesitated. "Posy, have you noticed any . . . incidents . . . lately?"

Posy looked down. "I hate telling on Savannah. You know I don't care two bits about her borrowing small things from the store."

"So she did take something?" Georgia's face was anxious.

Posy's sweet face was distressed. "It was nothing. It was a roll of tape from the checkout desk that was almost empty. Please—I'd like it to be a small gift for Savannah. You don't have to bring it back to me. She's seemed as if she was feeling so low lately." Then she flushed, realizing that Savannah had been low because Georgia hadn't been around. "I should run and get the supplies for the sign. We need to let everyone know there's been an accident."

"Murder! Murder!" corrected Miss Sissy.

"What makes you think this is murder, Miss Sissy?" asked Beatrice curiously. The old woman was suddenly silent, looking at her warily, and Beatrice asked, "Did you see or hear anything?"

"That Phyllis. Wicked!" Miss Sissy's eyes gleamed.

"Phyllis? Here? At the church?" Beatrice glanced around the parking lot and saw that Phyllis was most definitely not here now. So—was she here earlier? When Frank pitched down the staircase?

"Shh—Miss Sissy! Phyllis is driving in," said Georgia, waving her hand at the old woman. "We don't want her to think we were talking about her."

"Murder!" insisted Miss Sissy.

Beatrice said in a low voice, "You saw Phyllis here at the church, Miss Sissy. Is that right?"

Miss Sissy gave an emphatic nod.

"Today? You saw her here today?"

Miss Sissy emphatically shook her head no.

Beatrice sighed. "Today is all that matters, Miss Sissy. Frank died today." Miss Sissy could be very observant, but the problem was that she had all her days and nights mixed up and her head was basically a tremendous jumble. Beatrice looked up at the cars entering the parking lot. "Oh no," she said. "Martha Helmsley is pulling in."

"Posy would have been a good candidate to tell Martha about Frank," said Savannah in her analytical way. "But it looks as if she's out of earshot now."

Georgia looked pleadingly at Beatrice.

"Evil!" said Miss Sissy emphatically.

"I'll talk to her," said Beatrice quickly. She walked quickly toward Martha's car but paused for a moment when Phyllis called out to her, "Hi, Beatrice. Can you help me with some of this stuff for the show?"

"The show is canceled," said Beatrice. "Meadow is trying to find out a good time to reschedule it."

"What?" Phyllis asked.

"Just ask Georgia," said Beatrice, hurrying to catch up with Martha, who was now looking toward the church with a frown.

Martha was devastated to hear the news and immediately rushed over to join Ramsay, despite Beatrice's attempts to persuade her that she needed to go with her inside the sanctuary and wait for Ramsay to come out to talk with her.

"I can't believe it!" she said, gasping. "I just saw Frank a few hours ago!"

Ramsay climbed the stairs and said soothingly to Martha, "I'm so sorry. There's nothing we can do here, and our police process will likely only upset you. Why don't you and Beatrice go into the church for a little while? Once the state police are here, I can talk with you there. Right now I've got to secure the scene so that we can figure out what happened."

"So you don't know what happened? You're not sure?" asked Martha, tears falling down her face.

"All I know for certain right now is that Frank fell down the stairs," said Ramsay. "I don't know if it was an accident or not."

"Who would want to kill Frank?" asked Martha, bewildered. "Who?" she asked Ramsay and Beatrice.

"We don't know that it was murder," Ramsay reminded her. "That's one of the things we've got to find out." He gave Beatrice a pleading look.

"Martha, let's go sit for a while in the church sanctuary," said Beatrice. "I'm sure we can find out more information soon."

Wyatt joined them, quietly. As they sat in the sanctuary, Martha couldn't stop talking about Frank's death. "It was just a normal day," she said, a blank expression in her eyes. "Frank came by around lunchtime and we ate pimento cheese sandwiches. He told me what he was going to be working on next."

Beatrice suddenly remembered that Frank had told her at Jason's funeral that he knew who was behind his murder. Had he tried blackmailing the person? That would be a good reason for him to be pushed down a stone staircase. Could he have arranged to meet this person at the church to try to extort money from him? Aloud, she said, "Frank didn't say anything about meeting with anyone today? Or going to the church?"

Martha shook her head. "No. Not a word. As far as I was aware, he wasn't doing anything but working on an abstract painting today." Her hand clutched her throat. "And now he's lost his chance at sharing his work with the world. All that work he's done through the years. He wanted to have enough for a huge show, you see," she told Beatrice. "A one-man exhibition. And he was something of a perfectionist, so it could take him a while to finish a piece. But he was just on the point of being ready. I was trying to persuade him to go ahead and let me find someone who would host his show."

Beatrice said quietly, "I'd love to see his work sometime, Martha. Maybe you could still go ahead with a show. It might give you more of a sense of closure. And you know it's what Frank would have wanted."

Martha looked thoughtful. "That's a good idea, Beatrice. Thank you. I might have to look into doing that. I'd love for everyone to see what a talented artist he was."

Meadow came into the sanctuary and gave Martha a fierce hug. "I am so sorry!" she said in her big voice. "What an awful thing."

"How is it going outside?" asked Beatrice quietly.

Meadow said, "Posy's sign about the quilt show being canceled is working well and quilters and other attendees are turning around and heading back home. Miss Sissy is helping, too, although maybe in a more flamboyant way. She's shaking her cane at people and shouting about murder when they drive up. Wyatt said the basement room was free at the end of next week, so we'll shoot for that time to reschedule the quilt show."

"Have the state police arrived yet?" asked Beatrice.

"A car was just pulling in when I left," said Meadow.

"I was hoping to talk with Ramsay for a second," said Beatrice.

"Let me sit with Martha—I think you can catch him before he gets stuck in there with the other police," said Meadow.

Beatrice hurried out of the sanctuary and into the breezy night. She decided that she didn't want to be like Frank—she didn't want to know something that could put her in danger or get her killed. Investigating was intriguing, yes . . . but only to the point that you kept your wits about you and kept yourself out of trouble.

"Ramsay?" she said quickly. "There's one thing I've remembered that I thought you should know. Frank Helmsley told me at the funeral yesterday that he knew who killed Jason Gore."

Ramsay's face was grim. "I sort of thought that might have been the case. Blackmail sure sounds like a good way to supplement your income when you're relying on your mom to provide for everything. Did he give you any hints about what he knew?"

"No. And I did urge him to tell you what he knew."

"I'm sure he was real eager to do that," said Ramsay with a snort.

"Not especially, no. He said something like 'that was for him to know and for you to find out.' Do you suppose that he met his killer at the church to blackmail him?"

"Maybe. Of course, we don't know for sure if this is an accident or a murder. And it's a strange place to meet, since Frank should have known that there would be a gaggle of quilters here later today," said Ramsay. He gave a small wave to the SBI as the group headed toward them.

"Not if he were meeting the killer in the afternoon. He must have thought it would give him plenty of time—the quilting show wouldn't have started for hours and it wasn't like blackmailing someone was going to take much time," said Beatrice. "And everyone knows that Wyatt visits folks in the local hospitals on Tuesday afternoons." It seemed as though there were something else she was forgetting, too. She frowned, trying to remember.

"Good point," said Ramsay, nodding. "Thanks for telling me, Beatrice." And then he was swept away by the state police.

Chapter Ten

After a restless night, Beatrice decided to give up on sleeping by the time the clock hit five a.m. She started a load of laundry, put away the dishes in the dishwasher, and then looked down at Noo-noo, who was gazing up at her hopefully.

"Want to go for a walk?" asked Beatrice, and smiled as Noo-noo grinned up at her and gave a sharp bark to indicate her approval.

It was still dark out, so Beatrice grabbed a flashlight along with the leash. Although she was dragging a little from lack of sleep, Noo-noo seemed full of energy and darted ahead of her into the darkness.

There were so many unanswered questions about Frank Helmsley's death. Was he blackmailing Jason Gore's killer? Who was that person? Or was his death an accident? If it was, why was he even at the church at the time of his death?

Beatrice's walk had an aimless quality to it and she let Noo-noo lead the way. She soon found that Noo-noo had decided to lead her to Meadow and Ramsay's house. And Beatrice saw lights on. She knew that sometimes Ramsay couldn't sleep—and that he frequently got up very early, even if he *could* sleep.

Noo-noo trotted confidently over to the front door of the barn. Boris, probably hearing Noo-noo's toenails clicking on the driveway (no genius required, Beatrice thought with a sniff), put his great paws up on the windowsill by the door and grinned at them. This made Ramsay peer out the window, too, to see what Boris was so enchanted by. He gave a quick wave and moved to open the door.

"You're up awfully early, Beatrice," he said, motioning her to a chair around the kitchen table and bending to pet Noo-noo.

"Up early or never really fell asleep," said Beatrice. "And it looks as if you're in the same boat. You're dressed and everything." She gestured to Ramsay's uniform. "I guess Meadow and Ash are sleeping, though."

Ramsay nodded. "Although this is the time of day when Meadow usually wakes up, so I'm sure she'll be joining us soon."

As if waiting for her cue, Meadow said, "Are y'all

talking about me?" She put her hands on her pajama-clad hips and mock-glared at them before beaming. "So we're having breakfast? Omelets are in order. Something with some substance to it." Meadow started rummaging in the fridge and pulling out eggs, blocks of different cheeses, an onion, mushrooms, bacon, and spinach.

"Can I help you, Meadow?" asked Beatrice.

"Absolutely not! I'm the queen of this kitchen," said Meadow. She crouched to open the pots-and-pans cabinet.

"Won't we wake Ash up?" asked Beatrice. Considering what Piper said, Beatrice wasn't exactly eager to have a conversation with Ash right now. She had a feeling that she and Piper weren't on his favorite people list.

"That boy sleeps like there's no tomorrow," said Meadow with a snort. "Sometimes I'll come in here and rattle all my pots and pans just to see if I can raise him from the dead. Never any luck." She gave Beatrice a sidelong look. "And right now, what with all the things on his mind, I have a feeling that he isn't sleeping too great at night."

Ramsay looked curiously at Beatrice with his eyebrows raised.

Beatrice decided she wasn't going to touch that one. Instead she said, "Ramsay, did the state police give you any more information last night?"

Ramsay rubbed his eyes with both hands. "They did and they didn't. At first glance, they couldn't really say whether it was an accident or not. They did say Frank had some bruises that *could* be self-defense and the bruises looked recent. But they could just be from bumping around in his art studio. It sure looked as though he'd been drinking, although we'll have to get the results on that, too. He could have been a little drunk and taken a wrong step and pitched down the stairs."

"Pooh on that," said Meadow, gesticulating in the air with the frying pan she'd pulled out. "That doesn't even make any sense. Why on God's green earth would Frank Helmsley be wandering around at the church and suddenly decide to go down the basement stairs? I accept that he might have been drunk enough to fall, but I can't understand what he was doing there in the first place. He's no churchgoer. No, if he was at the church, he was up to something."

Beatrice nodded. "It does seem rather odd for it to be an accident. I'd have to say that somebody pushed him down those stairs—because he knew something about Jason's death."

Meadow cracked several eggs at once and opened them into a bowl with a flourish. "I'll tell you what we'll do, Beatrice. We'll head over to Martha's today."

Ramsay, resting his head in his hands, rubbed his temples as if they were starting to hurt. "Now what are you and Beatrice up to, Meadow? Y'all aren't the Bobb-sey Twins, you know. Somebody out there is danger-ous. You don't want to be messing with them."

Meadow put her hands on her wide hips and glared at Ramsay. "You just said that Frank's death could be an accident. There's certainly nothing dangerous about an accident. It's not like there's a gang of stone stair-cases skulking around and waiting to ambush people."

"I don't *know* if it's an accident yet. Maybe it's not. Either way, you and Beatrice don't need to be poking around where you don't belong." Ramsay poured him-self another cup of coffee and looked as though he wished it were a different type of beverage instead.

"Good!" said Meadow, yanking a spatula out of a nearby drawer. "Because we do belong at Martha's house. A quilting sister has suffered a terrible tragedy—no, *two* terrible tragedies. The very least we can do is to bring her solace. In the form of casseroles." She turned to Beatrice. "Isn't that right, Beatrice?"

"It *is* the Southern way," said Beatrice with a small smile.

"And while we're there expressing our condolences over iced tea, we'll be sure to find out if Frank was all bruised up when she saw him," said Meadow.

Ramsay rolled his eyes at Beatrice. "How do you plan to ask *that* in a sensitive way to the grieving mother?"

"I think what Meadow is saying is that we'll ask her

if Frank seemed completely normal to Martha when she saw him. Something like that," said Beatrice with a smile.

"I guess this means that we're not going to keep Martha on our list of suspects," said Meadow thoughtfully as she folded over an omelet. "Considering the fact that I really can't picture her being responsible for Frank's death."

"What?" Ramsay blinked as if he needed to go get some more sleep. "You thought Martha was behind Jason's death?"

"Sure, why not?" asked Meadow in a breezy voice.

"Because she was crazy about him, for one thing. She seemed devastated that he was killed."

"Yes, but Jason was supposed to be such a flirt. Apparently, he couldn't seem to help himself. Martha could have gotten fed up with Jason's behavior and . . . well, and finished him off." Meadow rummaged in the fridge for some milk.

"But if she murdered Jason, then who murdered Frank?" asked Ramsay.

"That's the problem with that theory, as I was saying," said Meadow. "Martha wouldn't have harmed a hair on Frank's head. So maybe there are two killers?" she asked hopefully.

Ramsay groaned. "God help me if there are two killers in this tiny town! No, Meadow, I think you'll just have to take Martha off your list, that's all."

Meadow had already made several omelets and placed them on the table and now she was whipping up pancake batter.

Beatrice's stomach growled as she put an omelet on one of the plates. "Is it wrong to be this hungry before six a.m.?"

A deep voice from across the room said, "Was there a breakfast feast planned for this morning and my invitation got lost in the mail?"

"Ash!" said Meadow in amazement at the tall, handsome man in plaid pajama bottoms and a white cotton T-shirt. "How on earth are you up at this hour? I've lost all credibility now—I just finished telling Beatrice that I could bang around in the kitchen all I wanted and I'd never wake you up."

Ash sleepily sat down at the large wooden kitchen table across from Beatrice. He smiled a greeting at her, which put her a bit more at ease. "It wasn't the noise that woke me up, though. It was the aroma of a delicious Southern-style breakfast." He squinted at the wall clock. "Maybe I can go nap for a little while after I eat."

A few minutes later, they were eating a feast of pancakes, sausage, fruit, and omelets. Beatrice was surprised how much she ate, considering how early in the day it still was. "Noo-noo," she said sadly, "maybe we'd best walk for another mile or two to work our breakfast off."

"Like you ever gain weight," scoffed Meadow. "Or, if you do, you clearly take it right back off again." She gave her own generous stomach a reproachful glare. "All right, so we have plans for today. We'll go to Miss Martha's house bearing gifts. What time? Right after lunch? Does that give us enough time to cook?"

Considering Beatrice wasn't even sure what she was going to make, this made her think for a moment. "I suppose I'll make my pimento cheese," she said doubtfully. Now she was feeling more insecure about her cooking than she usually did. At least the pimento cheese was something she regularly made and knew how to do.

"You mean your *fabulous* pimento cheese," said Meadow with a flourish. "Don't sell it short—it's great. And we're going to work on those cooking skills of yours, right? All you need is a little practice, since you're a bit rusty. Okay, I'll pick you up at about one o'clock."

Beatrice stood to go, clipping the leash back on Noonoo's collar. Ash said, "And tell Piper I said hi, if you see her." A shadow crossed his face before he quickly got up and moved to the coffeepot for another cup.

"You're so sweet to come by," said Martha. She looked as elegant as usual but had skipped her customary eye makeup or else it had been cried off. Her eyes were red from weeping and lack of sleep. She seemed genuinely happy to see them.

"We wish we could do more," said Beatrice. "Do you need anything? Need us to run to the store for you or something?" She glanced around. Ordinarily she'd have offered to help a friend clean up in preparation for the company that comes along with funerals, but Martha's stately home took tidiness to a new level. A few minutes later she glimpsed little June Bug scrubbing industriously at what Beatrice presumed must be a smudge. It was imperceptible from here. June Bug gave her a quick wave before resuming her work, even more enthusiastically than before.

"You know what I'd really like?" asked Martha. "I'd love for someone to sit down and talk with me for a few minutes. My nerves are—well, they've been better." She reached a shaking hand up to push stray strands of hair from her pale features.

Beatrice and Meadow exchanged glances. "We'd love to," said Beatrice.

"Let me just get us some drinks and cheese and crackers," murmured Martha. It seemed she was almost on autopilot. She'd always been an impeccable hostess.

"Certainly not," said Meadow hurrying to the kitchen. "I can find my way around any kitchen. And if I have any questions about where things are, then June Bug can point me in the right direction, I'm sure."

"Darling June Bug," agreed Martha in a tired voice.

Meadow bounded off to save the day with refreshments and Beatrice sat down on an antique settee that was actually more comfortable than it appeared. Martha said, "Everyone has been so kind. June Bug is busily freezing all types of foods—I won't have to cook for weeks. But no one wants to stop and talk. That's really what I'd like more than anything—a visit."

Beatrice said, "I'm sure they're not sure what to say. It's such a terrible thing to lose a child, even a grown-up one. None of us knows how to react."

Tears welled in Martha's eyes. She fought them back for a few moments before saying, "I know Frank wasn't perfect. But he was my son." She leaned forward in her chair to peer intently at Beatrice. "I thought more this morning about what you'd asked me last night. If Frank had said something unusual or mentioned something that had seemed out of place."

Beatrice drew in a swift breath and nodded. "Did something else occur to you?"

"It didn't seem strange at the time. But I was so very busy," said Martha. Although it wasn't a question, she said it with a pleading voice. "I was trying to get ready for the quilt show and doing several things at one time. I should have listened to Frank more. I wish I'd known that was the last time I was going to see him." She took a deep, shuddering breath and then continued. "He was full of bravado. But that was in keeping with Frank's usual way. He always had big plans."

"What were his big plans this time?" asked Beatrice.

"Well, he was unhappy with me for threatening to take away some of his income. I wanted to make him more independent," Martha said sadly. "Jason had advised me time and time again that that would be the best thing I could do for Frank—to help him stand on his own. Jason thought that not only would Frank be more productive in his studio if he had to be, but he'd also start setting up shows and finding ways to sell his art and make a living off it."

"What did Frank say?" asked Beatrice.

"He said that I didn't have to worry about him anymore. That he wouldn't really need my help—he had his own ways of making money. At the time, I thought he was just being childish and throwing something back in my face that wasn't really true." She shrugged and hesitated for a few moments before saying, "I also thought that he was a little tipsy and didn't know what he was saying."

So he had been drinking before going to the church. "Was that normal for Frank? Was he a heavy drinker?" asked Beatrice.

Martha thought about this. "I wouldn't have said so, no. Not ordinarily. He certainly drank. Sometimes I saw him looking . . . less than sober. He never drove that way, but Dappled Hills is perfect in that you can walk it so easily. I figured that maybe he drank a bit so that he could face a blank canvas or drank a bit so that he could face the fact that what he'd painted wasn't as good as what was in his head. But I wouldn't say that he drank all the time. And I knew he hadn't been painting yesterday, because he told me he needed to go buy more paints—I think he was hinting that he could use some extra money. But when I asked him if he did, that's when he launched into not needing my help as much anymore."

"Do you think that Frank could possibly have known who murdered Jason? He was at the retreat, bringing you the forgotten fabric. Could he have seen something when he went out into the store? Could he have been drinking because he was nervous about setting up a meeting with the murderer?" asked Beatrice. "Confronting him about Jason's death?"

Martha shook her head stubbornly. "I don't believe any of it. Frank's death was obviously a terrible accident. Why would Frank know anything about Jason's death?"

"Well . . ." Beatrice searched for the right words. "I'm only asking because I know that Frank was there with us at the quilt retreat that day. He might have seen something. Maybe he saw something that didn't even seem important at the time, but that he realized was key to the case afterward. Maybe he decided to approach that person and confront him." Beatrice decided to leave out the blackmailing part.

"Why would Frank do that, though? He wasn't really a confrontational person. I don't see him as some sort of vigilante." Martha held her hands out and looked bewildered.

No, Beatrice agreed with her. Frank was no vigilante. But she could certainly see him as a blackmailer . . . especially with a bit of alcohol in him to make him braver.

"It was all just a terrible accident," murmured Martha. She looked blankly at a painting across from her that Beatrice assumed Frank had painted. Although it wasn't the kind of thing that Beatrice ordinarily liked— it was very modern and had angry brushstrokes—she could see that he'd had talent.

"I was also wondering," said Beatrice carefully, "if you knew what made Jason return to Dappled Hills. After seven years, I was just a little curious why he came back."

Martha gave this a few moments of thoughtful consideration. "I think there were a few different reasons. His brother was here and he was his last living relative. I believe he wanted to improve his relationship with Eric, although I'm not sure that happened." Her green eyes had a real sadness in them. "I also think that he genuinely liked Dappled Hills and wanted to return. Maybe he felt he'd left the town on bad terms and wanted to win everyone over." She gave a rueful laugh. "He certainly won me over."

"Here we are," sang out Meadow brightly as she came in with a tray of refreshments. She suddenly frowned as she saw Martha looking lost. "I'm sure some tea and cookies will make us all feel a little bit better." She gave Beatrice a questioning look and Beatrice shook her head at her.

Martha seemed spent, so Beatrice and Meadow filled the quiet talking about quilting and admiring some of the quilts that Martha had carefully displayed on wooden quilt racks propped against a wall like a ladder. Martha gave short answers and nods for a while, but then seemed to get some strength back as Beatrice admired one vintage quilt in a log cabin pattern of dark blues and reds that Martha explained had been created by her grandmother.

Meadow was able to continue drawing Martha out from there as Beatrice collected their used plates and glasses, putting them back on the tray and walking into the kitchen with them. June Bug was in there, wearing a floral apron that was much too big for her. She was busily wiping down the outsides of the already-spotless cabinets, then started as she heard Beatrice and looked solemnly at her with her buggy eyes.

"I'll put these in the dishwasher," said Beatrice with a smile as June Bug moved as if to take the tray from her. She gave her a smile in return and picked back up with her scrubbing.

June Bug was hard to figure out. She was quiet and shy and had been mistaken by many to be rather dim-witted . . . but Beatrice believed that June Bug was always busy thinking, just as she was always busy at work. In fact, she didn't believe the little woman ever had an idle moment. She seemed to always be cleaning house, baking cakes, or quilting. Although June Bug was the newest member of the Village Quilters, Beatrice still rarely saw her—because her schedule was so hard to work around.

Beatrice said gently, "By the way, June Bug, I've enjoyed some of your cakes recently . . . at the quilt retreat and the funeral reception. You're an amazing cook."

June Bug kept scrubbing, but her round face flushed a little and her eyes danced as she glanced up at Beatrice.

"I was wondering if you could help me out a little. I know you're here at Martha's a lot."

June Bug froze, staring at Beatrice in concern. "Oh! Sorry. No more openings on my schedule."

"That's okay . . . it's all right," said Beatrice quickly in a soothing voice. "I don't need a housekeeper now, thanks. But I'm looking for some information about Frank—Martha's son. I figured, since you're here so often, that maybe you'd know something about him. Well, really, I wanted to know if you saw him on one particular day." Beatrice felt uncharacteristically tonguetied. But the little woman's buggy stare was a bit unsettling.

"When?" June Bug's face pinched as she focused.

"Yesterday, actually."

June Bug trotted over to the door and peered toward the living room, as if making sure they couldn't be overheard. Then she trotted back to Beatrice and gave her a solemn look. "You will find who is doing this." It wasn't a question. It was a statement of fact.

"I'll try." June Bug kept looking at her, so Beatrice amended it to "I will. Yes."

June Bug took a deep breath. "Mr. Helmsley was drinking here yesterday. Drinking Mrs. Helmsley's liquor. Right here in the kitchen." One of her eyes gave a small twitch of indignation, but she was moving on. "Then he got on the phone."

"Frank got on his cell phone?" asked Beatrice.

"The house phone," said June Bug, bobbing her head across the kitchen.

"Did you . . . did you hear what he said?" June Bug looked ashamed and Beatrice quickly added, "You could hardly help it, could you? He had no business being in here, anyway."

"He was asking someone to meet him." June Bug bowed her head and looked at her spotlessly scrubbed kitchen floor.

"Did he say where?"

"At the church." June Bug moved her white-tennis-shoe-clad foot over the floor, a bit nervously.

Beatrice nodded. "You probably didn't know this, but that's where Frank was found. There at the church."

June Bug looked even more startled. Although that

was difficult, considering that her protruding eyes always gave her that appearance.

"Ramsay is easy to talk with," said Beatrice gently. "Meadow's husband—you know him, right? He's a very kind man. You might want to let him know what you overheard. And if you think of anything else, let him know, too." She was about to rejoin Meadow and Martha in the living room but then remembered one other thing.

"June Bug, there was one thing I wanted to ask you about. Miss Sissy said that John Simmons was stalking Martha . . . uh, Mrs. Helmsley. Do you know anything about that? She said that you might."

June Bug twisted her cleaning rag between her hands.

"I won't tell anyone that you're talking about these things," said Beatrice softly. "It's up to you if you want to share them with Ramsay. But they will help me try to figure out who might be behind these crimes."

June Bug nodded, as if making up her mind about something. Then she blurted out, "He loves her. Keeps coming over here on funny excuses for visits. Mrs. Helmsley has me shoo him away."

The idea of little June Bug shooing away tall and spindly John Simmons made Beatrice's mouth twitch, but she was able to suppress the smile. June Bug looked so earnest. "So he kept dropping by uninvited? Anything else?"

June Bug hesitated. "When he saw me out running

errands, he'd ask me about Mrs. Helmsley—if she was doing all right. Sometimes, lately, he'd say bad things about Mr. Gore." June Bug looked sad. "I couldn't get away from him sometimes."

Beatrice gave her a smile. "Thanks so much, June Bug . . . you've been very helpful." The little woman glowed with the praise. "I hope you'll come to a guild meeting soon," said Beatrice. "I hear your quilts are really remarkable. I'm still learning—I'd love for you to give me some pointers on the project I'm working on now."

June Bug nodded shyly, a small smile tugging at her lips. "If I can. If I'm not working. I'll try."

Chapter Eleven

A few minutes later, Beatrice and Meadow climbed into Meadow's van. "I know Martha has a big house, but did you get lost in her kitchen?" asked Meadow. "I thought you were never coming back."

"I was talking to June Bug," said Beatrice, carefully snapping on her seat belt.

"Isn't June Bug marvelous? I mean, she hardly says a word and most of the time she stares at me with the most astonished look on her face, but those cakes! That cleaning! The quilts! She's something else. Let me tell you what I did. After I went to June Bug's house and saw those *magnificent* quilts everywhere—I snapped some pictures with my phone and sent them off to a quilt magazine."

"How were you able to do that without June Bug seeing what you were doing?" asked Beatrice, holding on to the door as Meadow pushed firmly on the accelerator.

"June Bug is very simple when it comes to technology," said Meadow. "I believe she thought I might be texting with my phone instead of taking pictures. But, Beatrice! Her home is just filled with these incredible quilts . . . all made from scraps of fabric. I knew *Quilting Today* magazine would be thrilled to see them. She's so insecure about her talent—tough to get her to the guild meetings, impossible to have her enter a quilt in a show. I figured this might be the best way to show her that she really does have some talent. If the magazine picks up on it. Hope they have the sense to do it. Anyway, tell me what June Bug told you in the kitchen." Meadow veered slightly off the road as she glanced at Beatrice before hurriedly correcting herself.

"She told me Frank was drinking Martha's alcohol when he visited her yesterday. And that she heard him arranging a visit with someone on the phone . . . at the church."

"Really?" Meadow's eyes grew wide. "Did she know who he was talking to?"

"She didn't seem to, no. But she's going to call me if she thinks of anything else. I tried to get her to talk to Ramsay about it, but she didn't seem real excited about doing that."

Meadow said glumly, "Great. Another person who

knows too much. Next thing you know, we'll be going to *her* funeral. Did June Bug say anything else?"

"She said that John Simmons dropped by a lot at Martha's house and that Martha would dispatch June Bug to dispense with him. He'd also say negative things about Jason Gore," said Beatrice.

"I could have told you that Martha avoided John and that he never seemed to be able to take a hint. And of *course* he was going to say negative things about Jason. He was his romantic rival, after all. John probably wanted to challenge him to a dual or something. You know—for the fair lady's hand." Meadow squinted at the road ahead of her. "Is that Miss Sissy?"

Sure enough, the old woman was standing by the side of the road, next to her ancient Lincoln. She shook her fist at them as they stopped the car and got out, and then descended from there into muttering.

"Won't your car start?" asked Meadow. Miss Sissy only glared at her as if not wanting to dignify that question with a response.

Beatrice climbed into the old Lincoln and tried starting the engine. It turned over but didn't start. "You've got gasoline, don't you?"

Another furious look from the old woman.

Beatrice said, "Meadow, I think the car is probably out of gas. If I stay here with Miss Sissy, could you grab a gas can at the station and bring it here?"

"Sure thing." Meadow jumped back in her van and took off down the road.

Miss Sissy examined her under hooded eyes.

"Miss Sissy," said Beatrice, "I was out to see Martha Helmsley. Meadow and I brought her some food since she's just lost her son."

"Frank. He's Frank." Miss Sissy gave her an exultant look, proud that she knew his name and Beatrice didn't.

Beatrice bit her tongue. "Anyway, it sounded like you've been by the church a bit lately, Miss Sissy, and I was wondering if you might have seen Frank there. Yesterday."

Miss Sissy's eyebrows met. "Frank Helmsley doesn't go to church. Wicked!"

"Yes, I know, but I was wondering if you *saw* him at the church, even though he doesn't usually attend."

"Never attends!"

"All right." Beatrice scanned the road for Meadow's car, even though she knew it was too early for her to be coming back.

"But I saw *him* there," said Miss Sissy coyly as if trying to lure Beatrice back to the conversation.

"You did." Beatrice stared at her. "Frank?"

"No. He doesn't attend!"

"Then who?" This was taking more patience than Beatrice was sure she was going to be able to muster.

Miss Sissy seemed to be talking to herself now. "In the bushes. He was in the bushes. Hiding."

"Who? Who was, Miss Sissy?"

Miss Sissy gave Beatrice a scornful look. "Boris!"

Beatrice threw up her hands in the air. "For heaven's sake." For a genius dog, Boris seemed to be running off a lot lately.

"Boris got lost," said Miss Sissy. "But Tony found him."

"Wait a minute. So Tony Brock was at the church, too?" Beatrice frowned.

"*Helping*. Tony was helping with Boris." The old woman glared at Beatrice as if she'd dare to suggest that Tony might be doing more at the crime scene than rescuing lost dogs.

Meadow drove up to them, grinning. "Got it!"

Good. Because Beatrice was ready to find out more about Tony's presence at the church yesterday.

Miss Sissy's car purred to life and soon she'd zoomed off down the road, speeding to wherever it was that she needed to go. Beatrice filled Meadow in on her conversation with Miss Sissy.

"Are you sure Miss Sissy had her days straight?" asked Meadow doubtfully.

"Well, you're never sure with Miss Sissy. But it was only yesterday. I'd never dream of asking her about something that happened a week ago. And Boris did get loose yesterday, didn't he? I know he showed up at the church after we discovered Frank there," said Beatrice.

"He's been very determined to set out on adventures for the past week," said Meadow, beaming at the thought of the dog. "With such a high intelligence level, I think he gets bored at the house."

"Anyway," said Beatrice through gritted teeth, "he was out of the house. How did he get back home again? Did Tony bring him back and he got out again later?"

"I'm not aware of Tony bringing him back, no. Do you think he might have taken Boris back home and just slipped him in the gate to our backyard? I wouldn't have realized it, if he'd done it and not rung our doorbell."

"Maybe. But even if he did, maybe he saw something at the church when he was there. I think I'm going to drop by the hardware store and pay a visit to Tony after I get back home."

Which she was definitely going to do. But when she got home and let Noo-noo out, she found that the fact that she hadn't slept last night was catching up with her. She decided to put her feet up for a few minutes and rest her eyes. Only for a few minutes.

Those few minutes stretched out longer than she thought, however, and when she sat up, flustered, to squint at the clock she saw that it was midafternoon already. Noo-noo was peacefully dozing beside her, never happier than when napping was a group activity.

She was going to see Tony; that was it. Beatrice hurried to get ready to leave the house again, trying to figure out how to phrase the question about Tony being at the church. It definitely didn't need to sound accusatory. What premise could she come up with for being at the hardware store? She glanced around, still patting her hair back in place. Lightbulbs. One could always use more lightbulbs.

There must have been, decided Beatrice as she walked into the store a few minutes later, many people in Dappled Hills who suddenly realized that they needed lightbulbs, because the store was crowded with customers. She could hear Tony patiently helping them as they searched for items and checked out. He smiled at her once and asked, "Need some help?"

She shook her head no and proceeded to peruse the lightbulbs for much longer than should have been required. Beatrice was hoping to catch Tony in a quiet moment. Surely there had to be one coming up soon.

Finally, to her immense relief, most of the customers had filed out. She grabbed her lightbulbs (she'd settled on an outdoor spotlight type of bulb, to justify the length of time she'd spent studying them) and headed for the cash register.

"Will this be all?" asked Tony with a smile. "You're Mrs. Coleman, aren't you? Piper's mom. I don't know that we really got all that properly introduced when I saw you last time. Of course, under the circumstances, that was understandable."

Oh dear. Was Beatrice now going to be grilling one of Piper's friends? She hadn't realized that they were friendly. Beatrice smiled back at him. He really had an attractive way about him, with his wide grin and his muscular frame. "That's right. You can call me Beatrice, though. Good to meet you. You've certainly got your hands full with this shop. You're the only one working today?"

They chatted for a moment or two about the popularity of hardware stores in small towns. Then Beatrice cautiously said, "Well, you certainly must be busy. I think you also help out Miss Sissy when you're not working here. Is that right?"

"That's right. I had an old granny that she reminds me a lot of. She was tough as nails, and funny. So I pitch in and help Miss Sissy out, every now and then. Visit with her, too." Tony put her lightbulbs in a bag.

Beatrice said, "It's funny because Miss Sissy ran out of gas earlier today and Meadow ran to get her a can while I stayed with her. Miss Sissy said she'd seen you at the church yesterday. Helping return Boris the dog, she said."

She could have sworn that she saw concern flash in Tony's eyes before he said steadily, "She might well have seen me. I do help Wyatt out some over at the church—do odd jobs for him, that kind of thing. And I did rescue Boris. Although he didn't care if he were rescued or not. Anyway, I was over there yesterday."

"Not at night, though?" asked Beatrice.

Tony shook his head.

"That must worry you to think that you were at the church around the time that the murderer must have been there?" asked Beatrice. "Did you see anyone or hear anything when you were there?"

"Not a thing," said Tony. But now he was looking off to the other side of the store as if wishing some customers that needed lots of help would come in. And his words just didn't seem to ring true.

As Beatrice was finally leaving the hardware store, clutching her lightbulbs and wondering if everyone in Dappled Hills had something to hide, she saw Piper walking in front of her. Actually, Piper was looking rather furtive herself. Maybe it was the influence of the town and all the secrets everyone seemed to have.

Trying not to scare her, Beatrice made a harrumphing coughing sound and Piper turned quickly to look behind her, nearly running into a streetlight in the process. "Oh," she said with relief, "hi, Mama." She glanced at Beatrice's paper bag. "Been shopping?"

"Just some lightbulbs—nothing very exciting," said Beatrice. "Want to have some fudge while we're out? My treat." They happened to be right next to a shop with fabulous homemade ice cream and fudge. Ordinarily, she'd be up for a little peanut butter and chocolate ice cream, but the chill in the air made her think that fudge might be a better choice.

Piper's shoulders relaxed. "You know, some chocolate fudge would really hit the spot right now."

Beatrice and Piper walked into the shop to the aroma of freshly baked fudge. The shop was very quiet with only the one employee working. She looked up from a book to help them. Beatrice got a peanut butter and chocolate fudge and Piper went with a mint chocolate chip fudge. The employee put the fudge on a bit of wax paper on a plate. Beatrice got some hot chocolates to go with them and also some waters, since she thought all the chocolate might make them thirsty.

They settled into a café table with two chairs near the window of the shop while the employee settled back into her book. A gusty wind blew against the window outside and Beatrice shivered, glad to be in the warmth of the shop.

The best tactic was to just wait and not push any topics. Piper obviously had something on her mind, but experience had taught Beatrice that it was better to let Piper bring up her worries herself. She tended to shut down if she felt like she was being interrogated. So Beatrice talked about visiting Martha and buying lightbulbs. Then she launched into the fact that she'd had to figure out where her winter sweaters were—and who would think it was possible to lose something in as tiny a cottage as she had? And Noo-noo had followed her around from room to room with such a worried expression on her face. Beatrice had been searching, in particular for a cardigan sweater that she'd only recently worn. Finally, she'd realized it was underneath the curled-up, napping kitten. Noo-noo had once again been completely unimpressed with the kitten's antics.

Finally, she was seeing a smile on Piper's face. "Poor Noo-noo," she said. "I don't know what you're going to do with that kitten. I guess you can't really keep her for good, can you?"

"I don't think Noo-noo would be excited about the kitten staying permanently with me," said Beatrice with a smile. "But now I've gotten the kitten's shots and I'll try to find a good home for her."

Piper nodded absently, as if she really hadn't been listening to what Beatrice was saying. Then she sighed. "Oh, Mama, I don't know what I'm doing with Ash. I saw him out today and it was just so awkward. He said hi, but he didn't know where to look. I didn't know how to react, either. I feel like I've really messed things up."

Beatrice said, "No one's perfect, sweetheart. I think the important thing is to know what you want before you talk with Ash again."

Piper nodded. "It's not fair to Ash otherwise. Like I said, I was so stunned the last time that I didn't know how to react or what to say or what to even think. Now I've got to figure out what it is exactly that I want so that there won't be any confusion between us."

Beatrice said cautiously, "Have you figured out what it is that you want?"

"Time. I think I want a little time—to spend time with Ash in bits and pieces. Usually, when we're visiting, it's all in a big chunk of time and then one of us gets on a plane for a month. It's not that I'm not interested in marrying Ash."

"Was that what he was asking?" asked Beatrice. She knew it wasn't, but she also knew that the underlying reason that Ash was moving to the area was that he was very serious about his relationship with Piper.

"No, no, of course not. And that's the thing—I was reacting to it as if it were a marriage proposal. But really, all that Ash was doing was trying to move back to North Carolina so that we *could* get closer. It was a big step for our relationship, though, and I felt it had really been sprung on me. I was worried that he'd move all this way for me, take a completely different type of job, make all these sacrifices, and then I wouldn't want the relationship to go any further." Piper shrugged. "That would be awful."

"I wonder," said Beatrice, "if Ash is still planning on moving, even though your relationship is stressed right now."

Piper looked startled. "I don't know." She looked down at her fudge. "I hope so. That would make things easier. At least, I guess it would." She looked hopelessly at Beatrice.

Beatrice took a deep breath. Her overwhelming instinct, whenever she was faced with a crisis of any kind, was to try to fix things. She'd learned, through the years, that some things were easier to fix than others—and that some things should actually be left alone, even if she felt she *could* fix them. She carefully said, "It mostly sounds like a misunderstanding, doesn't it? He thought you'd be thrilled by his surprise, but you've never been one for surprises. Ash took your reaction as a sign you weren't interested in making your relationship more permanent."

Piper nodded. Then her eyes filled with tears.

Beatrice started digging earnestly in her pocketbook. Why wasn't her pocketbook as well stocked as other women's purses she saw? Other women would have tissues, ibuprofen, and a water bottle. She seemed to have only an empty peppermint wrapper, a lipstick, and some loose change. Beatrice pulled off a couple of napkins from the table dispenser and thrust them at her daughter. "Piper, I'm so sorry. But I believe if y'all had a long talk, everything would be cleared up—if you wanted it to be."

Piper scrubbed at her face with the napkins as if she were impatient with the tears. "That's a very sensible idea, Mama, as always. But I want to let things cool off a little. You know? Sometimes it's easy to make things worse when you're trying to make them better. If I start apologizing and try to act excited about his new job, but he's still hurt and thinks I'm not being genuine . . ." Piper trailed off with a small shrug.

Beatrice realized, not for the first time, that she and

Piper could be a bit too analytical. "Okay, sweetie, if you think that's best."

Piper was suddenly eager to change the subject. "How are things with you and Wyatt? I'd like to think that at least one of us is having a successful relationship right now."

"Oh. It's fine. Everything is fine." Beatrice nodded but didn't meet Piper's gaze.

"That's not exactly a ringing endorsement, Mama."

"It *is* fine, it's just that he and I haven't really been able to spend any time together. We had a nice lunch, as I'd mentioned, but it was cut short by something he had to attend to at the church. Then I was going to cook an amazing supper for him, but *that* didn't go well, so I had to forget about asking Wyatt over for dinner." Beatrice gave an exasperated sigh.

Piper hid a smile. "It's not your fault that you've been out of the practice of cooking for a while."

"I know. But then I offered to help Wyatt set up at the quilt show. We were going to have supper then—but he got a phone call from a church member and had to cancel." Beatrice frowned. There was something funny about that, too, but she couldn't remember what it was.

"Oh no! And then when you met him at the church to help with the setup, you found a body. An evening together couldn't get much worse than that." Piper shook her head in amazement.

"So it's all fine . . . it's just that we really can't find

any time to see each other. And, naturally, he's been busy ministering to Martha because of the two deaths," said Beatrice.

"Was Martha okay today when you and Meadow saw her? She's always seemed so devoted to Frank. How awful that he had this accident right after Jason's death," said Piper.

Beatrice said very quietly, "It might not have been an accident at all. In fact, it almost certainly wasn't. Frank arranged to meet someone at the church yesterday—probably to blackmail him. Although he'd been drinking, it's also very likely that the person being blackmailed would have wanted to get rid of him." She glanced over at the shop employee, but she was deeply engrossed in her book. She'd have to get that title before she left.

Piper frowned at her. "You're not poking into these murders, are you? You know how incredibly dangerous that is. Remember what happened last time? And the time before that? And—"

"Yes, I remember," said Beatrice quickly. "I'm only interested, that's all." Very interested.

"Okay, as long as that's all it is. I can understand being curious. Here we are in this peaceful little town and suddenly we have this rash of violence." Piper paused. "What if Frank died for another reason, not blackmail? What if someone knew that *Frank* was the murderer and they killed him for revenge?"

Beatrice considered this. "I could see something like that happening in a fit of rage, maybe. But wouldn't it make so much more sense to simply tell Ramsay what you knew and have justice take its course? Not that I don't think Frank had motive to kill Jason—I do think he did. But . . ." Beatrice shook her head. "Besides, the only person who would have gotten that angry over Jason's death would have been Martha—and she wouldn't have hurt a hair on Frank's head."

"You know, I wonder if Eric Gore, Jason's brother, is on Ramsay's suspect radar," mused Piper.

"What would his motive be?" asked Beatrice. "Unless you're saying that he might have been upset enough over Jason's death to kill Frank. Was the family relationship complicated?"

"Isn't it always?" drawled Piper, giving her mom a mischievous smile. "I think Jason's actions really embarrassed Eric. It's hard to ever see him around town—it's almost like he's hiding."

"I don't know if he's *hiding*. It sounded to me as if he had a good excuse not to be around—a job in another town." Beatrice took a final bite of her fudge and immediately wished she had more.

"I guess that's true. I don't remember what he does for a living, but he couldn't make too much. The poor guy always seems to be wearing the same outfit whenever I see him and drives a really old car."

Beatrice said thoughtfully, "I believe Meadow said that he was an usher at the movie theater in Lenoir."

Piper frowned. "You're not thinking of going over there to question him, are you? It's not—"

Beatrice hurried to interrupt Piper before she heard again about the danger surrounding murder investigations. "Oh no. No, of course not. Only, I was just thinking that Meadow and I had mentioned wanting to see that new film. I'll have to check back with her and see if she still might want to go."

"What movie was it?" Piper looked rather suspicious.

"Hmm. Well, I can't remember the name of it, offhand."

"What type of film was it?" Piper's eyebrows were raised.

"I think it was a drama. Yes, I'm pretty sure it was a drama." Beatrice gave her daughter a weak smile.

Chapter Twelve

"A movie? When?" Meadow's voice boomed down the other end of the line. "What movie?" There was some howling in the background and Meadow said excitedly, "Did you hear that, Beatrice? Here, Boris, have a treat. I'm teaching Boris to sing! Have you ever seen videos of those singing dogs around Christmas? I thought I could make Boris go viral!"

Beatrice hadn't seen the videos, wasn't one hundred percent sure what *going viral* meant (although it sounded germy), and felt they were perhaps weaving off topic again.

"It doesn't really matter what movie we pick. I figured it would be a good time to talk to Jason's brother, Eric, since he's never really in Dappled Hills all that much. Whatever you want to see would be fine with me." Beatrice was already planning how to gingerly discover whether Eric had been in the vicinity of the church when Frank died.

"Well, usually I like costume dramas. Maybe something historical. Or even an adaptation of an Austen novel—something like that. Anything likely to be nominated for an Oscar for best costumes. Is there anything like that playing?" There was more howling in the background. "Good boy, Boris! Here's another treat."

Beatrice was starting to wonder if Boris was perhaps howling because his tummy hurt from all the treats. "I don't remember any costume dramas listed." She peered at the newspaper again, squinted, and then put her reading glasses on. "There looks to be a horror film, an animated children's film, a romantic comedy, and a documentary of some sort on global warming." She made a face at the paper. "I guess we can always leave a movie if we hate it."

"It's a lot of money to spend on something just to ask a question," said Meadow reasonably. "Especially for a movie we don't want to see. The *only* redeeming quality of such a field trip would be if we had a tub of buttered popcorn and movie candy."

Looking at the newspaper, Beatrice had to reluctantly agree with her.

Unfortunately, upon arriving at the theater in Lenoir, they found that Eric Gore didn't seem to recognize them. It was probably one of those things where you have trouble placing someone if he's not where he ordinarily is. He'd stared at them a bit when they introduced themselves until finally he said, "Oh, sure. Yes, I know y'all." He had a doubtful look on his face that contradicted his words.

Apparently, either there were no good movies out, or any new movies out, or else the citizens of Lenoir had no interest in seeing movies today, because Beatrice and Meadow appeared to be the only people at the theater. This must not have been considered out of the ordinary, either, because once Eric had sold them their tickets for *A Funny Thing About Love*, he courteously asked, "Will you be needing any popcorn or other concessions?" Apparently, Eric did everything at the movie theater on slow days—from selling tickets to starting the film. He possibly even cleaned the theater after the movie was over.

Meadow, who hadn't been excited about anything on this trip to the theater besides the food, gave an enthusiastic yes and Eric left the ticket booth, carefully locking the door behind him, and led the way to the concessions counter, where he fixed Meadow a bucket of popcorn so large that Beatrice was sure it could double as a bathtub for Noo-noo. They'd gotten to the theater in plenty of time before the start of the movie, so they loitered at the counter, getting napkins and straws for the equally mammoth-sized soft drinks they'd received.

Beatrice cleared her throat. "Eric, I just wanted to say again how sorry I was." When Eric looked momentarily confused, she hurried to add, "About your brother's death, I mean."

A swift and unfathomable look crossed his face. "Thanks. Although my brother and I weren't all that close, you know."

Beatrice blinked. There were people who liked to share information with people they barely knew. Beatrice knew this. But she was always amazed when she ran into one. She said, "It still must have been a shock."

"Not really," said Eric, with an unreadable expression on his face. "I mean—it wasn't a natural death. If he'd suddenly fallen over from a heart attack . . . now, *that* would have been a shock. But the fact that he finally annoyed someone enough to want to get rid of him for good? No, I can't say that surprises me at all." He took a bottle of cleaning solution and spritzed the counter with it, scrubbing at invisible spots with a paper towel.

Meadow, who seemed genetically designed not to be able to keep her thoughts to herself, coughed on a bit of popcorn. She took a few gulps of her drink and said, "You aren't surprised that your brother was murdered?" Her face was quite pink, either from the shock or from practically asphyxiating on the popcorn.

Eric said, "Think about it. And I know I'm not telling you anything you don't already know—the whole town knew what my brother had done before he left Dappled Hills seven years ago."

Meadow turned even pinker. She liked to pretend that Dappled Hills wasn't a gossipy town. "I don't know what you're talking about. What?"

Beatrice didn't want to dance around the issue, which was what Meadow would do. Meadow would take twenty minutes to argue that Dappled Hills had *not* talked about Jason Gore's fraud and that she was completely oblivious about the reasons he'd left town seven years earlier. "You mean about the fact that your brother committed fraud. And then left town right afterward."

Eric looked relieved. "You know, I'm glad to have somebody actually talk about it to me. For years people have crossed to the other side of the street to avoid talking to me because they didn't know what to say. It's been a little lonely." And standing there in his ill-fitting theater uniform, he seemed almost unbelievably awkward and insecure for a grown man.

Meadow seemed scandalized again. "Not in Dappled Hills! No one would do that—"

"Oh, for heaven's sake. Sure they would, Meadow! Sometimes it's easier to avoid a situation if you aren't sure how to handle it or what to say. Although," said Beatrice, turning to look at Eric thoughtfully, "you probably didn't help things, Eric, by spending most of your time here in Lenoir. Did you choose to work here because you knew you could avoid seeing people in Dappled Hills?"

His eyelashes fluttered several times in a row. "But I knew I'd run into Dappled Hills folks here," he said, looking away from Beatrice. "There's no theater in Dappled Hills. Everyone has to come here."

"But you'd be spared the daily, constant interaction with them that you'd have had if you'd worked at the grocery store there or the hardware store. If you worked in Dappled Hills, you'd see Dappled Hills people all day, every day. Working here was a way to escape, wasn't it?" asked Beatrice.

Meadow gaped at them, waiting for Eric's answer. Beatrice was sure she couldn't fathom someone hiding from Dappled Hills.

"But there was no reason for me to hide. I didn't do anything wrong," he said quietly in an unconvincing voice.

"I'm not saying that you did. But did you *feel* as if you had? Did you feel responsible for Jason's actions, even if you knew that you weren't?"

"I was embarrassed by him. And angry," he said. He took in a deep breath. "Dappled Hills was this great little town. Jason was always talking about it. Then he got greedy and decided to pull a scam. He ruined everything. I should have known," he said, almost to himself. "I should have known that he hadn't changed. He *couldn't* change."

"You followed him down to Dappled Hills, right?" asked Beatrice.

"He'd talked so much about it to our mother and me. It sounded like such a great town. The mountains, the people, the quaint downtown. Even the weather. I didn't have a job at the time and I remember what Jason said. He told me, 'Just as easy to be unemployed in Dappled Hills as it is in Lexington.' So I moved down here. He even helped me find some temporary work around town."

Meadow said, "When you say that he couldn't change—had he done something like this before, then? Had he . . . cheated people?"

Eric snorted and gave Meadow a disbelieving look. "Are you kidding? Jason was a con man. He'd always been a con man. Even when he was a kid. He could trick you out of a pack of chewing gum and you'd feel lucky for the privilege. That's the kind of guy he was. Everybody liked him—he could make people like him without any effort at all on his part. It used to drive me crazy when I was a little guy. He'd never study, never do his homework. I'd be working so hard, trying to memorize facts or learn vocabulary. Jason would charm the teachers and somehow he'd never get bad grades, even if his stuff was incomplete. He wouldn't make an A, but he'd have a good solid grade. And Mom would end up fussing at me because my grades would be lower than his." Eric gave a bitter laugh.

"Was it always kind of innocent stuff like that, then?" asked Beatrice.

"You mean instead of out-and-out fraud? There was some that was innocent. There was some that was just Jason trying to take advantage of a situation—usually with wealthy women and getting them to pay for various things for him. Sometimes he'd cheat at cards—and that could get dangerous because he was messing with the wrong people. Sometimes it would be more serious. He never seemed to get caught. I guess that's because people were too embarrassed to press charges. Mom always, always acted like everyone else was to blame. It was never Jason's fault. She'd never hear anything bad said about him." Eric knocked over the spray bottle of cleaner and roughly set it upright again. He glared at the bottle as if it were all its fault. "He was a charmer. Maybe that's how he got me to come down here."

"Did you think he'd changed, then? Did it seem like he had? He'd come to Dappled Hills, he'd met somebody, he was trying to be a regular guy?" asked Beatrice. "Someone who didn't con people?"

Meadow still gaped at Eric. She was always surprised by the dark side, the secret side of people.

Eric flushed. "I wanted to believe it. You don't know how great it was—it was somehow kind of flattering when he turned all his attention on you and tried to persuade you to do something. Yeah, I wanted it to be true. Mom and I both moved down here from Virginia. Maybe even *Jason* thought he'd changed. Maybe he thought that having Mom and me in town might help him keep on the straight and narrow. I mean—he was part of a church! I wanted to believe it was true. I bought in to it."

"And he hadn't changed," said Beatrice.

"He hadn't. At some point, I guess he started feeling that same old itch again. He needed to pull a con. That's what he was. He saw a mark and he couldn't help himself."

"That was Tony's grandfather?" asked Beatrice.

Eric nodded, looking tired and suddenly much older. "He convinced the old man that he could take his savings, invest them for him, and make him so much more money that Tony could go to the best colleges and he'd still have money left over for his retirement. He'd completely duped him. Tony's grandfather was dying to give him the money by the time Jason had worked his charm on him. Then Jason skipped town."

"How did you find out about this?" asked Beatrice. "I understood that Tony's grandfather was too embarrassed to talk about it or to press charges."

"Tony, of course," said Eric. He leaned his elbows on the counter as if he'd gotten too tired to really stand up. "Tony was a friend of mine, even though I'm older than he is. He told me all about it—and then he wasn't my friend anymore. He was incredibly hurt, desperate.

Couldn't believe his opportunity to get an education had been stolen from him. His grandfather never recovered . . . and neither did my mother. She was there when Tony told us what Jason had done. Mom—who never could hear bad things about Jason. She finally understood what he was and what he'd always been." Eric stopped and shook his head. "Mom never recovered from it and died a few months later. I think she died of a broken heart. And Jason didn't even come back for the funeral."

Meadow snorted. "Probably thought he'd go to jail if he came back."

"Right. But finally he caught on that nobody was going to charge him with anything and he comes waltzing back into town as if nothing has happened." Anger flared in Eric's eyes. "He returns to Dappled Hills like the conquering hero. Acting as if he hadn't done anything wrong . . . like he hadn't dumped a fiancée or stolen money or broken our mother's heart."

"Did you get in touch with him at all?" asked Beatrice.

"Are you kidding me? I was trying to keep my distance from him because I knew he'd pull some kind of con again. Now I knew that he was really incapable of change. The first time I saw him, I was in a restaurant downtown. I pretended I didn't even hear him when he greeted me. But yeah—he showed up at my door one night soon after he'd come back to town. He was all smiles, excited to see me. Gave me a huge hug. He was acting like he'd been away because he was off saving the world or something instead of letting the dust settle. When I told him I wanted nothing to do with him, that I'd felt like a pariah in the town since he left, he acted like he was hurt and shocked. Shocked!" Eric's face was scornful.

"Why do you think he came back after being gone for seven years?" asked Beatrice. "Doesn't it seem a little strange that he returned?"

Eric shrugged. "Not really. I'm sure he needed some money. Probably figured he could make some pretty easily here."

"Did he keep trying to get in touch with you?" asked Beatrice.

"A couple of times, he did. Called me on the phone—I hung up. Knocked on my door once—I didn't answer it." Eric shrugged. "It took him a while, but he got the message. Or maybe he was just busy . . . cozying up to the rich lady." His face was splotched with anger.

Beatrice said, "Were you anywhere around the church a couple of days ago? In the afternoon or evening?"

Eric said, "Are you kidding? I wouldn't go near the church if you paid me. Couldn't stand having half the town staring at me like I was one step away from Evil Incarnate."

Meadow couldn't keep quiet any longer. "They

wouldn't have done that! You didn't do anything, Eric. It was Jason. And he was already helping out at the church and doing things in the community. Everybody had welcomed him back to town."

"Not everybody," said Eric quickly. "Somebody wanted him dead."

Meadow opened her mouth and then shut it again. She couldn't really contest that.

"But no," he said to Beatrice, "I didn't go to church the other day. I didn't know Frank Helmsley. I didn't know most people in town." He looked at the clock. "And now I think you should see your movie. I need to get it started so we stay on schedule."

Beatrice and Meadow walked thoughtfully into the theater and watched *A Funny Thing About Love*, which Beatrice found neither funny nor really about love— mostly about infatuation. Meadow made a face at her about a third of the way through the movie after all the popcorn was gone. "I think I'm done," she said in her loud whisper. But this time the high volume of her whisper didn't matter, since they were the only ones in the theater.

Eric's anger somehow had the effect of making Beatrice exhausted. She could only imagine how *Eric* felt, carrying around that much pent-up anger and bitterness. Beatrice stayed awake as long as she could that night, hoping to make it to something like a regular bedtime. She really didn't want to wake up in the middle of the night again, feeling as though it were time to wake up. Beatrice worked on her quilt a bit, but she was so tired that she kept making errors, so she finally stopped. She looked at the clock. Eight o'clock. That was too early to turn in, but she'd have to or else she'd nod off in her chair.

Hours later—she wasn't sure how many—Beatrice awoke to the sound of Noo-noo giving a low growl. Beatrice sat straight up in bed, instantly awake. It was an ominous warning that made the tiny hairs on the back of Beatrice's neck stand on end. She slid her legs out of bed into the chilliness of the room, instinctively grabbed her robe to wrap it around her, and hurried into the tiny living room.

Noo-noo was standing at the front door, giving that same low growl—and her hair was also standing on end. The kitten also started growling and backing away. Beatrice hurried to the door, paused, then switched on the outside lights and peeked outside, almost dreading what she might see.

And she saw . . . nothing. Beatrice peered around, looking for some sign of an intruder. All she saw was her quiet yard, her car, and shadows thrown from the trees in the weak light of a crescent moon. She turned off the lights and reached down to pet Noo-noo.

"Are you on edge, too, Noo-noo?" she asked, smoothing down the corgi's fur. "It's okay. Did you hear a deer, maybe? That could be a scary sound . . . all that crashing around."

But Noo-noo stayed alert, intently staring at the door. Beatrice looked outside again. The little dog seemed so sure that something was out there that Beatrice felt bad about not giving it credence. Still, she saw nothing. She gave Noo-noo another pat and said, "Keep guarding for me, okay, girl? I'm going to try to get more sleep."

After spending the next forty-five minutes tossing and turning, Beatrice walked back to the living room to retrieve the big book that Ramsay had lent her to read. That was sure to put her to sleep. Noo-noo still stayed sentry at the front door.

Chapter Thirteen

When Beatrice walked out to get her paper the next morning, she saw what must have made Noo-noo so upset the night before. Her heart pounded as she stared at the four slashed tires on her car.

Beatrice hurried back into her cottage and shut and locked the door behind her, trembling. Then she took a deep, steadying breath. She was fine. It was only a warning. And that's what she felt sure it was—a warning. This was no teenage prankster out for a night of reckless vandalism. This was somebody who was letting her know she was getting too close to the truth—and to back off.

"Noo-noo, I'm sorry I didn't believe you," she said swiftly, bending down to rub the corgi. Noo-noo gave her a soulful look that informed her that gratitude was best expressed in the form of a dog treat. She followed Beatrice into the kitchen, where Beatrice took a treat from the canister on her counter and tossed it to the dog. Then Beatrice dialed Ramsay's number.

Minutes later, Ramsay and Meadow were both in her driveway. Meadow had insisted that Ramsay take her with him to Beatrice's house. She was still in her plaid pajamas and bright green bathrobe and looked like a distressed Christmas ornament. "Beatrice, I can't believe this. Who on earth would do such a thing?" she asked. Then she promptly burst into tears. Boris, whom Meadow had also apparently insisted on coming, looked sorrowfully at Meadow as he hung out the police cruiser's back window.

Ramsay sighed and looked up at the heavens for strength. Then he put an arm around Meadow. "There, there. It's all going to be fine. You'll see. Let's go in Beatrice's house and pay Noo-noo a visit. Boris, too." He raised his eyebrows at Beatrice, asking permission.

"I can make us all some coffee," said Beatrice kindly. Which, for some reason, made Meadow cry even harder.

It took a few minutes, but finally Meadow settled down a bit and was able to drink her cup of steaming hot Guatemalan coffee—Beatrice's favorite. The turning point was when an alarmed Noo-noo put her head on Meadow's leg to comfort her. That made Meadow give a small laugh through her tears and she reached down to scratch behind Noo-noo's ears. The kitten watched them from her safe perch on top of a bookshelf.

"So, are you going out there?" Meadow asked Ramsay. "You'll take measurements of footprints and fingerprints and look for clues as to who would have done such a thing to our Beatrice?"

Ramsay gave his wife a startled look. "Meadow, I can't launch a full forensics investigation into what's basically a prank. I'd have to call in the state police, and they'd think I'd lost my mind."

Meadow frowned at him. "Of course you can. This is Beatrice. And it's clear that whoever did this is also responsible for two murders. Maybe there's something at the scene to tie the crimes together."

Beatrice jumped in. "Meadow, it's sweet of you to feel that way. The truth is, though, that Ramsay is right. This isn't a murder—it's vandalism. It's costly, and I'm reporting it. But there's no evidence that it's anything other than that and Ramsay can't spend a lot of time and energy on this when there is a murderer to remove from the streets." Still, she shivered as she thought about the darkness last night and Noo-noo's growling and her vigil at the front door.

"Well," said Meadow, giving Ramsay an angry look, "I still say they're obviously connected. And here you are, living all by yourself with killers surrounding you on all sides."

Ramsay squinted at her. "On all sides? We live on that side, and Beatrice's daughter lives just across the street. And Miss Sissy. Although I guess Miss Sissy could be considered a bit homicidal, if you take her driving into account."

Meadow ignored him. "It's dangerous. That's what I'm saying. And Ramsay clearly hasn't had enough of his coffee this morning or he'd agree with me. That's why I want to lend Boris to you for a while. Until this investigation is through and the murderer is in jail somewhere far away."

Beatrice tried to keep her expression neutral. But she was pretty sure the last thing she needed was Boris in her tiny cottage—knocking down small tables and scavenging for treats in her little kitchen. And what would the poor kitten think?

"It might be a good idea," said Ramsay. "I'm not saying there's necessarily malicious intent here, but you just never know. Noo-noo is a big help, too, of course, but Boris might make someone . . . well, think twice."

Boris grinned, tongue lolling out. She could have sworn he winked at her. Beatrice had the strong feeling that Ramsay was simply hoping to keep Boris from being underfoot at the Downey household for the next couple of days.

"I guess it wouldn't do any harm," she said, somewhat ungraciously. Then, as an afterthought, "Thank you."

Now that the guard dog assignment was settled, Meadow turned to say indignantly to Ramsay, "And shame on you for saying that there were pranksters in Dappled Hills when you know there's no such thing! Aren't murderers bad enough without having pranksters, too? Why don't you accept that one person did all three crimes?"

Ramsay rolled his eyes at Meadow. Meadow was apparently taking the recent Dappled Hills crime wave very poorly. Instead of answering her, Ramsay said, "Beatrice, let me replace those tires for you. I can call over to the automotive shop and ask if they have your car's size in stock. Then I can bring them here and put them on."

"Or have Ash put them on," suggested Meadow.

Beatrice said gloomily, "There's no point in your lugging tires over here to put them on the car, Ramsay, although I appreciate the offer. It's not far to get it towed. Then they can put them on for me while I wait."

Ramsay said cautiously, "I'm not saying that this act of vandalism *is* connected with the recent murders, but if they *are* . . . they clearly would function as a warning of some kind. Do you have any idea, Beatrice, why someone might try to warn you off this case? You're not still digging around, are you?" His kind face was concerned. "You know my thoughts on that."

"I—" Beatrice looked helplessly over at Meadow. She didn't want to claim involvement in any type of investigation, but she somehow didn't feel capable of lying to Ramsay, either. Meadow was, rather unhelpfully, messing with Boris's collar and determinedly looking away from Beatrice.

Finally, she continued. "I'm not digging, Ramsay. But as I'm going around town, doing my regular business, I'm asking questions. I can't seem to help it. The puzzle underneath these crimes fascinates me somehow. I used to feel the same way when I was curator in Atlanta. We'd get some fabulous piece in and I couldn't wait to uncover the story behind it." Beatrice shrugged.

Meadow decided to pipe up. "She has a gift," she stated stoutly.

Ramsay ignored this. He urged, "Tell me what you found out. Was there anything that you can think of that might have made the murderer uncomfortable enough to do something like this . . . if he *did* do something like this?"

"I wouldn't have said that I knew very much," said Beatrice, spreading out her hands in front of her. She frowned and considered the question. "No, there's nothing that I feel that I know that's particularly important or dangerous for me to know. The only thing that really stood out was Frank Helmsley telling me he knew who did it. But I told you about that—unfortunately, after he'd already been silenced."

"Just be very careful, Beatrice," said Ramsay, looking solemn. "Be aware of your surroundings when you're out and about. And stop digging around, since it's possible you might be getting close to the killer."

"And let Boris and Noo-noo work hard as the best guard dogs ever!" said Meadow fiercely, giving her massive beast a tight hug before they left to head back home.

After they left, Beatrice got ready and called the repair shop as soon as they opened. Before long, they sent a tow truck over and gave her a lift to the shop to wait for the tires to be replaced. She sat in a narrow wood-paneled room in a folding chair with old copies of car magazines offered as reading material on rickety card tables. She briefly considered the coffee and then realized that the slightly burned smell in the room came from the coffeepot. Since the shop just opened, Beatrice wasn't sure exactly what this meant. Had the coffee been sitting on the burner since the day before?

Being that this was a small town, the mechanics asked Beatrice a lot of questions that she didn't have the answers to. She had a feeling that news would quickly spread around Dappled Hills that she'd been the victim of a prank.

When her cell phone rang, she jumped. It was Piper.

"Mama! Are you okay? Were you scared to death this morning when you saw your tires? Where are you now?"

Well, she hadn't expected the mechanics to spread

word *that* fast. "You know about the tires?" she asked weakly.

"Meadow called me."

She should have known that Meadow's network was a lot faster than anything at the auto body shop.

"I'm fine," Beatrice said firmly. "And yes—it did shake me up at first. Last night was a little scary, too, with Noo-noo growling like that. Poor dog. I was convinced she'd been spooked by a deer, but she knew all along that someone was out there." She gave a shiver and then sternly told herself to buck up.

"Do you want me to stay with you for a while? Maybe for the week? I'd be happy to do that." Piper's voice was still anxious despite her attempts to sound strong.

"Absolutely not," said Beatrice, this time with a lot more authority. She had a picture in her mind of the two of them trying to share space in the tiny cottage with two dogs and a kitten. Pulling guard duty with a rolling pin. It didn't bear thinking about. "Besides," she said in a lighter tone, "didn't you hear that I had a special alarm system put in? It's supposed to be foolproof."

Now there was a hint of a smile in Piper's voice. "You mean Boris the Great? Are you sure Boris has time to be a guard dog? The way Meadow tells it, Boris might be busy writing a dissertation on molecular physics."

"At least I'll have two very bright dogs who are light

sleepers. I'll be fine." Something occurred to her, though. If she knew Piper, and she was sure she did, then she was probably avoiding the whole Ash situation. Hoping it would get better, but not doing anything to make it better. "There is one thing you could do for me, though. It's a little backed up at the shop here," she fibbed. "Could you run by Meadow's house and pick up Boris's dog food? I swear I remember that he was on a special diet now. Supposed to help him lose weight, I think." Not surprising, considering how many times he raided Beatrice's kitchen.

"Meadow's house?" Piper's voice sounded a bit faint. Beatrice didn't think it had anything to do with their cell phone connection.

"That's right. I could do it myself, but I'm just not sure how long I'm going to be here. . . ."

"No worries, Mama. I'll run by there now."

Beatrice could imagine that Piper was squaring her shoulders, preparing to charge into battle.

"I appreciate it, sweetie. See you soon." Beatrice hung up and wondered if she should feel guilty for interfering and pushing the issue a little. She found that she didn't feel guilty at all. Boris *did* need his special dog food. And Beatrice might be stuck here for a while at the shop. If she didn't get that food over to the house, goodness knew what Boris might do in her kitchen in his desperation.

The door to the narrow room opened and a blast of cool air from the repair bays made Beatrice look up. John Simmons walked in. The tall, lean man gave her a small smile of greeting but didn't seem to be able to place her as someone he knew. No wonder—whenever Martha was anywhere in the vicinity, John was always completely focused on her. A volcano could erupt in Dappled Hills and John would only be aware of Martha's presence.

Beatrice cleared her throat. "I think you're Martha's friend. Is that right? I'm Beatrice Coleman—I'm also a friend of Martha's . . . a quilting friend."

John's thin face creased in a smile that reached up to his startlingly blue eyes behind his rather scholarly-looking glasses. "That's right. How are you, Beatrice? It's probably been a very strange week for you, hasn't it?"

"Even stranger than you know. I'm here at the shop because my car was vandalized. All four tires were slashed." Beatrice grimaced.

John's face registered shock. "I can't believe it." He held up a thin hand in apology and quickly added, "I mean, it's not that I don't believe you, Beatrice. Sorry, that came out wrong. It's only that it's so difficult for me to wrap my head around the idea of someone doing something like that here in Dappled Hills. I've lived here my entire life and I can't recall any vandalism at all."

"I know. Meadow Downey seems to take it as a personal affront that something like this could happen here. But it did."

John leaned forward, studying Beatrice gravely. "Did Ramsay think it was some sort of teenage prank? I wouldn't have said we even really had enough teens in town to carry out something like this."

"Ramsay did mention that it could be a prank. Although I told him that it felt like a warning," said Beatrice, carefully watching John for a reaction.

He drew in a shallow gasp. "A warning? For what? You think you're in some kind of danger?" His bright blue eyes displayed a sudden doubt. Doubt for what? Was he beginning to think that Beatrice was a bit nutty?

"Well, I thought it might be the murderer trying to warn me off from figuring out who's behind these crimes," said Beatrice.

"Crimes?" John put a slight emphasis on the *s*. "You mean Frank?" His high forehead creased in concentration. "But Martha told me . . . that Frank's death was an accident. An *awful* accident," he hurried to add, as if he hadn't expressed that enough the first time. "Martha said . . . well, she said . . ."

"That Frank had been drinking and fell down the stairs." Beatrice nodded. "And that *could* have happened. But then you have to ask yourself why Frank Helmsley, with absolutely no religious interest, would be at the church."

John Simmons's eyes showed complete lack of creativity of any kind as they steadily looked into Beatrice's.

Clearly, he wasn't going to be able to draw any conclusions. "The only reason that I could come up with is that someone thought that maybe I was figuring out who was behind these deaths and wanted to warn me to back off," said Beatrice.

"That's awful," murmured John. "Who could do such a thing?"

"I was wondering that myself. Do you have any ideas, John? You've been in Dappled Hills for a long time. Who can you think of who would want Jason Gore and Frank Helmsley out of the way?"

John's face flushed at Jason's name. There seemed to be some unresolved feelings there. "Well, Jason—he was a bad guy. You might not have realized that, considering that you're new in town. But he wasn't what he seemed. He acted like he was Mr. Dappled Hills—everyone's best friend. Like some kind of goodwill ambassador for the town." John's mouth twisted with scorn.

"I'm surprised that Martha would have spent so much time with him, considering how he was," said Beatrice delicately.

His expression softened a bit at the mention of Martha. He said, "Martha is a wonderful, sensitive lady. But she hates to see the bad in people, and that causes her problems sometimes."

Beatrice reflected that Martha seemed to very quickly see the bad in Phyllis. "So, if Jason was such a bad guy, you can probably think of some likely suspects. Anybody in particular?"

John gave her a curious look. "I'm starting to realize why someone might have wanted to give you a warning." Then he looked down at his lap and at his long, spindly hands clasped neatly together. "Isn't it usually family who are the first suspects in these types of crimes? I know Jason's brother and he weren't especially close. It seems like perhaps the police should consider him."

"What makes you think they weren't close?" asked Beatrice.

"I was actually around when Jason first returned to Dappled Hills a few months ago. I was having a coffee with Martha downtown and Eric was in line getting a muffin or something. Jason came through the door all smiles, acting as if he owned the town and Dappled Hills was going to be delighted to see him." John snorted. "He didn't exactly get a warm reaction from his brother, if that's what he thought he was getting. Eric looked nauseated. He grabbed his muffin and got out of there without saying a word to his brother."

"What did Martha say about it?" asked Beatrice. "Did she notice what was going on between those two?"

John held out his hands in a helpless gesture. "Martha had a big blind spot when it came to Jason. The only thing she noticed was that Jason was back in town. Next thing I knew, she was putting on some lipstick and enthusiastically welcoming Jason. Which was a lot more of the kind of greeting he was looking for. He came over to our table and gave us a bunch of smooth talk. Acted as if we'd all be delighted to see him back in town . . . as if his own brother hadn't given him the cold shoulder just a few minutes before."

"Didn't Martha know why Jason had left town to begin with?" asked Beatrice.

"If she didn't before, she sure did when I filled her in after Jason finally left. But she acted as if I were making all that stuff up—because I wanted Martha all to myself. At that point, I could tell from the look on her face that she was interested in him."

Beatrice studied John as he became lost in his memories. He muttered, as if almost to himself, "I just don't get it."

"What don't you get?" asked Beatrice.

"What she saw in him. He was all talk, all slick, insincere, toothy grins. Flashy. Nothing genuine about the man. His own brother wouldn't talk to him after he'd been gone for seven years!" John gave Beatrice a bewildered look.

"Going back to Jason's brother. How did he act after Jason left town? Why do you think he might be behind all this?" asked Beatrice.

"How did he act? How do you think he acted? He was completely humiliated. Plus, Eric was scraping by on this tiny salary and couldn't come up with the cash to leave Dappled Hills. Not only that, but he was also left to care for his mother, who took a turn for the worse when the Golden Boy left town."

Beatrice said, "So you're saying that he was stuck in a town that he felt might associate him with his brother's fraud."

"Exactly. He was embarrassed by Jason but couldn't move. And his poor mother went downhill fast. I was on the church committee to help bring food to her—she'd been a very loyal congregant. Every time I showed up at their door with a casserole, Eric could never bring himself to look at me. His mother passed away only a few weeks later. Jason didn't come to the funeral—I guess he figured he might get arrested if he showed his face so soon after skipping town. What I remember about that funeral was Eric's face. Most of the time when you go to a funeral, the family looks upset—they're grieving. You could tell that Eric Gore was grieving, but that's the emotion that was underneath it all. On the top was anger. He was furious about the whole situation. I almost felt as if he were mad at all of us, too—that Dappled Hills' citizens were resentful about the entire situation and just putting up with the Gores to be nice."

John shook his head and continued. "It wasn't that

way at all. But that seemed to be how Eric felt about it because shortly after the funeral, Eric disappeared."

"Disappeared?"

"Not *really*. But for all intents and purposes. He stopped going to church, stopped going to town functions. Bolted in and out of the grocery store as fast as he could. Got a job in Lenoir. He stopped interacting with Dappled Hills," said John.

"So you think Eric wanted to get rid of Jason?" Beatrice glanced out the glass door of the shop's waiting room and saw a mechanic heading in their direction.

"Of course," said John impatiently. "Why wouldn't he? Eric has been suffering—he lost his mother, he's lived on a shoestring, he's been completely humiliated, and then his brother comes back into town as if nothing were wrong. It was bound to make him furious."

The mechanic was pausing to pull out a towel to wipe off his hands. Beatrice said quickly, "But Eric was in Lenoir, working, when his brother was killed."

John raised his eyebrows. "No, he wasn't. Is that what he's been saying? I saw him in downtown Dappled Hills myself. He was walking into the hardware store when I got out of my car that day. He was most definitely on the scene. I remember that day clearly. He was there."

And so were you, thought Beatrice, remembering John's anger at how undeserving Jason Gore was of Martha's affection. She hesitated, and then said, "I know you're helping at the church a lot. Were you there the day that Frank died?"

John looked her right in the eye. "No. I was at home. Although I wish I could have been there for Martha during such a terrible ordeal."

Beatrice stopped herself from correcting John by saying that Martha had suffered through *two* ordeals. She didn't want to raise John's blood pressure again.

Chapter Fourteen

Beatrice had optimistically sprung for a more expensive set of tires for the car and was pleased that they were guaranteed for nearly a hundred thousand miles. The mechanic said, "Yep, these should last you a good long time, especially seeing as how you're mostly driving around town. As long as no punks go slashing them again."

Beatrice didn't think any punks were actually involved in the slashing. She hadn't noticed any punks in the Dappled Hills area, as a matter of fact. She was pretty sure that the murderer had punctured her tires and that he, or she, wouldn't do it again—he'd take his warning to the next level.

As she started up her car, Beatrice remembered that she needed some more needles and decided to run by the Patchwork Cottage on the way home from the garage.

She greeted Posy as she walked into the shop, and then noticed Savannah sitting on the store's sofa, across from a napping Miss Sissy. Savannah was flipping idly through a quilting magazine in a most un-Savannah-like manner. She looked a little lost. Her face brightened when she spotted Beatrice.

"How's it going, Savannah?" asked Beatrice.

Savannah seemed eager for the company and nearly spilled her cup of lemonade in her haste to scoot over and make room for Beatrice on the sofa. "Everything's good! It's all good, Beatrice." Then, to Beatrice's dismay, she burst into tears.

Beatrice reached over to squeeze Savannah's hand. "It's all right, Savannah. Everything will be okay."

Savannah reached into her incredibly organized pocketbook for a tissue and scrubbed her tears away with a vengeance. "Silly!" Savannah muttered reproachfully to herself. "Silly to cry." She took a deep breath and managed to regain control again. Then she said simply to Beatrice, "I miss Georgia. That's all. I can't seem to adjust to the change."

Beatrice said soothingly, "I'm sure you must. But you know she's just pet-sitting while her friend is away. She's going to be back with you, soon."

Savannah's brow furrowed. "Do you really think so, Beatrice? Because she didn't have to *stay* there to take care of Snuffy and Mr. Shadow. She could have simply gone over there a few times a day." Savannah shook her head. "I don't think she's coming back. She wanted a break from me and I think she's liking it by herself. And it's . . . very quiet at the house. I've spent almost as much time at the Patchwork Cottage lately as Miss Sissy."

The sound of her name somehow reached through Miss Sissy's subconscious, jolting her out of sleep. "Foolishness!" she spat, blinking in confusion. She looked sternly at Beatrice. "Thought I saw you coming out of the hardware store."

Miss Sissy could certainly be stealthy when she wanted to be. Beatrice hadn't noticed anyone at all when she'd left the store. "I did."

"Talking to Tony?" The old woman's gaze was sharp.

"Yes." Beatrice hesitated before deciding she might as well bring up her concerns with Miss Sissy. She frequently seemed to know more about what was going on around town than she let on. "We were talking about him being at the church the afternoon that Frank died."

"Tony is a *good boy*." Miss Sissy's eyes narrowed.

Savannah rolled her eyes in sympathy at Beatrice.

"He said that he didn't see anything," said Beatrice. She shrugged. "But it seems as if he probably would have seen *something* while he was there working and finding the missing Boris. Considering the timing of Frank's death. I know you're friends—if Tony tells you anything that might be helpful, could you let me know?"

Miss Sissy gave her an icy glare, turned slightly in her chair, and fell promptly back to sleep again.

This actually put a small smile on Savannah's face. Beatrice cleared her throat. "Getting back to our conversation about Georgia. You clearly miss her very much. What do you think you could do to encourage her to come back?"

Savannah gave her a startled look, and then she frowned furiously as she considered the question. "I could try to give her more space," she said slowly. "Not fuss as much at her disorganization. And maybe . . ." Savannah rolled her eyes. "Well, I've been thinking that maybe I should let Georgia have that pet." She sighed. "It's just that they're so messy when you're trying to train them and everything."

Beatrice felt a grin spread across her face as she was suddenly struck by an excellent idea. "What if you tried out a kitten for a while—to see if you liked it, while Georgia's gone? That way, if being a pet owner really drives you up a wall, you can return it and she wouldn't even have to know. She wouldn't have an opportunity to get attached to it."

Savannah said, "Well . . . I guess. It's the house-training part. You know—the mess." Savannah gave a small shudder at the thought. "I'd have to go find a litter box and clean up any messes. And worry about the furniture getting scratched up."

"You probably don't know this, but I recently took

in a little gray stray kitten. She came looking for me one frosty night and I let her in. Noo-noo isn't delighted with her, so I didn't want it to be a long-term solution, but I felt I could keep her for a while until I figured out what to do with her. She's even had her shots. And I've never seen her scratch at the furniture. If you'd like, you can come home with me now and meet her."

Savannah still hesitated. Beatrice added, "What's more, she's already been litter box trained. She seems like a very smart kitty. Come on, I'll take you there. And I'll drive you back to your house when you're ready . . . are you on your bike?" Savannah ordinarily rode her bicycle everywhere.

Savannah nodded and then sighed. "All right, Beatrice. I'll meet her. But that's all I'm promising."

Five minutes later, they walked into Beatrice's living room. Noo-noo and Boris barked joyfully at their arrival, and Savannah made a face as the dogs leaped around the small space. "Now, remember, we're not talking about dogs, Savannah. I know they're a little formidable right now—they're just excited that we're here. I bet the kitty is curled up on my bed. She's usually very sweet and wants to quietly cuddle. No jumping from her."

Sure enough, that's where she was. She was curled up in a fluffy ball on the end of Beatrice's bed, tail wrapped around her face, sound asleep despite all the carrying-on from the dogs in the living room. She woke up, sleepily revealing her cobalt blue eyes, and stretched on the bed, arching her back. Then the kitten flew into a frenzy of bathing, washing its face with vigor.

Savannah gave a little gasp. "Oh!" She seemed mesmerized by the kitten.

Beatrice pulled a cat toy out from her closet and dangled the feathery bird-looking contraption over the kitten. She crouched down like a miniature hunter, watching the toy intently before leaping up to box it with both paws.

"She's the cutest thing!" said Savannah breathlessly.

And she was. The kitten acted as if she were a star performer. She sparkled and preened and tumbled around and was the cutest thing ever. It was almost as if she knew she was auditioning for a permanent home. What's more—she seemed to really like Savannah. She purred and rubbed up against her, and Savannah uncertainly reached out her hand to pet her.

"Could I . . . maybe take her home with me?" asked Savannah. "Just for a while. Just to see how she does there. And how *I* do. You won't miss her really badly?" she asked Beatrice, looking anxious.

"I'm sure I will miss her antics a little. But Noo-noo isn't quite as fond of the kitty as I am. And Noo-noo came first. I can visit her at your house if I miss her too much," said Beatrice with a smile.

Savannah reached out a little timidly and gingerly picked up the kitten. It immediately curled itself against her chest and Savannah rested her cheek against its fluffy fur.

"I'll drive you and kitty to your house. And I'll send the litter box and some food with you," said Beatrice.

"And the toy. Could we bring the toy, too?" asked Savannah. "She seemed as if she really liked that feathery toy."

"Naturally. The toy, too."

"Noo-noo won't miss the toy?" asked Savannah with concern.

"Oh no. Dogs don't like these types of toys," explained Beatrice. It was obvious that Savannah had no experience with animals whatsoever. Who knew how this experiment might turn out?

"Does she have a name?" asked Savannah? "What have you been calling her?"

"You know, I haven't even gotten that far with my little visitor. I've been calling her 'the kitty' or 'the kitten' whenever I've been talking about her to other people. She and I haven't spent that much time together with everything going on. Besides, I had a feeling that whoever became her new owner might want to name her themselves."

On the way to Savannah's house, Beatrice made some small talk as she drove and Savannah cradled the kitten against her. "I guess the rescheduled quilt show will be coming up soon."

Savannah said a bit sourly, "Yes. That Phyllis brought

by some flyers on the rescheduled date while I was at the Patchwork Cottage. Trying to advertise it, I guess."

Beatrice said, "I believe you weren't much in favor of Phyllis becoming part of the Village Quilters."

Now Savannah made a face. "Certainly not. No. I don't think she'd fit into our group at all."

"Is there anything in particular that makes you feel that way?" asked Beatrice delicately.

Savannah hesitated and then said, "I've never been crazy about Phyllis. At first I thought I was simply being unfair because she was such a good quilter and she was with the Cut-Ups. But then I noticed all the subtle, mean things she did through the years. She isn't very nice. And life's too short to spend with people who aren't nice. Our guild has such wonderful ladies in it that I didn't want to see that changed."

"Mean things," mused Beatrice. "Was there anything in particular that you can point out? As an example, maybe?"

Savannah pressed her lips together in a thin line and then said reluctantly, "I spent a little time in the shop right before the quilting retreat started."

Probably looking for small things to swipe. Poor Savannah.

"Anyway," Savannah continued, "while I was in the shop, being very quiet, you know, I saw Phyllis deliberately set her shears down in the shop. She even glanced around her while she did it—she was being very surreptitious, you know. Then, the next thing I know, Phyllis is blaming Martha Helmsley for stealing her shears! She'd set her up. It was very petty."

"Why didn't you say anything at the retreat? Why didn't you call Phyllis out for it?" Beatrice pulled into Savannah's driveway.

Savannah flushed and looked flustered. "I don't know. I was surprised when she accused Martha. And I was confused about what she was doing. Plus, I didn't want to publicly contradict Phyllis like that."

And she likely didn't want to admit that she was skulking around the shop, thought Beatrice.

Savannah said quickly, "I did confront Phyllis about it later . . . after the body was found and all. I talked to her after the funeral, as a matter of fact. I told her it was ugly what she'd done to Martha. A member of her own guild! I thought that was especially disloyal to a fellow sister quilter. It certainly seemed to show her true character."

Beatrice put the car in park and turned in her seat to stare at Savannah. "What did Phyllis say in response?"

"She cried," said Savannah a little scornfully. "She was very sorry she got caught being mean, is what I thought. Not sorry she did it. Not at all."

"But did she say anything in her own defense?" asked Beatrice.

Savannah absently rubbed the kitten's soft fur. "She said it was petty of her. But then, when it was used as a murder weapon . . . she didn't want to admit that she'd laid the shears down deliberately. She thought the police might get strange ideas. She'd only done it to try to make Martha look bad. Which didn't succeed!"

Beatrice helped Savannah get the kitten and the kitten's things settled in her house. Savannah kept cheerily remarking on the kitten and asking her questions about her, but Beatrice listened and answered automatically, her mind mulling over the information Savannah had given her. Why *had* Phyllis laid those shears down?

She drove back to her cottage on her springy new tires and pulled into her driveway to see Boris and Noo-noo peering out the picture window on the front of the house. Boris immediately started barking, with Noo-noo taking up the chorus. "Even though they clearly see it's me," muttered Beatrice. Still, she figured that no one would be sneaking up on the house in the middle of the night—not with those two around.

Beatrice was fumbling with her keys when she heard a car pull up. She turned around to see Piper and raised her hand to wave at her.

"Nice tires, Mama," said Piper as she got out of her car with a plastic bag. She came over to give Beatrice a tight hug. "I hate that this happened to you. Scares me to death to think of someone sneaking over here in the middle of the night. However did they get past Noo-noo?"

Beatrice waved her hand. "It wasn't Noo-noo's fault—it was mine. She was growling like crazy and I looked outside, didn't see anything, and went back to bed. But I sure will pay attention next time." She finally got the right key in the lock and opened the front door. Boris leaped around as if he were a puppy and Noo-noo stood very close to Beatrice's leg, as if claiming her territory.

"I'm hoping there won't be a next time. Especially with two dogs over here putting up an alarm. You'll call Ramsay, even if it's the middle of the night, right? If the dogs start making another ruckus?" Piper followed her mother inside. "Or the kitten, maybe."

"Of course I will." Beatrice made a face at the thought, though. She really detested waking people up with phone calls. It was such a scary thing, hearing a phone ring in the middle of the night. No good calls ever came at three a.m. "Although I won't get any kind of an alarm from the kitten. Savannah has taken her home with her."

"What? Oh, that's wonderful news! Georgia will be so excited to hear that. She's been telling me nonstop about how terrific Mr. Shadow and Snuffy are—you know, the cat and the dog she's pet-sitting."

Beatrice said, "But Savannah is only *trying out* the kitty, so please don't let Georgia know. The idea is that Savannah is going to see if she and the kitty get along and if she can tolerate the kind of chores that go along with pet ownership. Then, if for some reason it doesn't work out, Georgia won't be the wiser."

"I see," said Piper slowly. "Great idea. It would be awful if Georgia got attached to the kitty and then Savannah realized that she just wasn't cut out to be a pet owner. Although I have a feeling that the kitten is going to win Savannah over."

"She seemed pretty smitten," said Beatrice with a smile. "We'll keep our fingers crossed. That sure would solve a couple of problems—I could find the kitten a great home, and Savannah and Georgia would be back on good terms again."

"Right. I'll keep my fingers crossed that it works out. Okay, I've got Boris's special food, clearly." Piper lifted the plastic bag over her head as the massive dog stood up on his back paws to sniff the bag. "And his favorite toys."

"Does he have a dog bed or anything?" Beatrice took the dog food and carried it into the kitchen to put it on top of her fridge. It should be safe there. Maybe.

"He does, but Meadow says he never sleeps in it. And sometimes, apparently, he pushes his way into their bedroom to take up half their bed." Piper shrugged. "So you might get a visitor in the middle of the night."

"Oh no. No, I don't think so. Unless Boris can turn door handles, I do believe that he'll be camped out in the living room with Noo-noo." Beatrice put her hands on her hips and gave Boris a repressive look. He drooled at her, grinning.

"Maybe doorknobs aren't a problem for Boris. Considering he's a genius and all." Piper winked at Beatrice and they both laughed as they relaxed into Beatrice's cushy sofa. Boris trotted into the kitchen to sit at attention, staring at his dog food on the top of the fridge.

Beatrice watched him. "Maybe I should get a child-proof lock and stick his food in a cabinet," she said, frowning.

"The funny thing is that Meadow doesn't seem like she thinks Boris has behavior issues at *all*. She's only thinking of the fact that he's helping you keep an eye on the cottage," said Piper.

"So, was it Meadow who gave you Boris's things?" asked Beatrice. She felt a small pang.

Piper took a sudden interest in her hands, which were folded on her lap. "Sort of. I mean—Ash opened the door originally. But he was on his way out, so Meadow was the one who put everything in a bag for me."

"Did Ash . . . say anything?"

Piper put a determinedly cheerful smile on her face. "He did say hi. Then, after I explained why I was there, he called for Meadow." She looked down at her hands again. "I think that I must really have hurt his feelings. But, by this time, I'd thought we'd be back together again as if nothing had happened."

"I suppose that sometimes it takes a little longer to put things right," said Beatrice softly. "And it does sound as if Ash has been busy. I guess he's been trying to set things up here, right? A place to live? All the logistics that come with moving?"

"I guess," said Piper miserably. "I really don't know what he's been doing, since he's not actually speaking to me. Meadow would tell me, if I asked her."

"Right. Although that would open up a whole other can of worms. I'm sure that Meadow is homing in on the fact that something is wrong between you two. She was getting a hint of it earlier. And you should know Meadow well enough to realize that once something like this is on her radar, she's going to try to fix it. She's a matchmaker extraordinaire." Beatrice shook her head at the thought of Meadow trying to help with the problem.

"Her heart's in the right place," said Piper. She gave a short laugh. "At this point, maybe I do need that kind of intervention. Otherwise, Ash will end up flying back to California to get things straightened out on that end and we'll still have this misunderstanding between us."

"*Is* it a misunderstanding?"

"It is," said Piper. "I do really want to continue our relationship. I want it to grow and see where it leads us. It was a shock, that's all. It seemed like everything was suddenly a rush to a finish line that I hadn't even visualized yet."

"I'm sure it will all work out," said Beatrice, leaning over to squeeze Piper's arm. "Why don't you call him and ask to meet him for coffee? You could mention that when you saw him today you realized how much you missed him. Something like that."

"I think I will," said Piper. "Otherwise, there's no telling how long this might go on. But I won't try to meet with him today—it looked as if he was heading out for a while." Piper sighed. "I wish I could change the way I am. I know that I'm too set on a routine and that I don't handle change well. I wish I could handle it easier somehow."

"We'll, it's hard to adapt to change. And it's also hard to change *ourselves*," said Beatrice. She remembered her conversation with Wyatt and abruptly asked Piper, "Do you think it's really possible for people to change?"

"Sure I do," said Piper immediately. "Absolutely. You hear about it every day."

"Do you?" Beatrice was pretty sure that she didn't.

"Yes. Think about all the news stories for the area. Someone falls on hard times, develops an addiction or some other problem, and next thing you know . . . they're breaking into cars or something. Maybe a few years before that, they were upstanding citizens who paid their taxes and drove carpools and cut their grass and were good neighbors." Piper shrugged. "They've changed. Big-time."

"Well . . . yes. That's very true. Those are stories about people who adapt poorly to a situation, though. Their change is happening because of a change in their circumstances. I guess what I'm talking about is a change for the *better*. Can someone change their personality or habits for better ones? For the long-term?"

Piper gave her a thoughtful look. "You mean like my good intentions to be more adaptable?"

"Right. And that probably should be my goal, too— go with the flow and be more adaptable. And what about someone like Jason Gore? Maybe he resolved to be a better person than he'd been the last time he lived in Dappled Hills. Did he genuinely change?"

"If he was a better person, wouldn't he still be alive?" asked Piper.

Beatrice leaned back on the sofa, resting her head on its cushiness, and stared thoughtfully at the ceiling. "Maybe. But I don't think we can say that for sure, Piper. Maybe the reason he was murdered has to do with his behavior two years ago. Maybe someone didn't *like* seeing him happy, seeing him changed."

"Or *was* he even changed?" said Piper. "After all, we're talking about some pretty big changes. It could be that he was back in the game again—that he was being a con man. If it's tough for me to master small changes, how hard would it be to completely change . . . from someone who is dishonest to honest?"

"I know what you mean. But I think . . . I'd like to

think . . . that Jason did change. And that it was something from his past that caught up with him. Although I'm the first to realize it's tough to make any kind of personal change or even to develop a habit. You know how I can't seem to sit still for more than a few minutes before leaping up to unload the dishwasher or do something around the house? Or check my e-mail? I made a resolution that I was going to try to relax more . . . not to be so restless," said Beatrice, glancing sideways at her daughter.

"You did?" Piper looked startled. "I didn't realize that."

"See? That's how successful that's been." Beatrice made a face.

Chapter Fifteen

After Piper left, Beatrice tried to make everything as ordinary and routine as possible. Well, despite the fact that a tremendous dog was shadowing her the entire time and a small, indignant one was trailing them.

She folded laundry, she washed and put away the few dirty dishes. She trimmed back the last of the Knock Out roses that were still evident in fall. She filled her birdfeeders. Doing everyday, normal activities made her feel a lot more relaxed. Apparently, it *was* upsetting to have someone slash all your tires. Expensive, too.

By the time it was midafternoon, she picked up her quilt to try to make some headway. She paused. The double wedding ring pattern was a real trial. But it was lovely. She hadn't been sure she could do it justice, with her current skill level. The truth was, though, if she put some extra time into it and really focused, it wasn't as hard as she'd made it out to be. And really—it would be a work of art when she was done, worthy of handing down to any children that Piper and Ash might have. Beatrice frowned at herself. Putting the cart before the horse . . . heavens, she sounded like Meadow. Piper and Ash needed to start talking to each other first.

Beatrice turned on the lamp on the table next to her and worked until she'd finished one block. True, it was a block that she'd started a different day, but it still felt good to realize that she had *finished* something she started. Beatrice decided that she really liked the colors of the fabrics that she'd chosen for the quilt. The warmth of the jewel tones added to the comforting quality of the quilt. She hadn't interrupted her quilting to do something else; she'd focused on the task at hand. Beatrice realized that she'd gotten multitasking down pat. . . . What she needed to learn how to do was *single*-tasking.

There was a light tap on her front door and Boris and Noo-noo immediately jumped into a cacophony of barking. She gave a small smile. No chance of anyone sneaking up on her with those two around. Still feeling the need to exercise some caution, though, Beatrice peered out the side window. There she saw an apologetic-looking Tony, who raised his hand in a small wave and a grim-looking Miss Sissy with hair coming pretty much completely out of her bun. Beatrice unlocked the door. There went her quiet afternoon. But she'd accomplished so much she didn't even care.

Miss Sissy trotted right in and headed for Beatrice's kitchen. The old woman was about as bad as Boris when it came to kitchen raids. Tony scratched the side of his forehead with one hand—in the other he was carrying a plastic bag. "Ah, Mrs. Coleman. Sorry about this. I went over for my visit with Miss Sissy and she was bound and determined to come see you. Wouldn't hear no for an answer."

Beatrice sighed. "She could have just walked over—it's not far. She didn't have to make you come out of your way."

"You know how Miss Sissy is," said Tony in a low voice. "She gets things stuck in her head. For some reason, she wanted me to come along with her. Plus, she had something she wanted to give you." He nodded down to the black garbage bag he was holding.

"Please have a seat, then," said Beatrice, gesturing to her sofa. "I'll get us something to drink."

"I'm fine," said Tony hurriedly. "I have a drink in the car that I've been drinking."

Miss Sissy came back in from the kitchen with a plateful of pretzels, apple slices, and cheese crackers.

"Did you make us a snack, Miss Sissy?" asked Beatrice in surprise.

Miss Sissy glared at her.

"I think Miss Sissy planned on that being her snack,"

said Tony with a smile. "Which is fine," he added quickly, putting his hand up to stop Beatrice from getting up to bring in some food. "I ate a big lunch this afternoon."

"I do recall Miss Sissy being territorial over her food," muttered Beatrice as Miss Sissy busied herself by putting the plate on the coffee table and spreading out a paper towel on her lap. Once she was done, she fixed Beatrice with an intense stare. "They didn't hurt you, did they?" she barked at Beatrice.

Beatrice blinked at her. "They?"

"Bad guys. The ones who broke your tires." Miss Sissy stuffed an apple slice and a couple of pretzels in her mouth.

"Hurt me? No, I never even saw them," said Beatrice.

"Didn't matter if you saw them or not. Tires still broken." The old woman studied Beatrice as if trying to figure something out. Boris put his huge head against Miss Sissy's spindly hand and she gave him a stern look before patting him.

"Well, that's certainly true. I'm sure it won't happen again. And now, as you see, I've got Boris here to keep an eye out for me. With Boris and Noo-noo, I should be in good shape," said Beatrice. She was a little worried that Miss Sissy was planning to take up a guard post to look out for bad guys "breaking" tires. That wouldn't do at all. Miss Sissy was a raging insomniac and would wander around the cottage all night, eating. She'd rather take her chances with the murderer.

Miss Sissy gave her a canny look, then gestured to the black garbage bag that Tony still held. He silently handed it over to her. She opened it up and pulled out the most beautiful double wedding ring quilt that Beatrice had ever seen. Beatrice couldn't hold back a gasp of admiration when she saw it. It was everything she felt her quilt-in-progress wasn't—skillfully curved hand piecing, with beautifully coordinating arcs of multicolored and multipatterned scraps with perfectly scalloped edges.

"Thought you might be sad. About the people breaking your tires," said Miss Sissy gruffly. "I wanted you to have this."

"You made this? It must have taken forever to finish this, Miss Sissy."

Miss Sissy ran a gnarled hand over the quilt. "It was supposed to be mine. When I got married. But I didn't marry. Never. And maybe you'll marry again." The old woman looked curiously at Beatrice as if she was hoping to coax an admission from her.

Beatrice asked softly, "Are you sure you want me to have this, Miss Sissy?"

This earned her a glare in response. "Of course. That's why I brought it over to you." She continued frowning at her under beetling brows until Beatrice said, "Thank you, Miss Sissy. I don't know what to say. I'll treasure it."

Tony had been patiently listening to their conversation. Miss Sissy suddenly swung around in her seat and pointed at him. "He's a *good* guy," she said firmly to Beatrice. "A *good* guy! Fixes tires, doesn't break them."

Fortunately, Beatrice had known the old woman long enough to be used to her non sequiturs. And when Miss Sissy had a favorite, she'd hear nothing but good things said of them. It was exactly the same with Wyatt, who also came by for visits with the old woman.

Beatrice gave her a reassuring smile. "Oh, I know he's a good guy, Miss Sissy."

"He was at the church that day. That day that man died. Helping. He was helping at the church. Tell her." Miss Sissy now pointed a long, crooked finger at Beatrice as she prompted Tony.

Tony sighed and said to Beatrice, "Miss Sissy is determined for me to clear my name. I was over at the church—probably when Frank died. Wyatt is a good man and he gives me odd jobs to do over there for extra money. I was there that whole afternoon. I did leave, though, when the police came."

She nodded. "Did you see anything that day? Anything unusual?"

"Wish I had. But all I saw that was unusual was Frank. I mean, seeing Frank at church was really out of the ordinary . . . the guy never set foot on the church grounds as far as I knew," said Tony. They watched as Miss Sissy polished off the plate of food.

"Frank wasn't talking to anyone at the time you saw him? He was just standing there? Surely that looked a little suspicious." Beatrice frowned.

"Well, his cover story was probably that he was planning on painting a picture of the church," said Tony. "Once he caught sight of me, he started busily taking pictures of the church from different angles. You know— like he was going to paint the scene later. I was trying to make sure he wasn't up to anything strange, so the next time I walked by, I looked for him. It was twenty or thirty minutes later, though, and I didn't see him."

"He was probably at the bottom of the staircase by then." Beatrice rubbed her forehead. Who had he met at the church?

"Well, Miss Sissy, I guess we should be heading back to your house. Was there anything else you wanted to ask? I know you wanted to check on Beatrice as well as have me explain what I saw at the church." Tony stood up.

Miss Sissy fixed Beatrice with a solemn stare. "He was there. There! Not Tony!"

Beatrice gave Miss Sissy a moment to froth before she asked patiently, "Miss Sissy, who was there? Where? The church?"

"Church. The man. The man who likes going to church."

Miss Sissy's complete incapacity to learn names did get frustrating. Beatrice took a deep breath. "A man who likes going to church was at the church. I'm guessing when Frank Helmsley died?"

Tony squinted a little in concentration. "Do you mean John Simmons, Miss Sissy? Tall, skinny guy? Wears glasses? Older?"

Miss Sissy clapped her hands. "John Simmons! Yes! John Simmons. The one who stalks her. That June Bug knows."

"John was at the church the day that Frank died?" Beatrice studied Miss Sissy. The old woman was very observant, but did she really keep track of the days? Most days she spent sleeping in a chair in Posy's shop.

"He was. Careless man. Jumped in front of Posy's car when she was driving me to the store." Miss Sissy's eyes were scornful.

"Well, it's certainly good to know who might have had the opportunity to do such an awful thing," said Beatrice in a soothing way. The last thing she needed was an agitated Miss Sissy in her house.

Miss Sissy glared at her. "Wickedness!"

Tony leaned forward in his seat and gently said, "Miss Sissy, I've got a few things to take care of at my house this afternoon. Is it okay if we go ahead and leave?"

She gave a birdlike bob of her head and moved spryly toward the door.

Beatrice said, "Well, I certainly appreciate your coming by. A . . . nice surprise," she said a bit awkwardly.

Tony gave her a smile. He opened the door for Miss Sissy and then followed her out on the porch after saying good-bye to Beatrice.

Beatrice was reaching to lock the door when Miss Sissy popped her head back in and said sternly, "Nice boy!"

The sun always seemed as if it went down faster in the fall. One minute, Beatrice was wondering if she had the energy to go out and rake a few leaves out of a bed in the backyard. The next, she looked outside and it was already so dark that she decided it would need to wait for another day.

It wasn't only the dark. Beatrice felt weary from the day. One of these suspects was lying to her. He or she was bent on scaring her away with a quick bit of vicious vandalism. And now she had Piper to worry about in addition to the case. Tony had been both at the church and near enough to the quilting retreat to easily run in, kill Jason Gore, and hurry back out again.

Beatrice turned on a small lamp behind her sofa and sat down, still mulling it all over. Yes, Tony could easily have committed both crimes—he was on the scene of both and certainly had plenty of motivation. He had his own, promising future stolen from him. What if that had been eating him up over the years until he felt he *had* to act when Jason carelessly came back into town? And then he'd been forced to act again when Frank let him know that he'd seen him?

Still, somehow she couldn't picture it. Tony seemed so easygoing. If he was the killer, he was a real cold-hearted one who wasn't troubled at all by killing. He just didn't seem to fit the bill . . . and Beatrice really hoped he didn't.

What about John Simmons? Miss Sissy sure seemed to have it in for him. Again, he appeared to be a very upstanding man in the community. He volunteered frequently at the church. His only fault was that he had been blindly determined for too many years to woo Martha Helmsley, even if she didn't want to be wooed.

Except—he was on the scene for both murders, as well. And he was so single-mindedly determined to end up with Martha that Beatrice could easily see him eliminating anything that got in his way—even if it meant murder. She remembered that anger in John's eyes when he said that Jason didn't deserve Martha's love. Had that anger, that desperation pushed him to the limit? Maybe she could ask Wyatt if he knew if John had any legitimate business at the church that afternoon.

Beatrice leaned her head back until she was looking right up at the ceiling. Yes, thwarted love could definitely be a motive for murder. But John Simmons wasn't the only thwarted lover. There was also Phyllis

Stitt. By all accounts, she'd been head over heels in love with Jason Gore a couple of years ago. Jason had jilted Phyllis in a spectacular manner . . . as he fled town after defrauding at least one of Dappled Hills' citizens. Phyllis had to have been furious and humiliated. In a town this small, everyone would have known that Jason had dumped her. She seemed to be over it—but was that just an act? Martha Helmsley hadn't thought Phyllis had gotten over it.

And—Phyllis hadn't been alone in her anger and humiliation. Eric Gore had practically disappeared from town, he'd been so embarrassed by his brother's behavior. His anger was certainly not over . . . nor did he seem to want to try to hide it. He'd clearly felt that he couldn't show his face in his own town again—to the point where he'd found a job in another town. Eric also seemed to blame his brother for their mother's death. That fury, coupled with Jason's smiling, easy reentry into Dappled Hills, was certainly enough to motivate him to kill his brother.

There was something there, thought Beatrice, frowning up at her ceiling. Then she realized. The brief moment of interaction between Phyllis and Eric Gore that she'd seen at Jason's funeral reception at Martha's house. There had been a recognition between the two of them of some kind. Not only that—Miss Sissy had said something about Eric and Phyllis at the funeral reception, hadn't she? Not that Miss Sissy was the most reliable of witnesses. Of course, those two would have known each other fairly well a couple of years ago. . . . Phyllis was engaged to Eric's brother. But surely there wouldn't have been that glimpse of friendliness, al-most of intimacy, there—would there? If Eric was the type to get so completely humiliated over his brother's behavior, then wouldn't he barely be able to look Phyl-lis in the eye? After all, his brother subjected Phyllis to the same treatment . . . or worse.

Beatrice thought back to the day of the retreat. Those *had* been Phyllis's shears that were used for the murder weapon. Phyllis had been a central figure that day. She'd lost her shears. Actually—she *hadn't* lost her shears, according to Savannah. Phyllis had purpose-fully laid them down. She'd blamed Martha. She'd wanted to look for the shears with Beatrice. Because of Phyllis losing her shears, she'd been responsible for both the fact that the murderer had a weapon and that the body was discovered.

Beatrice was having a hard time remembering how often Phyllis had left the back room, though. If she'd had time to murder Jason, it sure hadn't been very much time. And then to calmly go back into the retreat without so much as labored breath? She wasn't that young a woman.

Beatrice felt as if there were something else that she was missing. She cast her mind back to the day of Frank's murder and thought again about the canceled supper plans. Hadn't Wyatt said there'd been some-thing odd about the visit he made that evening?

She reached for the phone and dialed Wyatt's num-ber. He picked up and she talked with him for a few minutes about the rescheduled quilt show and possible dates for them to have a coffee or dinner out. Then Be-atrice said, "I actually wanted to ask you about the din-ner we were going to have the evening of Frank's death."

"I'm sorry I had to cancel, Beatrice. It was just that I got that phone call—"

"Oh, I know. Of course you had to go . . . that's not what I was worried about. It's simply that when I met up with you at the quilt show, you said that it had been an odd visit. I was wondering what you meant by that," said Beatrice.

Wyatt said, "It was a prank of some kind, I guess. When I arrived at the lady's house, she was completely confused and said that she'd never called me. I was thinking that maybe there was a real rash of pranks going on in Dappled Hills—what with your tires being slashed and that phone call. But then, as I was pulling away from her house, I got a *genuine* phone call from someone who needed a hospital visit. That's why it took me so long to get back to the church."

Beatrice said slowly, "Do you think it's possible that someone made that call to lure you away from the church so that they could meet privately with Frank Helmsley?"

Wyatt's voice now sounded startled. "I hadn't thought about that. She could have, I guess."

"It was a woman's voice, then?"

"That's right," said Wyatt.

"Did you recognize the voice?"

Wyatt said slowly, "No. It was sort of hoarse, gruff. Thinking back, I suppose the woman must have been trying to disguise her voice."

"Also—one other thing I wanted to ask you. Was John Simmons at the church on legitimate business the day that Frank Helmsley died?"

Wyatt considered this. "He was, actually. He was in the church office that afternoon to work on a computer problem we were having. He's pretty good with computers and he doesn't mind helping us with ours from time to time."

Then Wyatt sighed. "Beatrice, I'm sorry—it looks like I'm getting another call in. I'm going to try to talk with you later and we can plan our meal out."

Beatrice was just putting the phone down when it suddenly rang, jarring Beatrice from her thoughts and startling her. "Hello?" she asked.

"Hey, uh . . . it's Meadow." The voice on the other end actually didn't sound much like Meadow.

"Oh, hey. Listen, I was thinking about something with the case and—"

Meadow blurted, "Do you know what's going on with Ash and Piper? I swear to goodness, what's wrong with those children? Here they were, acting all grown up, developing a nice relationship, and then they blow it!"

"I don't know if they're *blowing* it, per se. I think they're having a minor misunderstanding, that's all," said Beatrice in as calming a voice as she could muster.

"I want to wring my Ash's neck," said Meadow. She sounded about as angry with Ash as Beatrice had ever heard Meadow get mad.

"The foolishness!" Now Meadow was starting to sound distressingly like Miss Sissy. "Piper acted like she was trying to set up time to talk with Ash and all he could do was come up with excuses." Meadow said in a deep, Ash-like voice, " 'I've got an appointment with my Realtor. I've got a human resources meeting at the college.' Pooh!"

"I'm sure he does have all those things to do, Meadow. After all, he's about to move clear across the country. Think of what a logistical nightmare that would be. He's probably simply trying to spare Piper from getting involved in that mess. It's all very important business for him to be working on."

"What's more important than our future grandchildren?" bellowed Meadow, sounding wounded.

Beatrice took a deep breath. "Now, Meadow, we're getting ahead of ourselves. It's just a spat. Spats happen. Give it time. Listen—I'm glad you called because I was thinking about the case and was trying to figure something out."

"How is my sweet Boris?" asked Meadow. "Are you feeling more protected over there now? During your investigation?"

Beatrice glanced over at Boris, who was sprawled out on his back, tongue lolling out of his mouth. "Definitely. Much more protected. He and Noo-noo are doing a great job protecting the house. But what I wanted to ask you about was the retreat. Can you remember back to that day and tell me what Phyllis's actions were?"

"Phyllis's actions were most annoying that day, that's what. Losing the shears, making us all look for them, picking on Martha. Trying to bulldoze her way into the illustrious Village Quilters guild. It was all a pain."

"That's the part I remember. But I'm talking about the times she went into the shop area. Do you remember much about that?" Beatrice remembered that Phyllis said later that she'd gone out to use the restroom or to get something to eat. Had she, though?

"As I recall, Phyllis never left the room," said Meadow. "That got on my nerves, as a matter of fact. I kept thinking, 'Hey. If you lost your scissors, go out and look for them.' I thought she'd likely left them in her car or something. The only time she actually left the room was to finally go looking for the things with you. Or join you after you'd left to find them. Whatever."

"You're sure about this?" asked Beatrice.

"Of course I'm sure. That's why I was annoyed." Meadow sounded annoyed even now, but Beatrice realized that she was still distressed over the Piper-Ash problem.

"This isn't what she told me," said Beatrice thoughtfully.

"What?"

"It's not what Phyllis told me happened on the day of the retreat. She told me that she got refreshments or went to the restroom or something. I can't remember exactly what she said, but the upshot was basically that she left the room." Beatrice rubbed the side of her face as she tried to remember exactly what was said.

Meadow sounded impatient. "Does it matter? So she didn't leave the room. Maybe *she* didn't even remember exactly what happened that afternoon. After all, she was obsessed with her silly shears. Maybe all she could think about was where the scissors were."

"If she didn't leave the room, then why didn't she say so, though? Surely that would have provided her with more of an alibi and put her under less suspicion. What if she *knew* what was going on out there, didn't want to see it taking place or interrupt it, and then lied because she knew that it was more natural to have left the room during that time? Everyone left at some point or other except for Phyllis. Think of all the delicious food out there."

Meadow said, "But if she *didn't* leave the room, then

how could she be involved in Jason's murder? It's not as if Jason's body were found in Posy's back room."

"She could be involved with the murder if she had a partner. If Phyllis had a partner, she could even distract us all in the back room with her allegations and her arguments—glue us to her, so to speak, to see what crazy thing she's going to throw out there next. We're distracted, her partner kills Jason Gore, and then she leads me to the body." Beatrice felt breathless again. It was starting to make sense to her.

"Who would this partner be?" Meadow's voice was baffled. "Are you saying she hired a hit man or something? Here in Dappled Hills?"

"No, definitely not a hit man. I'm thinking that her partner was Eric Gore."

There was a stunned silence on the other end of the line. Then Meadow said, "Beatrice, you haven't been sipping the cooking sherry, have you? That doesn't even make any sense. We just saw Eric at the theater. . . . You know how he is. He wants to pretend he's on a separate planet from everyone in Dappled Hills because he's so incredibly embarrassed over his brother's deceptions. And that includes Phyllis! For heaven's sake. Jason jilted Phyllis—I'm sure Eric can't even be in the same room as Phyllis without wanting to escape. Didn't you see him at the funeral reception?"

"I did. I did see him at the funeral reception. That's the whole point. The two of them seemed to have a real connection. And even Miss Sissy commented on it—we just didn't understand what she was talking about. We thought she was saying that Phyllis and Jason had gone out with each other, but she meant *Eric* and Phyllis were a couple."

"Well . . . but this is Miss Sissy we're talking about. You know how befuddled she can be," said Meadow.

"Look, never mind. I'll keep mulling it over. Thanks," said Beatrice. Her head was starting to pound.

"What are we going to do?" Meadow's voice was agitated again.

"Do? Well, there's no real evidence that Phyllis had anything to do with this. *Or* Eric. We can't go to Ramsay at this point, because he'd think that we were nuts. But maybe, if we can somehow surprise them? Trap them into a confession somehow . . . ?"

"No, no, Beatrice! I mean do about Piper and Ash. The heck with Phyllis and Eric!" Meadow spluttered in her fury.

"We're going to do nothing at all, Meadow. Nothing. They're two grown-ups, trying to work through a temporary speed bump in their relationship, and that's all it is. We'll sit tight and when they work things out, as I'm convinced they will, then you and I will share a bottle of wine and celebrate." Beatrice got up and walked into her kitchen, peering into her refrigerator. How long had it been since she'd last eaten? It must have been a while.

Meadow was making grumbling mumbles on her end of the line.

"Now I probably need to go. The sun is getting ready to go down and I have no idea what I'm going to eat for supper." Beatrice surveyed the contents of her fridge. "At this point, it's looking like baked beans and cheese on crackers."

"The very reason I gave you that food processor and the other equipment, Beatrice!" fussed Meadow before hanging up.

Chapter Sixteen

Cheese and crackers was, in fact, the very supper she was sitting down to eat, ten minutes later, when there was a knock at her door. Beatrice sighed, wondering if there was some sort of conspiracy to keep her from having a full meal that day. And the number of visits and phone calls. They were certainly extraordinary. Then it struck her that it might be Piper out there, coming to tell her that things with Ash hadn't gone well. Beatrice was headed uneasily to her front door just as there was a second tap.

Phyllis stood on her front porch and smiled when she saw her peeking out. She held up a hand with papers in them and said, loud enough to be heard through the door, "I've got flyers on the rescheduled quilt show, if you could hand those out to the Village Quilters and around town. Meadow thought you'd help out. And I brought by a pie for you, too—I heard what happened to you last night. Frightening!"

Beatrice hesitated. She had no proof that Phyllis was part of these murders, no matter how much sense it made. She'd come by on quilt show business, after all. Beatrice slowly opened the door.

Phyllis stepped in. She was bundled up in a big coat and gloves. Beatrice said in surprise, "Is it getting that cold out there, then? I know it's windy."

"Oh, I've always been cold-natured," said Phyllis a bit carelessly.

Beatrice turned to look curiously behind her at Noo-noo and Boris. Usually, whenever people came to the door, the dogs would be cavorting around them in delight, practically knocking them down in their enthusiasm. Now both dogs crouched on the door, staring intently at Phyllis. Noo-noo made a low growl in her throat, which Boris echoed. Boris showed his teeth and a chill went up Beatrice's spine. Now she just wanted to get Phyllis out of there as soon as possible. Phyllis must have been the one responsible for slashing her tires. It was the only possible explanation for Noo-noo's unusual behavior. And Boris had been on the scene when Frank's body was discovered. Had Boris seen Phyllis there? Or possibly smelled her scent?

"I'd ask you to sit down, but I'm actually about to go out," said Beatrice. Noo-noo's growls got louder and Beatrice turned to see the corgi's fur standing up on the back of her neck. Boris was so focused on Phyllis that he was completely ignoring the fact that there was a pie within easy reach of his tremendous head. "Sorry about the dogs," she said with a small laugh. "They're not feeling friendly today, I guess. Thanks for bringing by the flyers and the pie, though. That's very kind of you." She kept standing and made a slight gesture to the door.

"Well, dogs are like people, aren't they?" said Phyllis in her cheerful voice. "They're entitled to an off day, too. I just love dogs." She reached out a hand and Noonoo gave a sharp warning bark. Phyllis drew back her hand, looking startled. Her eyes narrowed.

"Sorry," repeated Beatrice. "It's probably better if we cut our time short. Thanks for coming by, though. Maybe we can visit another time." She fidgeted with the flyers that Phyllis held.

"Is that the quilt you're working on now?" asked Phyllis, completely ignoring Beatrice's attempts to move her toward the door. "It's beautiful. That's a very tough pattern, you know. The double wedding ring. I really struggled the first time I tried to do one. Were you working on this quilt the day of the retreat? Because I don't remember it."

Beatrice said slowly, "It's the same one. But I have trouble remembering that day, too. For good reason, I guess, right? After all, it was a very stressful day. I was trying to remember your movements that afternoon. You mentioned that you'd left the back room for refreshments or a drink or the restroom, or something. But Meadow staunchly states that you never left the room. And, come to think of it, I don't remember your doing so."

Phyllis's cheery smile disappeared and she rapidly put her hand into her coat and pulled out a knife. "Back up," she said darkly. "Get away from this door." She opened Beatrice's front door and the dogs ran out, as if Phyllis was leaving. As soon as the dogs were out on the porch, Phyllis slammed the door shut.

Noo-noo and Boris were barking and whining outside the door. Beatrice raised her hands up and looked levelly at Phyllis, backing toward the kitchen as Phyllis was gesturing for her to do. "You don't want to do this." Phyllis advanced slowly toward her until they ended up in Beatrice's small kitchen. A better place for Beatrice, since at least there was a shot at getting her hands on a knife at some point.

"What am I doing?" she asked saucily, but there was a combination of fear and fury in her narrowed eyes.

"You're wanting to get rid of me. And the way the dogs are acting makes me think that you were the one last night who slashed my tires. As a warning." Beatrice swallowed, feeling the dryness of her mouth.

"Which, clearly, didn't work." Phyllis frowned. "Was Boris here last night?"

"Boris is picking up on Noo-noo's signals." Beatrice paused. "And he may also be aware that you were responsible for Frank's death. After all, he would probably have been able to place your scent at the scene of the crime. You know . . . you can't get away with this, Phyllis. Are you seriously thinking of murdering me with a knife? Think of all the evidence you'll leave behind in the process. Here you are in my house. And I've just gotten off the phone with Chief Clover," she fibbed. "Giving him all the reasons why I thought you were behind this."

"Did you?" Phyllis made a fake surprised look. "That's funny. Because I don't hear any police sirens. I don't believe you called him at all. After all, there's absolutely no proof that I had anything to do with it. You stated yourself that I was in the back room the entire time during the retreat, except when you and I left to find my shears."

"Your conveniently missing shears. You didn't leave the room on purpose . . . because you didn't want to see a murder in action. Jason Gore still must have had at least a small hold on you, even after all this time. You worked with a partner. Jason's brother, Eric." Beatrice's legs felt weak as she looked at Phyllis's knife, but she tried to look strong and confident.

Boris and Noo-noo were scratching at the front door, whining, and giving small, frantic barks. Maybe Miss Sissy or Piper would notice the dogs out there and call the police. Probably not, though—they weren't being that loud. The sound might not carry that far.

Phyllis blinked at the mention of Eric. She gave a breathless laugh. "Eric Gore? He's practically a hermit. He's never even around town. . . . How are you figuring that he and I would partner up in anything?"

Beatrice spread out her hands in front of her, trying to make sure they didn't shake in the process. "It really makes a lot of sense. There seemed to be a connection between the two of you at the funeral reception, which is what made me think of it. As a matter of fact, Miss Sissy even alluded to the fact that you two were seeing each other—not that anyone really listened to her. And it makes sense. After all, you were both deceived by Jason. You would have known each other pretty well as future brother- and sister-in-law. Jason's actions would have felt like a betrayal to both of you, and it's only natural that you would have sought each other out to talk about it."

"No one has seen me together with Eric. No one!" Phyllis's fingers gripped tighter around the knife and Beatrice felt her heart pound harder. Glancing around, she couldn't see any knives lying on the counter or in the sink.

"There's no point in really denying it now, is there? Not to me, anyway. I also noticed that there seemed to be an attempt to make Martha a suspect in Jason's murder. I kept hearing rumors that Martha might be mad that Jason flirted with other women. Finally, though, I realized that all the rumors came from the same source." Beatrice looked levelly at Phyllis. It wasn't as if Phyllis was going to let her walk out of this situation and just promise not to tell. She started mentally canvassing her kitchen, trying to think what she could possibly use to either knock Phyllis out, or at least to knock the knife out of her hand. "I had seen Jason being friendly with a woman in front of the Patchwork Cottage the day of the retreat, but I would have said he was only being attentive . . . not flirting. I'm sure the two of you felt pretty vengeful to Jason, considering how he'd treated you a couple of years ago. Even if he'd changed."

Phyllis's face was furious now. "You've got it all wrong. After I found out the way he was, I didn't *want* him back. He hadn't changed a lick, believe me."

And then Beatrice realized she *had* gotten it all wrong. "You and Eric fell in love, didn't you? It's not just that you were partnering with Eric to enact revenge on Jason. You and Eric started a relationship after Jason left town. But Eric has never had the money to have Jason's lifestyle."

"Neither did Jason," said Phyllis quickly. "He just scammed people to get money. I should know—he scammed me out of mine, too. I bought Jason a car, I bought him clothes, furniture, art. It put me into terrible debt and I've never recovered. Can you imagine Eric and me getting married? We wouldn't have had two pennies to rub together. He'd be working at the movie theater and I'd be a wedding coordinator, like . . . once a month. Not enough money to really even live on and we'd never see each other."

"So your idea was to kill Jason. Eric, as Jason's only living relative, would inherit his money. Then the two of you could be comfortable. But didn't you think everyone would be suspicious? You'd have even more motive than if you were merely trying to take revenge on an ex-fiancé," said Beatrice.

"Don't you guess we'd have thought that through? Eric and I are *already* married, by the way. We got married in South Carolina a couple of weeks ago. We weren't going to stick around Dappled Hills and have everyone's suspicious eyes on us until our dying days, no. We were going to leave town separately, and no one would have been the wiser." Phyllis stopped short. "What am I saying?" she said with a short laugh. "We *are* going to leave town separately with no one the wiser. That's still the plan. I just have to shut you up first."

Beatrice's heart pounded so loud that she felt sure that Phyllis should be able to hear it plainly. She quickly changed the subject. Boris and Noo-noo continued scratching and jumping at the front door. Noo-noo gave a sharp, alarmed bark. "What I don't totally understand is what happened with Frank Helmsley. It sounded to me like he knew something about what happened to Jason. Did he try to blackmail Eric?"

Phyllis said, "Frank was in and out of the Patchwork Cottage. I guess he was smoking or something. Why on earth was he sticking around? Maybe he was waiting for the chance to ask his mother for money . . . again." She snorted at her own joke. "Whatever it was that he was doing, he seemed to be nosing around like he knew something was up."

There was a noise behind them and Eric was suddenly in the kitchen with them. "Wanted to make sure everything was okay in here. You were supposed to let me know when it was over. What's up?" He only briefly glanced at Beatrice. It was as if she were already gone to him. Beatrice felt a chill going up her spine.

"It's taking longer than I thought. The dogs." Phyllis's eyes were huge in her pale face. "How did you get past them?"

Eric held up his hand, which had hot dogs in it. "I came prepared. At least, I was prepared against the corgi. That big dog . . . well, lucky it was hungry."

"What are you doing here, Eric? It's going to look weird—our two cars being here. No one even knows anything about us . . . except for her."

"I told you—I was worried about you."

"You don't think I can hold my own against an old woman?" Phyllis asked indignantly.

Beatrice gritted her teeth. Phyllis must only be a decade younger than she was. Let her believe what she wanted.

"Just go, okay?" pleaded Phyllis. "Nobody probably saw you come here. If you stick around, that might change. I'll let you know when I'm out of here. Promise."

While they were debating the point, Beatrice's gaze latched onto the clunky food processor that Meadow had given her. She'd put the container up in the cabinets, but the bulky processor wouldn't fit in there with the top. It would hurt to be hit by that thing. Really hurt. But she had no hope against both Eric and Phyllis.

"Okay. Be careful," said Eric, reaching over to give Phyllis a small hug. You'd think Phyllis were about to go on a long road trip instead of about to commit murder.

Eric made his way past the barking dogs, with some difficulty this time, if the scuffling sounds were any indication.

Beatrice cleared her throat. "So Frank actually witnessed Jason's murder."

"No, he saw Eric leaving the shop, though. And then he found out that Jason was dead, not long after, and drew his own conclusions. What other business would Eric have had in the quilt shop?"

"And he tried to blackmail Eric."

"It must have been the first time in his life that he ever motivated himself to make money." Phyllis gave an unpleasant laugh.

"And you met him at the church." Beatrice looked at her levelly.

"Me?" Phyllis looked startled that Beatrice had figured it out.

"Sure, why not?" Beatrice tried moving imperceptibly sideways toward the counter. "You made a prank call to Wyatt to lure him away from the church. Eric spoke to Frank on the phone that afternoon, right? He must have been able to tell that Frank was completely intoxicated. According to Martha's housekeeper, Frank was even drinking Martha's alcohol. Frank demanded to speak to Eric late that afternoon, didn't he? Knowing how Frank was, he probably didn't listen to reason, either. Eric wasn't even in town, was he?"

"Working," said Phyllis, eyes narrowed. "In Lenoir."

"The day that Meadow and I were at that theater, it was so quiet that Eric was the only employee we saw. He took our ticket money, helped us at the concession stand, and started our movie for us. It's not as if no one would notice if he left. And it would be obvious he had no alibi during the time of the murder if he'd locked up the movie theater and driven off to Dappled Hills. So you offered to meet Frank in Eric's place—and silence him," said Beatrice. She leaned back against the counter in her narrow kitchen.

Beatrice continued. "What choice did you have, when Frank was being so unreasonable? Maybe the fact that Frank sounded so slurred and unsteady made you feel better about pushing him down the stairs. He was practically falling down the stairs on his own, wasn't he? He was so intoxicated that it might even have passed as an accident."

Beatrice noticed the pie that Phyllis brought over was still on the counter next to the heavy food processor. She rested her hip against the side of the counter and put her hand casually on her hip. "But then I started getting a little close, didn't I? It must have been worrying you both, having me go to Lenoir to talk to Eric there. The slashed tires were a warning, weren't they?"

"One you didn't heed," grated Phyllis. "Why couldn't you simply have backed off? There was no need for you to get involved in this at all. It wasn't any of your business."

She moved closer and Beatrice took a deep breath. She knocked the pie to the floor and instead of watching the pie's movement, Beatrice watched Phyllis watch the pie. Phyllis leaned over just a little as if to catch the pie . . . and Beatrice awkwardly twisted to grab the heavy food processor, pull it to the edge of the counter, and drop it on the back of Phyllis's head and neck.

Chapter Seventeen

Phyllis was definitely not knocked out, but she was hurt. She dropped the knife as she fell—it skidded toward the kitchen door leading into the living room and front door. Beatrice ran to grab it but knew that there were plenty of other potential weapons in her kitchen—she needed to get out of the house. Where were her keys?

Phyllis groaned in the kitchen and Beatrice shot a harried glance her way . . . and saw her struggling to her knees. Beatrice spun around frantically. Her keys? Where were they? Finally, shaking, she spotted them on a table near the front door, partially obscured by the Dappled Hills newspaper. She grabbed them, fumbled them, grabbed them again as Phyllis rose to her feet and staggered her way.

Both dogs were barking outside the front door. Beatrice yanked the door open and they bolted inside, spotted Phyllis, and started snarling at her. "Come on, guys," called Beatrice, "let's go for a ride."

But the dogs wouldn't budge. All the calling, all the begging, all the promises of treats wouldn't move them. Beatrice hurried toward the car. They loved to ride—maybe they'd hop in the car if they heard the motor running and her calling them. She had to believe that if Phyllis was determined to kill her, she wouldn't hesitate to get rid of Boris and Noo-noo.

Beatrice tried to hit the unlock button but couldn't see which one it was in the dark. She ended up hitting the panic button on the key fob instead. The car fell into a frenzy of honking . . . just as two different sets of headlights pulled into her driveway. Could it be Eric returning? And someone else?

She hit the button again and the doors unlocked. Beatrice yanked open the car door, climbed inside—and heard, "Mama?"

Beatrice was looking into Piper's worried face and heard Ash call behind them, "Piper? Beatrice? What's going on?"

Phyllis exploded out of the house, waving one of Beatrice's kitchen knives in front of her. Noo-noo was nipping at her heels in true corgi herding fashion and Boris leaped around her, making it difficult for Phyllis to move forward.

"Phyllis?" breathed Piper, staring disbelievingly at the wild-looking figure in front of them.

"She tried to kill me," said Beatrice simply. Her hands trembled as they wrapped around the steering wheel for support.

"Did she?" asked Ash, glaring at Phyllis through narrowed eyes. Phyllis made a slashing gesture with her knife. "Oh, I think we're shutting this down right now."

"Ash, be careful. You don't know what she's capable of," said Beatrice.

"Or what I'm capable of," said a calm voice behind them, and they whirled around to see Eric standing behind them with a gun. "I saw the two cars headed in this direction and thought I should make sure everything was okay."

"Oh, Eric," said Phyllis tearfully. "It's not okay. Can we tie them up and leave town real quick or something? What's the best thing to do?"

"We *could* do that. Except that as soon as they were discovered, they'd have every cop in North Carolina following us . . . the son of a police chief, after all. I'm thinking we shut them up more permanently."

Phyllis didn't look so sure. "What? Three people and two dogs? Because I don't think the dogs are going to be happy about this." She gave a nervous glance at Noo-noo and Boris, who were still snarling at both her and Eric.

"I don't think *I'm* going to be too happy about this," came Ramsay's stern voice behind them, and Beatrice turned to see him training a gun on Eric's back. Miss

Sissy, looking rather wild, and Wyatt were right behind him. "Don't turn around, Eric. Drop the gun. Drop it. Then put your hands up as far as you can."

Relief flooded Beatrice's body and suddenly she felt as if her legs wouldn't support her any longer. She slumped in her car and Wyatt hurried over to pull her into his arms as Noo-noo and Boris bounded joyfully around Ramsay while he took Phyllis and Eric into custody.

Minutes later when they were all back inside the house, Miss Sissy's eyes were full of a fierce pride. "I called Wyatt and the police! Called them!"

As Ramsay booked Phyllis and Eric, Beatrice and the others gathered in her small living room. She'd brought out wine for everyone and they were all gratefully drinking a glass—even Miss Sissy, who was reliving with enjoyment the fact that she helped save the day.

Piper, who had collapsed, shaking in Ash's arms, the moment that Ramsay took control of the situation, said, "What made you decide to call, Miss Sissy? All the cars coming down the street?"

Miss Sissy pointed a skinny, bent finger toward Boris and Noo-noo, who were now eating rawhide treats. "Them! Barking! They were scared . . . terrified! Called the police!"

Beatrice threw Boris and Noo-noo another treat and gave Miss Sissy a hug. Piper continued shivering in the protective circle of Ash's arms.

*   *   *

It wasn't long before Meadow joined them, clucking over them all—but shooting pleased looks at the reconciled Piper and Ash. "Ramsay called me," she said breathlessly as she ran in and hugged everyone. "What a horrid, horrid person that Phyllis is! And Eric . . . a monster. A monster. In our own Dappled Hills!" Meadow was so anxious that she seemed physically incapable of sitting still. Finally, unable to stand doing nothing, Meadow said, "I'm going to make us all something to eat. Wait. Ash, what happened to the food I sent you over here with?"

Ash looked puzzled, and then said, "Ah. That's right—you wanted me to bring over food. I left it in the car, Mom. You know—after I saw that Phyllis was holding a knife on Beatrice and Piper. It kind of slipped my mind."

Meadow waved her hand dismissively. "Doesn't matter. It's cold enough outside for the casserole to have kept. I'll heat it up real well and then we can have a little something to eat." She bustled out the front door, nearly running into Ramsay as he was on his way in. Meadow gave him an especially tight hug.

"It's okay, Meadow; it's okay," said Ramsay tiredly. "Everyone is safe. Now I need to get a statement from everybody."

It didn't take very long for them to relate the events in the order they happened. Miss Sissy interrupted every now and again with "wickedness!"

Once they'd finished, Ramsay snapped his notebook shut. "All right. Guess I'd better get back and start processing this."

Meadow, working to warm the food up in the kitchen, stepped out into the living room, face red. "You certainly will *not*! You're going to fill us in on what's going on. I've just spent ten minutes cleaning pie off Beatrice's floor—pie she had to throw there to get away from the maniacal Phyllis. Tell us what they've said."

Ramsay sat back down again. "Well, they did confess. That's something."

"What choice did they have? After all, you caught them red-handed. And Phyllis basically confessed to Beatrice, right?" said Meadow.

"A full confession is still much better than working with someone who is uncooperative. Besides, we didn't have any actual evidence against them, otherwise." Ramsay rubbed his forehead as if he was getting a big headache.

Beatrice said, "How about the fact that Phyllis's story didn't add up . . . or kept changing? She told me that she left the back room at the retreat. Then she admitted that she hadn't. She was the one who set up the crime with her shears. And she and Eric are already married—could you prove that? Look it up in the records somewhere?"

"It's no crime to get married," said Ramsay gently. "But you were good to pick up on the fact that her story wasn't adding up. And you're right—the fact that those two got married gave them some additional motive. Eric and Phyllis believed that, with Jason out of the way, they'd end up living a more financially comfortable life."

Beatrice said quietly, "I think we might find there was more than one motive here. Phyllis basically came out and said it was all financial. But Eric is a different story. Eric was more about revenge. He seemed to blame Jason for their mother's death . . . that she'd died of a broken heart. He and Phyllis had a lot in common, though, and I think that's what powered their relationship."

"Who slashed your tires?" asked Wyatt. "Did you find out which of them was behind it? Was it a warning to you, like you were thinking?"

"That was Phyllis. Which was why Noo-noo got so upset when Phyllis visited tonight. And yes, it was a way for her to warn me off."

Meadow came out of the kitchen with food and plates. "And then Boris followed Noo-noo's lead. Brilliant!"

"Actually," admitted Beatrice, "that was very intuitive of Boris, I have to say. It might also have helped that he was on the scene of Frank's murder. He might have caught Phyllis's scent there. He changed from a completely placid, happy dog to a menacing brute.

And then for both dogs to keep barking and scratching and making a racket outside the front door . . . well, they saved the day, didn't they? They made Miss Sissy call Ramsay."

Miss Sissy looked pleased with herself. "Called the police. Called them."

Beatrice saw that Wyatt was being very quiet. She reached over and held his hand and he gave her hand a tight squeeze.

Meadow clapped her hands together. "I almost forgot. Did you hear that Martha is setting up an art auction? John's been helping her put it together. They really do make a nice couple, now that Martha has capitulated and everything. She's renting out that empty store in downtown. Frank had tons of completed paintings and sculptures, apparently. Who knows why he was so funny about sharing it with the world? Anyway, she's holding an auction and the proceeds are going to charity."

Wyatt smiled at her. "That's a great way to celebrate his life."

"Isn't it? I thought that was really nice. And we all wondered if he were just totally mooching off his mother and not really accomplishing anything in his studio. All the while, he was actually working pretty hard." Meadow shrugged and took a big bite of her casserole. A dark look passed over her face. "Phyllis and Eric won't get Jason's money now, will they? That wouldn't be right."

"No, criminals can't benefit financially from their crimes," said Ramsay. "But those two wouldn't have, anyway. They made assumptions that were completely incorrect. Counted their chickens before they hatched."

Beatrice said, "Jason didn't leave Eric his money?"

"Well, the will is being executed right now. What will surprise Eric and Phyllis is that Jason left only a smattering of money to his brother, anyway. In fact, we just notified Tony Brock this afternoon that he was the recipient of the bulk of Jason Gore's assets. Along with some other people that Jason had some shady dealings with in Dappled Hills." Ramsay grinned at the stunned look on their faces. "That's right. Looks like Jason was trying to set things right with people he took advantage of. And Tony was surprised and gratified to learn this."

Now a smile was pulling at Wyatt's mouth. Beatrice said, "So maybe people *can* change for the better. They can have real regrets and move on and become better people."

"But what if . . ." Wyatt hesitated. "What if Jason hadn't died so suddenly? Or what if Tony had predeceased him? Would Jason have continued living off Tony's grandfather's money?"

"As a matter of fact, I believe that Jason was working on a way to repay Tony. We found a letter in Jason's home . . . a letter that sounded as if it was going to accompany a check of considerable size." Ramsay smiled at Wyatt, who seemed to be more at peace every second in Beatrice's small living room.

Ramsay snapped his fingers. "Beatrice, are you enjoying *The Brothers Karamazov*? Meant to ask you about it the other day."

Beatrice nodded. "Very much. Can I hang on to it for a while longer?"

Ramsay looked pleased. "Of course you can, Beatrice. I'm glad you're getting as much out of it as I have." He glanced over at Meadow, who was still beaming at Piper and Ash sitting close together on the sofa, holding hands. "We should probably head on home, Meadow. It's been a long day . . . for all of us."

Ash asked Piper, "Want to go grab an ice cream downtown? I think we've got an hour before they close."

Piper smiled at him. "Sounds great."

Meadow teared up a bit, watching them, and fumbled in her pocketbook for a tissue. "All right, Ramsay, I'm coming. I'll join you in a second." Ramsay left and Meadow said, breathlessly, "That went better than I thought! Oh, Beatrice, I'm so thrilled they're back together!"

Remembering that their two different sets of headlights had arrived simultaneously, Beatrice asked, "Did you arrange for them to get here at the same time?"

"It was easy. I asked Ash to bring you some food,

since you admitted you were having cheese and crackers. And I called up Piper and told her that I'd talked to you and I thought you were uneasy from the tire slashing incident and needed some company." Meadow was practically dancing in her excitement. "And now they're off to get ice cream. It worked. It really worked."

"Maybe a little life-threatening incident was the perfect catalyst to show them life is too short for misunderstandings," mused Beatrice.

"Maybe so. Well, I guess I should catch up with Ramsay. Oh, Beatrice, did you get the information on the rescheduled quilt show?"

Beatrice said dryly, "Yes, I think I've got all the info I need. Phyllis brought me plenty of flyers."

There was a small toot of the horn outside and Meadow said quickly, "Better run. See you tomorrow, Beatrice." She grabbed Boris, now back to his happy-go-lucky self, and left.

Only Wyatt remained and he stood to leave, as well. "I'm going to leave you to get some rest. After the day you've had, I think you need it." He enveloped her in his arms, giving her a tight hug and a kiss on her temple as he pulled away. "Say, what book was Ramsay referring to?" he asked curiously. "I'm always looking for something else to read."

Beatrice grinned and pointed to the tome on the end table near the armchair. Wyatt picked it up, hefting it because of its weight, and flipped through it, eyebrows raised. "What makes *The Brothers Karamazov* so good?" he asked.

"The fact," said Beatrice with a smile, "that it helps put me to sleep."

The rescheduled date for the quilt show seemed to work out well this time. Not only did all the quilters show up, but the response from the community was such that they'd had to quickly allow the overflow of people into an adjoining basement room and Beatrice helped Wyatt and Meadow to move the refreshments into that room to help disperse the number of people.

Shy June Bug was present, wearing a turquoise top with black pants . . . and an anxious expression. She kept darting out to the kitchen to bring more food out. Beatrice finally put a firm but gentle hand on her arm. "June Bug, the refreshment table is just fine. Why not relax for a few minutes and walk around to see all the wonderful quilts?"

June Bug flushed a little. "They *are* wonderful. I just don't know what *mine* is doing here. When I see all those beautiful quilts, it makes me feel like I have no business at all being here."

Meadow joined them in time to hear that last bit. She gaped at June Bug. "No business *being* here? Are you kidding? We were all staring in silent wonder at your scrappy quilt a few minutes ago. It's innovative, unique. We're all agog. Come on over—you really need to see how everyone's reacting to it." And she dragged a wide-eyed June Bug off.

"Did Meadow kidnap June Bug?" asked Piper, grinning.

"She sure did," said Beatrice with a sigh. "That poor woman. But at least Meadow has a distraction—she's been so focused on you and Ash lately."

Piper flushed a little and laughed. "True. Although I'm glad that she cared so much. And glad that she ended up intervening like she did."

Martha was at the quilt show, still looking tired, but glowing at John's attention. "In times of stress, I tend to do a lot of quilting," she said to Beatrice as they stood in front of Martha's quilt with its grandmother's flower garden pattern. "A couple of nights I found I couldn't really sleep at all and working on this quilt was such a solace to me." She smiled at John, beside her. "As John has been in many ways."

Beatrice heard Wyatt's voice, swelling to be heard over the throng of people. "Thanks so much for coming out tonight. Our judges have made a decision." He squinted at the paper that an older woman handed to him, and then put on his reading glasses. "Best of Show goes to . . . June Bug Frost!"

Meadow whooped and Beatrice and the rest of the quilters cheered and applauded. June Bug's eyes danced and she blushed as she took her ribbon.

Best Traditional quilt went to Martha and there was

again thunderous applause from the group . . . as well as a proud hug from John.

Piper met up with Beatrice a little later at the refreshments table. Beatrice was happy to see Piper once again looking happy and relaxed. They moved to a corner to get out of the way of the crowd approaching the food. "I'm so glad everything is better between you and Ash," said Beatrice.

Piper said, "Me, too. When he and I weren't together, I realized how much Ash has come to mean to me."

"Did y'all get a chance to have a long talk? To work everything out?" asked Beatrice.

Piper nodded. "He started out apologizing for everything . . . said he was sorry that he'd been pushy and hadn't moved slowly enough. I had to cut him off so that *I* could apologize—and explain that it's just really tough for me to suddenly adjust to big changes . . . but that I was working on it. That I didn't mean that I didn't see a future for us together."

Beatrice gave her a hug. "I'm so glad you had a chance to talk it out."

Piper gave a rueful laugh. "And then he immediately asked me if I wanted to go tour the college where he just got accepted and help him find a house to rent! He was just kidding, but to both of our surprises, I immediately said yes. So maybe I'm getting over that hurdle."

"Well, thank goodness Meadow barged in and contrived a way to get you both together," said Beatrice. "Although I never thought I'd be saying something like that."

"You or me, either!" said Piper. "I'm not sure whether to hug her or to strangle her."

"Maybe, under the circumstances, a hug would be better," said Beatrice with a chuckle.

Several mornings later, Beatrice poured herself a coffee and looked at the food processor, now sitting back up in its usual position on the counter. She was never going to use it. It had actually already more than served its purpose, helping defend her against Phyllis. She didn't see herself cooking that many meals for Wyatt— maybe some omelets. Maybe they could enjoy some tomato soups with grilled cheese sandwiches. Did it matter?

She put it in a cloth tote bag. Piper, on the other hand, had always been interested in cooking and would probably love a nice food processor. She really *would* cook Ash some nice meals. She got a warm feeling thinking of the two of them together. It was wonderful that they were on the road to working everything out.

There was a light tap on her front door and Beatrice sighed. It had to be Meadow. No one else ever visited Beatrice this early. She called, "I'm coming. Be right there!" and put on more coffee to perk. Might as well, if she had visitors.

It was indeed Meadow at the door, but she'd also brought Georgia along with her. Georgia put a hand over her mouth when she saw Beatrice. "You just woke up. I'm sorry—we shouldn't have come this early."

Meadow waved her hand dismissively. "Pooh! It's not early. Beatrice simply doesn't get dressed until later. We frequently have morning coffees together, don't we, Beatrice?"

"We certainly do," said Beatrice, a bit dryly. "Come on in, y'all."

They were helping themselves to coffee in the kitchen when Georgia couldn't contain herself anymore. "Beatrice," she said, bubbling with excitement, "I can't thank you enough for persuading Savannah to take in Smoke!"

"Smoke?"

"That's what we named her—Smoke. Your little gray kitten," said Georgia.

"You mean *your* little gray kitten. If you and Savannah both like her, she's all yours," said Beatrice with a grin. "And Noo-noo will be vastly relieved."

"I *do* like her . . . we both do. In fact, I think Savannah has fallen in love with her. Smoke is all she talks about! I don't know how you did it—I've never seen anything like it."

Beatrice said, "Oh, it wasn't me. It was Smoke. He really showed off for Savannah when she came by to visit. You should have seen how absolutely adorable he was."

Georgia smiled and took a sip of her coffee. "You know, I've always felt a little . . . smothered, by Savannah. In the nicest way, of course. But now, not only do we have the pet I've wanted for years, but Savannah's attention has been diverted to Smoke and away from me. It's wonderful. I'm back home but have a little space. It's been terrific the last few days—really nice."

Beatrice and Meadow smiled at Georgia.

Meadow snapped her fingers. "I almost forgot to tell y'all. Remember how I sent off those pictures of June Bug's amazing scrappy quilts? Guess what. *Quilting Today* magazine is going to interview June Bug for their next issue! Isn't that wonderful? I thought June Bug was going to faint dead away when I told her. But she deserves it . . . those scrap quilts of hers are pure genius."

Beatrice said, "Good. Maybe that will help her develop some confidence in her work."

"It's hard to imagine how she's so insecure about her quilting," said Georgia. "Everything she makes is gorgeous."

"It *did* seem to help her develop confidence," said Meadow, beaming. "Because when I asked her for the umpteenth millionth time to enter one of her quilts in the show, she finally agreed to!"

"Good work, Meadow!" said Beatrice, lifting her coffee cup in a toast.

Later that morning, after Meadow and Georgia had left, Beatrice was opening her front door with the plan of heading to the store when she stopped short at seeing Wyatt there. Not only was it a surprise to see him there, but he was holding a large picnic basket. He smiled warmly at Beatrice, eyes crinkling at the edges. "It's such a beautiful day. Can you believe it's nearly seventy degrees? I thought I might be able to persuade you to have a picnic lunch with me."

A picnic—just the two of them. Away from the bustling church activities and the pull of the parishioners. On a gloriously beautiful day. Looking at Wyatt's kind face, feeling the warmth of the day, spotting what looked like some delicious egg salad sandwiches in the basket . . . Beatrice smiled and said, "I'd love to."

Quilting Tips

To keep blocks from slipping when you're sewing them together, spray starch on them.

Running your needle and thread through a folded dryer sheet before hand-piecing helps prevent knots.

Sharpen your rotary cutters by cutting through a folded piece of aluminum foil several times.

To keep from accidentally cutting through fabric when you're snipping threads, use blunt-tipped children's scissors.

Scrubbing fabric with an old pair of nylon hose will help remove chalk markings.

Recipes

Here are some favorite Southern dishes in Meadow's recipe box. She's convinced that Beatrice could easily cook them, if she just set her mind to it.

Boris, epicurean that he is, has also sampled these recipes. Meadow can't get mad at him for grabbing food off the counter. His hankering for shrimp pasta and skill in acquiring it simply demonstrates his good taste and advanced thinking skills, after all.

Easy, Corny Corn Bread

1 c. cornmeal
2 beaten eggs
1 c. milk
1 large can cream-style corn
¼ c. vegetable oil
1 finely chopped medium onion
8 oz. shredded sharp cheddar cheese

Preheat the oven to 350 degrees. Grease a casserole dish. Combine all the ingredients except the cheese. Pour half the batter into the greased dish and then sprinkle cheese on the top of the batter. Add the remaining batter on top. Bake at 350 degrees for 40 minutes.

Simple Shrimp Pasta

8 oz. angel-hair pasta
1 lb. medium shrimp, peeled and deveined
1 c. green peas (thawed if frozen)
5 oz. garlic and herbs cream cheese spread
2 tsp. butter
2.5 oz. can sliced mushrooms
2 Tbsp. milk
¾ tsp. dried dill weed or 2 tsp. fresh

Cook the pasta according to package instructions. Cook the peeled shrimp and mushrooms in butter. Sprinkle dill weed on top of the shrimp. When the shrimp are halfway cooked, add the garlic and herbs cream cheese spread and milk and heat this until it's melted, stirring constantly. Stir in the peas to the shrimp mixture and cook it until it's heated through. Spoon the shrimp mixture on top of the cooked pasta to serve.

Garlic Cheese Grits

4 c. water
1¼ tsp. salt
1 c. uncooked quick-cooking grits
1½ c. (6 oz.) shredded extra-sharp cheddar cheese (divided)
1 Tbsp. butter
¾ c. milk
2 tsp. garlic powder
1 tsp. Tabasco sauce
2 large eggs
Cooking spray

Preheat the oven to 350 degrees. Boil water and salt. Gradually add the grits while stirring (They will spit at you when they get hot, so look out!). Cover and simmer the grits until they thicken—about 8 minutes. Take the pot off the heat. Add one cup of the cheese and the butter, stirring to melt the cheese. Combine milk, garlic powder, Tabasco sauce, and eggs and whisk. Stir the milk mixture into the grits mixture. Cover an 8-inch baking dish with spray. Then pour the grits in. Bake this uncovered for 45 minutes. Then put the rest of the cheese on top and cook 15 minutes more. Let the grits stand 10 minutes before serving.

Chicken Crescent Rolls

6 oz. cooked, chopped chicken
4 oz. light cream cheese, softened
½ c. chopped mushroom
2 Tbsp. diced green onion
1 package crescent rolls (can of 8)
1 Tbsp. melted butter
¾ c. seasoned croutons, crushed

Preheat the oven to 375 degrees. Combine the chopped chicken, chopped mushroom, green onion, and softened cream cheese in a bowl. Unfold the crescent rolls into rectangles. Separate them until there are two rectangles (perforations pinched together) to form a larger rectangle (there will be four rectangles, total). Add a ½ cup dollop of the chicken mixture to the center of each of the four rectangles.

Pull the dough up over the mixture and pinch the dough closed. Drizzle this with melted butter and sprinkle it with crushed croutons. Bake this on a cookie sheet for 12 to 15 minutes at 375 degrees, covering it loosely with aluminum foil until the last five minutes.

Turn the page for a sneak peek at the next Southern Quilting mystery by Elizabeth Craig, coming from Obsidian in June 2015.

"Isn't it wonderful to have a wedding to plan? I don't know *when* I've been so thrilled." Meadow Downey gave a most un-Meadowlike squeal to emphasize the point.

Her friend Beatrice Coleman gave her a repressive look. But she couldn't hold back a grin. "Especially when it's not one's own."

"Well, but for you it's practically a family wedding," continued Meadow. "Wyatt's sister is finally tying the knot after fifty years. It's all very exciting."

Meadow and Beatrice were following up on Meadow's resolution to work in more exercise by walking their dogs through their neighborhood in the tiny mountain town of Dappled Hills, North Carolina, where they lived. Now that it was April, the air had warmed enough that a morning walk required only a light sweater. The dogwoods were blooming, daffodils were waving in the breeze, and the women could feast on the view of the rolling Blue Ridge Mountains returning to vibrant life after the starkness of winter.

Meadow was wrestling with her gigantic beast, Boris, while Beatrice was taking an easy stroll with her corgi, Noo-noo. With Meadow always a couple of yards ahead of Beatrice because Boris pulled her along at great speed, Beatrice wasn't sure if the walk could be considered a success. Or if it really could be termed a walk at all.

"It really is," said Beatrice. "Although I would hardly call it a family wedding, Meadow. I haven't even properly met Harper. And Wyatt and I are only just starting to date. It's not as if we're married."

Meadow completely ignored this detail, continuing on with her line of thought and yanking back on Boris's halter as he tried to race off after a terrified squirrel. "Can you imagine? Marrying at fifty. She'd have to be very set in her ways, don't you think? It sure would be tough trying to train a man at that point in your life. Actually," she said in a ruminating voice, "I can't imagine trying to train a man at *any* point in life. You can see what a disaster my training of Ramsay was."

Ramsay was Meadow's long-suffering husband and the police chief of Dappled Hills, North Carolina. He seemed very housebroken to Beatrice. Yes, he had a fondness for losing his reading glasses, writing poetry, and quoting *Walden* a bit much. But he was kind and hardworking. And even seemed to pick up after himself.

"Harper was just waiting for the perfect match, that's all. Wyatt is so happy for her. He felt terrible that she and I haven't met each other, so he invited Harper and her fiancé, Daniel, to have supper with us tonight at his house," said Beatrice.

"What are you bringing to the dinner party?" asked Meadow a little breathlessly. Beatrice wasn't sure if the breathlessness was due to the fact that she was always trying to persuade Beatrice to win Wyatt's heart through food—or the fact that Boris was pulling her along as if she were waterskiing.

Beatrice's already brisk walk turned into more of a jog. Noo-noo gave her a despairing look as if her short corgi legs couldn't possibly keep pace. "I'm not cooking anything," said Beatrice, slowly. "I'm just bringing a bottle of wine."

"But it's the perfect opportunity for you to impress Wyatt with your culinary skills," said Meadow, disappointed. "A bottle of wine just shows you know how to shop." She neatly sidestepped a puddle left by a brief spring shower from earlier that morning. Meadow finally reined in Boris as he skidded to a stop to inspect a mailbox that apparently smelled fascinating. Beatrice gave a grateful sigh as she slowed to a walk and completely caught up with Meadow again. Noo-noo, tongue hanging out and panting, seemed relieved as well.

"I think we're keeping it really low-key, actually." Beatrice shrugged. "And my culinary skills are nothing to brag about, as you know."

"A low-key dinner party?" asked Meadow. She sounded a bit scandalized.

"It's not even a *dinner party*. It's really just supper. That way I can meet Harper and her fiancé and we can have a nice evening together."

"I think it's a little odd that you haven't been introduced to Harper before now. After all, she does go to church quite a bit," said Meadow.

"I'm still pretty new to town, you know. Besides, I don't know everyone who goes to church and there was no real reason for Wyatt to have introduced me to his sister before we started dating. Harper doesn't live in town, anyway."

"She doesn't, but she doesn't live far from Dappled Hills, either. Just let me know how it goes," said Meadow. "I'm curious about Daniel. I know he grew up here, but he was gone for so long. It's been ages since I've last seen him. I remember him as a serious kid. He's younger than I am, but is the same age as my youngest sister. He was very smart and kind of quiet. The kind of kid who always had good manners when speaking with adults. He's a lawyer, isn't he? Not that we don't have enough of those around town." Meadow rolled her eyes.

"He is, but I think he works pro bono half the time. Daniel sounds like a good guy."

"Well, be sure to give me the scoop. I'm interested in his best man, too—I've been hearing some gossip lately about Trevor Garber." Meadow waggled her eyebrows in what was supposed to be a telling manner.

"Considering this is Dappled Hills, I can't say I'm surprised. Everyone seems to know everything around here. What are you hearing about Daniel's best man?"

"I hear he's behaving sort of out of character. And rumors"—here Meadow dropped her voice into her usual loud whisper, as if someone could hear them out on the quiet road—"that he might be having an affair." Then she jerked forward abruptly as Boris took off at a full gallop again.

"I doubt I'll hear much about that at supper tonight," said Beatrice, jogging ahead again. But you never knew. Not in Dappled Hills.

Meadow gave a gasping laugh as Boris dragged her forward. "Do you think I'm really getting exercise doing this? It feels like I'm just being pulled along. If I put roller skates on, I bet I'd end up across town in minutes."

"Whatever you're doing, it's exertion, all right." Beatrice smiled ruefully as Meadow went flying forward again. Beatrice decided she and Noo-noo were done with running to catch up and instead ambled toward their friends.

Eventually Meadow was able to tighten her grip on the leash and slow Boris down to a more leisurely pace. When Beatrice caught up with them, she gave Beatrice a curious look. "Have you been able to see much of Wyatt these last few weeks? It seems like he's been in charge of tons of activities at the church lately."

Beatrice cleared her throat. "We've seen each other, yes. Maybe not as much as I'd like to, but I understand about how busy he's been. And, when you're a minister, you're never really off. There are always people to visit—folks in hospitals, things like that. It's sort of the point of the job."

"I'm guessing," said Meadow archly, giving Beatrice a sideways glance, "that the best way for you to spend more time with him is probably by spending more time at the church. Right? Volunteering there, helping set up events, attending events. That sort of thing. After all, you're the one who's retired. So, technically, you have more free time."

Beatrice admired a row of azalea bushes as they walked past. She'd have to take a more scenic walk with Noo-noo tomorrow. This one was flying by. "Technically I *do* have more free time," said Beatrice. She was amazed lately how the days seemed to just disappear with a puff. Retirement was growing on her. But Meadow had a point, and it was one that Beatrice had been considering, too. The only thing that was really holding her back was the thought that a lot of extra socializing was going to be in order if she really started spending time at the church. Beatrice didn't mind a little socializing, but always quickly felt as though she wanted to retreat. She thought longingly of her hammock and her book.

"It's something to think about, anyway," said Meadow. She was fond of planting ideas in people's heads. "Although I'll miss seeing you if you spend more time with Wyatt. The sacrifices I make! Well, I'm sure tonight there'll be lots of talk of wedding planning. I hope it will be a beautiful wedding. Although the other night on TV, I saw this really horrifying show. It was sort of like watching a train wreck—I couldn't seem to pull myself away from it. It was called *Worst Wedding Day Disasters Ever!* and there was everything from a typhoon to the groom not showing up to a deer running into the ceremony and charging around the sanctuary. Scary stuff!"

"Well, none of that is going to happen during Harper and Daniel's wedding next month. When was the last time you saw a typhoon here in North Carolina? Daniel sounds too responsible to skip out on his own wedding. And I'll personally ensure that the door to the